FIVE HIEROGLYPHS

BY STEPHEN T. PERSON

FIVE HIEROGLYPHS

A NOVEL

STEPHEN T. PERSON

ILLUSTRATED BY JORDAN STOVKA

ISBN 13: 978-1-63489-621-4

Library of Congress Catalog Number has been applied for.
Printed in the United States of America
First Printing: 2023
27   26   25   24   23   5   4   3   2   1

Illustrations by Jordan Stovka
Cover design by Steven Meyer-Rassow
Interior design by Vivian Steckline

Wise Ink Creative Publishing
807 Broadway St. NE, Suite 46
Minneapolis, MN 55413
wiseink.com

To order, visit itascabooks.com or call 1-800-901-3480.
Reseller discounts available. Visit StephenTPerson.com.

To Suzanne Scherr

ACKNOWLEDGMENTS

I THANK MY FRIEND Suzanne Scherr for urging me to begin this novel, and for her steady encouragement along the way. She was also kind enough to read an early draft, as did Zoë Woodruff, and I thank them both for their helpful feedback. My thanks also to my family and friends for their words of encouragement and support—with special thanks to Patricia Person, Amy Townsley, and Cliff Baptiste.

It was a pleasure working with Amy Quale and her team at Wise Ink—copyeditor Kellie M. Hultgren, book designer Vivian Steckline, and production editor Chelsey Burden. I am grateful for their guidance and expertise.

My thanks also to cover designer Steven Meyer-Rassow, and to illustrator Jordan Stovka for her commitment and dedication, especially during the first five hard months of the coronavirus pandemic as she worked to transform my torrents of emailed notes and sketches into the artwork that illuminates this story.

S. T. P.

Contents

THE SEVEN WONDERS OF THE ANCIENT WORLD

· ✦ ·

THE GREAT PYRAMID OF GIZA (PYRAMID OF KHUFU)
Giza, Egypt
ca. 2560 BC

THE PHAROS OF ALEXANDRIA
Alexandria, Egypt
ca. 280 BC

THE HANGING GARDENS OF BABYLON
South of Baghdad, Iraq
ca. 600 BC

THE COLOSSUS OF RHODES
Rhodes, Greece
ca. 280 BC

THE MAUSOLEUM AT HALICARNASSUS
Bodrum, Turkey
ca. 350 BC

THE TEMPLE OF ARTEMIS
Ephesus, Turkey
ca. 325 BC

THE STATUE OF ZEUS
Olympia, Greece
ca. 430 BC

CHARACTERS

· ✦ ·

DANTE RIVERA, a high school student

NORA RIVERA, his sister

GRANDMA (EMMA BROOKS), his grandmother

ALISON FINE, his substitute teacher

DYLLIS KIRBY, a reporter

MARSHALL REYES, tour planner and concierge

RAYMOND MISHKY, a retired museum employee

PROFESSOR JASPER JAMES, an anthropologist

DOCTOR PETER SACKVILLE, an Egyptologist

MONICA DEUSS, tour organizer

BARONESS RENATE VON WEBER, companion to Monica Deuss

CHEF WERNER, the baroness's chef

MED, an Egyptian boy

OTTO, an Alexandrian aide

SARA GAMAL, a dealer of antiquities

RIGGIO AND JERRIE, hired agents

"ANCIENT LIGHT," a prominent Alexandrian

ABBOT, Saints Constantine and Helen Monastery

FATHER DOMINICK, a monk

Tour Guests & Crew of *Modestine*

· ✦ ·

Nikkos Nicolaides, captain

Lieutenant Regan, communications officer

Eyüp, boatswain

Doctor Ali Khalil, guest lecturer on the Hanging Gardens

David Dickenson, *The New York Times*

Deirdre Rao, *The Independent*

Torrie Benet, *The Travel Show*

Dick Stewart, *Travel + Leisure Magazine*

Michael Scott, *Condé Nast Traveler*

Michelle Reinhart, Travel Channel

Donna Miranda, in-flight airline magazines

PROLOGUE

THE PRUSSIAN GENTLEMAN PACED inside his tent, weighing whether to break camp or to extend his dig another week.

Seven more days of toil in this heat? he asked himself. *Seven more nights in the territory of this hostile pasha?*

No, he judged.

But his excavations at the remote, mud-brick ruins of Babylon had begun to yield more than he had dared to imagine. In his hand he held one find—a tiny baboon amulet—turning it once, twice, a third time. He deemed it to be no less important—or confounding—than the large avian mosaic his team had uncovered.

Neither belongs to Babylonian culture, he told himself. *What more is here? So we will stay. Two more days, perhaps three.*

He had not foreseen the haboob that had developed to the west—a billowing sandstorm pushing across the arid landscape of Ottoman Iraq toward the Euphrates River and his camp. Now it came in, eerily silent, yet charged and strangely alive, even as it shrouded the late-afternoon sun and muffled the sounds of the clandestine dig.

"What is this?" the gentleman murmured as his tent's door-flap shuddered, then clapped with a beat his heart began to match. "The air . . . So close."

He stepped out into the dry soup of sand and dust that had engulfed his camp and drew his silk scarf to his face. Through the amber haze he scanned the site to locate his two aides, but he made out only indistinct huddles of the men and beasts he had hired— twelve laborers, six guards, and thirty-two camels. Some of the men grumbled. Some, like the camels, were stoic.

He judged every one a malingerer.

"Colonel!" he barked at the idling clumps. "Doctor!"

The colonel, retired from the Prussian army, emerged from one of the huddles, coughing. Next, the British archaeologist stepped out from behind a stack of excavated bricks and bolted after the colonel, brushing the sand from his jacket fussily.

"Why do the men stop working, Colonel?" the gentleman demanded as the two drew up.

"It's impossible to breathe in this stuff, sir, much less work in it."

"I hired you to carry this out quickly," the gentleman snapped. "If you cannot do that, then leave us." He turned to the archaeologist. "How much is left, Doctor?"

"We've removed the last pieces of the mosaic terrace, and we've dismantled the little wall around it. If you're agreeable to staying longer, it would be worth our while," he added, gesturing toward six partially excavated areas outside the wall. "More mosaics, sir, I believe."

"With respect, Doctor," said the colonel, "we don't know yet if they're mosaics. We've only identified some edges."

"Oh, they are," said the gentleman, almost to himself.

He feels them, too, thought the archaeologist. *Even this rigid man can feel them.* Aloud, he gushed, "And over there, sir, the top of a fountain. We found it this morning as well. But it will take us most of tomorrow to reveal it all. It's extraordinary."

The gentleman looked to the fountain and then to the Euphrates, whose waters would have fed it and given it life for centuries. He looked back at the fountain and watched, through the gritty air, as a lone wading bird, an ibis, alighted on its gracefully curved rim.

"Your decision, sir? Will we stay?"

"No," said the gentleman, his voice distant as he studied the white-and-black bird that now studied him back. "I sense something here that wants us gone, Doctor. We will leave the fountain. And those smaller mosaics, too. We break camp today."

"Then we must be grateful for what we can take," said the archaeologist. "The big mosaic and the wall bricks are of immense importance. Your amulet, too."

"Just finish your work, Doctor. Colonel, tell the men to cover the fountain. We leave at dusk."

"Three hours," the archaeologist muttered to the colonel as they withdrew. "Impossible."

But the order to end the dig recharged the workers. In a burst of chatter and resolve, they set about wrapping the remaining slabs of the big mosaic, the tiled terrace floor it rested in, and the bulky glazed bricks of the low wall that surrounded it.

The archaeologist worked furiously to keep pace, inspecting, tagging, and recording each piece, and though the air was suffocating, it seemed to transport him. As his work concluded, he sat down heavily on his overstuffed bag and made a final entry in his journal.

> *O, back two millennia, through the timeless haboob, to Babylon. Here beside the River Euphrates, inside the city's great walls, stood the verdant Wonder.*

From this air, I know the Hanging Gardens' terraces, trees, and flowers once tended by Amytis, wife of Nebuchadnezzar. From this air, I hear the songs and conversations of ancient nights and days and the fountain that invites them. May others listen, too, when passing this way, this place of peace.

He looked at the mound that now covered the ancient fountain, telling himself it was fitting to leave it. He turned the page to begin a sketch from memory, but was startled by a chorus of shouts and groaning camels.

"Doctor!" he heard the gentleman call. "Come!"

He shot up to join the departing caravan, breathing in the particled air, revering it, and this time did not brush it from his jacket or shake it from the pages. He stuffed the journal into his bag as he ran, unaware that the bag had torn. The force of his hands pushed another of his journals through the tear to the ground.

It was only after the caravan emerged from the haboob that he discovered the journal was missing, and with it the maps he had drawn of the dig's location. He clutched the precious remaining journal and wept, knowing that the sands had already claimed the other and that he would likely never see the whole of the fountain or the six mosaics they had left behind.

Still, they had the big mosaic and wall bricks, and he was content with that achievement—until it struck him that something else might have fallen from his bag. He thrust his hands into it, searching for the velvet pouch that held seven small tesserae from a detail of the mosaic. When his fingertips felt the pouch, he gave a cry of relief, knowing that when the great mosaic terrace was reassembled in its new home in Prussia, it would not be whole, would not come alive, without those little stones.

· ✦ ·

OLYMPIA, GREECE, NOVEMBER 2004

At a centuries-old monastery in the south of Greece, a heavyset man in his early seventies, dressed in a suit of Egyptian linen, approached a compact, domed pavilion that stood alone in an olive grove. He stopped at the edge of the pavilion and then breathed out slowly, satisfied that it had been looked after by the monks and his friend the abbot. He sat down on a bench under the orange and azure twilight sky, wanting to absorb the atmosphere around him, and to be reassured by it.

"A man has died," he whispered in Arabic. "A desperate little man in America. So be it. The piece he stole from us will yet be recovered. So be it," he repeated, this time in English.

His contemplation was interrupted by the arrival of the abbot, a tall, slim man with a benign demeanor. With him was a beefy monk named Father Dominick, who carried several small wooden bowls.

"You look troubled," said the abbot. "More so than I have seen you in many years."

"Yes," the visitor agreed. He embraced the abbot and gave Father Dominick an apologetic smile.

"Not this time, then," Father Dominick remarked without judgment. He withdrew with the little bowls, leaving the old friends alone.

"Each visit in recent years," said the abbot, "you depart without performing what you know you must. If you were to shed the burden of your responsibilities, you would find peace. Both for yourself and your family. We are not young. You should not resist this."

"We are of different faiths," replied the visitor, "but may I ask for your prayers?"

"Of course. You will return to Egypt now, to Alexandria?"

"Yes."

"Until next time, then."

The visitor nodded and walked from the pavilion to his waiting limousine, satisfied with his decision to keep his responsibilities for a time longer.

1

CHICAGO

IN THE HUMBOLDT PARK neighborhood of Chicago's West
Side, Dante Rivera awoke to the sounds of his grandmother's
kitchen—her coffee machine's gurgles, her metal cabinet doors'
clicks, and her soulful voice accompanying Earth, Wind & Fire on
the radio as she began breakfast. He pushed the blanket from his
chest, relieved that it was Saturday. Weekends meant time to be
alone with his thoughts when he awoke, and later on to read or
draw. But they also brought his grandmother's admonitions that
he should get out of the house, get some air, do something. And
comments about his moodiness and what she called his "growing
pains."

"How can that be," he had once argued, "when I'm practically
the smallest one in my class?"

"Well, you're too much within yourself," Grandma had answered. "You're turning seventeen, and you need to snap out of it."

Now he was thinking that she was right. *In six months, I graduate. In nine months, I'll be in college. Or not, because shouldn't you figure out who you are first? Who you want to be?*

But on this November morning in 2018, his thoughts were on an image that had come to him when he awoke. It was just the latest of many that had been coming to him since he was ten. "Big deal," his fourteen-year-old sister Nora had said when he first told her about them. "Everyone gets cool thoughts like that, when you're half asleep and half awake, coming out of a dream."

But these were not the vaporous trails of a dream. Some were still images and others moving tableaux. "Like a scene in a movie," he'd told her. They were vivid and did not evaporate, and they presented themselves without any thought on his part, at any time of day, even if he was in midsentence. Sometimes they were troubling, but mostly they were benign. Always, they came true. Sooner or later, what he saw would happen.

In time, Nora had come to believe him.

He called them "pictures." He dared not call them premonitions because that sounded supernatural. But they worried him enough that he had begun to push them away and pray that they wouldn't turn into something more, or arrive nonstop.

In quiet moments, something else might come, too: a dim memory of a night at home when he was very young—of his mother's screams and of his terror at hearing them. And then of being closed off in the dark, and the bewilderment he felt later on when she and his father were no longer there.

Grandma insisted that he had imagined the screams. "Dante, your mother died in a car accident," she had told him. "You were three. And your father left after that. You should put it out of your mind, that's all."

So, on this morning, he put aside thoughts of the past and focused on the picture that had come. It was a display case, in a cavernous space . . . and inside the case, a large, glazed brick, ancient in appearance, broken in two . . . and on its surface, a design . . . and on its underside, a lump with a mark on it.

He was relieved that the picture wasn't unsettling, but he thought it odd to see an old, oversized brick, isolated and without context.

It's probably because I have an architecture tour today, he thought.

Whoo-wheet? The soft whistle from downstairs pulled him from his reverie. It was Grandma, asking him and Nora if they were awake.

He returned the call and hauled himself out of bed, put on the flannel robe that fell formlessly over his slight frame, and made his way down to the kitchen. Grandma saw his gentle smile and ran her hand through his hair playfully.

"Eat, please," she ordered when Nora came down, took a section of the newspaper, and began reading aloud. "We have to meet Dante's teacher."

"Miss Fine," said Dante. "But she wants us to call her Alison."

Nora continued to read aloud, adding running commentary, but Dante didn't hear. As he ate, his thoughts were on the architectural river tour Alison had invited them on. He had read up on Chicago's renowned buildings and skyscrapers and knew that Alison was the most popular guide. He had seen a profile of her on TV and knew that her tour would be as interesting as her classes when she substituted at school, especially when she spoke about music, ancient history, or astronomy.

Weeks earlier, when he had told her he hoped to do the tour one day, she had invited him and his family to be her guests. He remembered having to tell her that it would be just him and his grandmother and sister because his mother had died and his father was gone.

Grandma's voice brought him back. "Did you hear me? Go and get dressed, or we'll miss that boat."

Dante rose from the table but saw that Nora had become quiet, her breathing labored. He knew what it meant. Born prematurely at just twenty-eight weeks, she had a chronic asthmalike condition.

"Not up to going," she said.

"I'll call Alison," said Dante. "We can go another time."

"No. It's the last weekend before the tours close for the winter. You can tell us about it when you get back."

Dante went back upstairs to change and gave his globe a spin, wondering where he'd be in a year. He placed his finger on Egypt, half a world away. "The Great Pyramid is fifty stories high and more than four thousand years older than our own skyscrapers," he remembered Alison saying. She had also said that the night sky was wonderfully vivid and alive once you got out of the city, and that ancient civilizations spoke to us every day. She had said these things in a way that told him she knew him, and understood his hunger to know what books and maps and museums could only hint at.

· ✦ ·

DANTE CAUGHT AN INBOUND train and walked to East Wacker Drive, where *Chicago's First Lady* was berthed. Alison spotted him from the ship's bridge and pointed to the gangway with her silver-knobbed walking stick. Alison Fine was a widely recognized personality in Chicago, as much for her signature walking stick, unruly silver-blond hair, and spirited blue eyes as for her award-winning work in education and the arts. In addition to her part-time work with the river tours and substitute teaching at Dante's school, she played bassoon with the Lyric Opera of Chicago and ran the prestigious Fine Discoveries Foundation.

Alison liked to tell her students that her antique stick was made of calamander, a prized wood of hazel-brown with black stripes that was related to ebony. When she once invited Dante to hold it, he marveled at its weight and its grain, which she called "deep, smoky, and mysterious." The stick was always with her, an extension of her lyrical spirit, and a barometer of her mood as well. It was often used to punctuate a point, but sometimes it seemed to have a will and a power of its own.

Now, from the dock, Dante watched the stick move toward him in a slow arc as she called, "Where's the rest of you?"

"At home," he answered. "It's just me."

He smiled when the stick motioned him forward.

"I saved you a good spot," she said as she led him to the ship's bow. "So, your grandmother and sister—too cold for them?"

"My sister didn't feel well," he told her.

"Poor thing. Well, we have a minute before we get underway. Is there anything you'd like me to highlight? A favorite building?"

"The Tribune Tower. I like the old stone fragments and artifacts they've embedded into the front of it. There's a piece from the Great Wall of China, the Taj Mahal, Petra . . . One hundred and forty-nine of them. Lincoln's tomb, the Berlin Wall—"

"For real. But I have to stop you there. I need to get up to my perch."

Dante felt the rumble of the *First Lady*'s engines as she eased away from her berth and made a slow turn to take them down the Chicago River through the heart of the city. Alison stood on the bridge, poised to begin.

"Welcome," she said, into her microphone. She spoke with an authoritative whisper, as if bursting to share a secret. Already, with just a word, she had drawn the passengers in.

Over the next ninety minutes she highlighted the city's landmark buildings, telling their stories with such color that Dante began to see them as people, each with a personality, each in a handsome suit of stone, brick, steel, or glass.

"By the end of the nineteenth century, Chicago was the nation's hub of corn, wheat, and meat," she said with a laugh. "The push was to build upward, beyond the limits imposed by thick walls of brick and stone, which could support structures only so high."

Chicago pioneered the use of steel to create taller and taller buildings, she explained. Their rigid frames—skeletons, she called them—bore the weight. She pointed to them with her stick as if bestowing knighthoods: the Wrigley Building with its glazed terra-cotta walls and noble clock tower; the twin "corncob" towers of Marina City with their condos that had no right angles; the Merchandise Mart, so big that it once had its own zip code. And more than twenty more, including the Civic Opera Building, which Alison admitted was her favorite. It loomed above them like an enormous chair, a hybrid of the art nouveau and deco styles.

"Isn't it wonderful?" she said. "The real wonder, though, is that they allow me in there from time to time to play my bassoon with the Lyric Opera."

Now the boat was nearly back to its berth and there was one important building Alison hadn't mentioned. Dante assumed she had forgotten, but when he looked up he found her looking at him, her stick raised upright, its silver knob flashing in the sun.

"And now, the Gothic-style masterpiece off our port beam," she announced. "The Tribune Tower."

Dante stood, anxious to hear her words, but stiffened when he saw that the stick was no longer pointing at the building but at him.

"Young man, please come up."

As he made his way to the bridge, he heard her explain that the Tribune Tower's design was inspired by the Button Tower of Rouen Cathedral and that it was completed after just two years of work in 1925. He heard her say that now, almost one hundred years later, the *Chicago Tribune* had moved out and work was underway to turn the building into condos.

"And another thing about this building," she said, "but I'll need the help of one of my students." She handed Dante her mic and asked him to name some of the artifacts embedded in the building's façade.

Which he did. More than thirty, ending with, "And the Great Pyramid."

The passengers applauded, and Dante beamed.

"Finally, folks, a word about a mystery artifact—the so-called Hillwood Stone," she said as they docked. "You may remember the newspaper story about that infamous brick around fourteen years ago. Well, it was never embedded into the façade—the owner has never come forward. But it's on display in the Tribune Tower's lobby, ever since the man who offered it to the Trib for examination was found dead a couple of hours later from a still-unexplained fall from his motel balcony. We have this lovely old brick, this orphan, but we know nothing about its lineage. So, where does it rightfully belong? Question mark," she concluded. "Thank you for your attention, and good day."

"I've never heard of the Hillwood Stone," Dante told her as they descended from the bridge.

"No? A reporter friend of mine at the *Chicago Tribune* actually wrote the story."

"Who?"

"Dyllis Kirby. She's the Turkish bureau chief for CNN in Istanbul now. Anyway, she covered crime at the time for the Trib. The stone—it's actually a baked-mud brick, and very ancient—was thought to have been stolen from a museum in Washington, DC. The Hillwood Estate, once the home of the heiress Marjorie Merriweather Post."

"So the Trib didn't buy it?"

"No; the man—a guy named Mishky—had no papers to prove he owned it. He was a security guard at Hillwood. Seems he must have taken the brick just before he retired, and then driven around half the country trying to sell it to museums. The Trib offered to study it, but wouldn't pay him. And right after he returned to his motel room, he fell and died. According to Dyllis's story, a house-keeper saw someone outside Mishky's room in the hallway around the time of his death. And the people at the Trib said that Mishky had been referred to them by some guy he met at a bar the night before. . . . Oh, and it seems there was a note on Mishky's night-stand that went missing, according to the housekeeper. There was a lot of speculation that he might have been pushed off his balcony."

"So, no one knows who did it?"

"Nope. Neither of the two 'persons of interest' was ever appre-hended, as far as I know. And Hillwood denied that the brick was part of its collection." She laughed, saying, "I remember a quote from Dyllis's article. A Hillwood spokesperson told her, 'We don't collect rocks, Miss Kirby.' So, it remains a cold case to this day, fourteen years later."

Dante thought it best not to tell Alison about the picture that had come to him earlier in the morning. "You said the brick's on display in the lobby? I've never been inside."

"We can walk over and see it if you want. The lobby's still open to visitors, despite all the construction."

When they reached the building, Dante ran ahead to the en-trance, barely glancing at the façade's embedded artifacts or up at the gargoyles and flying buttresses he knew so well. Alison caught up to him in the lobby and pointed out its mammoth topograph-ical map of North America, explaining as she walked that it was made from shredded currency and plaster, until she realized that Dante had come to a stop well behind her.

He looked at her expectantly, recognizing the space from his picture that morning, and knowing what he would soon see.

"Well," she said, "I guess that big, wonderful map up there can do that to a person."

"The Hillwood Stone," he said, walking over to her.

"Yes?"

"It's over that way, right? In a display case."

"Yes, but, I thought you hadn't been here."

"I haven't," he said, striding toward it.

At the display case, Dante gazed at the notorious object but said nothing.

"Can you believe the color?" said Alison, breaking the silence. "That beautiful yellow glaze?"

He heard her voice only faintly. He was thinking about the brick's underside, about the mark he had seen there—perhaps a wax seal with an owner's mark. He turned to her, wanting to tell her but not sure he could. *It's enough that I told her where the brick is*, he told himself. *What will she think if I say I've seen the bottom of it?*

"Anyway," she said, "it's big—what, about eighteen inches long and ten inches tall and deep? And those rough, unglazed ends suggest that it must have been part of something larger. Likely a wall."

"That's what I think, too," he said, brightening. "The sign here says Mesopotamian, but with a question mark. I wonder if it's from the Hanging Gardens of Babylon."

"Well, that little mosaic on the top does look like reeds, which are plentiful in the marshes of southeastern Iraq, not far from the ruins of ancient Babylon. Did you know that people used to make pens from them? Anyway, the Hanging Gardens were constructed by King Nebuchadnezzar the Second, and that period is known for large wall tiles of lions and other animals in low relief—bas-relief, it's called. But I don't think the Babylonians created mosaics like this. Not that I'm aware of, at least. Just look at the intricacy of the tesserae, and the fine colors and glazing. So I'd say the brick is probably not from the Hanging Gardens. It probably came later."

"But if it is, it would be the only thing that survived," he said. "There's nothing left of that Ancient Wonder, right? Not even in a museum."

"I don't really know," she admitted. "So, you're into the wonders? I'm reading up on them myself."

"I learned about them from my grandfather back when he was alive. And I did a term paper this year on ancient Egypt. Their writing. But look at the break in the brick . . ."

"According to my reporter friend, the damage was probably caused by the guy who tried to sell it here. Some fragments from the brick were found in his motel room. . . . Hey, are you hungry? I'm always starving after a tour—let's get something to eat."

As they walked to a café she liked, Dante told her that he had studied Egyptian hieroglyphs since grade school and had created stories and poems with them. (He didn't mention that they often helped him express his feelings better than speaking or writing in English could.)

"I saw your paper while I was subbing for another teacher," Alison told him. "About the discovery of the Rosetta Stone in the Nile Delta, and how the hieroglyphs on it were deciphered . . . and how they can represent sounds as well as literal pictures of things. It was so well written. You know, a lot of students get distracted by sensational details—like writing only about the people of Pompeii getting buried alive under the volcanic ash from Mount Vesuvius, and not about their daily lives . . . their stories . . . which we're still learning about from the amazing things being excavated there. It's so easy to get caught up in the spectacle part. I despair," she sighed. "But your paper . . . yes, so well written."

· ✦ ·

THAT EVENING, ALISON DECIDED to call Dante's grandmother.

"Mrs. Brooks, it's Alison Fine, Dante's substitute teacher."

"Oh, of course. Alison. I remember you from a couple of school things last year. Call me Emma."

"Yes, and I'm sorry you weren't able to join us on the *First Lady*. I'd be happy to have you and Nora visit anytime, and Dante too if he'd like to go again. You know, I'm just so impressed with him.

His curiosity, his maturity. I wanted to discuss an opportunity I have for him."

"Yes, he's an old soul, as they say. He does work hard in school—"

"He does, he really excels. And maybe you know this, but outside of teaching, I work through the Fine Discoveries Foundation to inspire exceptional students through hands-on discovery."

Dante's grandmother said nothing.

Surely she's heard of my foundation, Alison told herself. "Well, we've been to places like Stonehenge, Angkor Wat, Easter Island, Mont-Saint-Michel," she went on. "Mrs. Brooks—Emma, I wonder if you'd allow Dante to join a cruise with me next June. To the Mediterranean, to the sites of the Seven Wonders of the Ancient World. It's a cruise that's being put together by a European organization. I've been invited to lecture, and I'll be evaluating it as a potential future offering by my foundation. And Dante said that he was interested in the wonders. Anyway, I can bring a guest, so Dante could help evaluate it, too, as a student. It's for a week. Oh, dear, I'm out of breath. I'm sorry."

Again, no answer. *Too strong, Alison, as usual*, she thought.

"Now, these Seven Wonders are where, exactly?" asked Emma.

"The first two are in Egypt: the Great Pyramid of Giza and the Pharos of Alexandria, the ancient lighthouse. Then we board a cruise ship and head into the Mediterranean Sea to where the rest of the wonders were—"

"Where they *were*?"

"I hear you. Yes, they're gone now, or in ruins, except for the Great Pyramid. But it's the history, you see. And the rare opportunity to visit all seven of the sites in one trip. So exciting, especially if I can make them come alive for the guests. That will be my job."

"I see. I guess you could call it a tour of the imagination."

"The organizers aren't sure it will work either. But that's what this is about. It's a pilot cruise to test the concept. If all goes well, they'll open it up to the public."

"Well, I suppose it'll be successful if you're narrating. Dante enjoys your classes. He likes you very much."

Heartened, Alison added, "Even though this is just a test cruise, we'll have a tour director. He's someone I've worked with at the foundation. Dante will be well chaperoned."

"Maybe you can send me some information," said Emma.

"Sure. What else?"

"Well, Dante's never been away from home. That would be a concern."

"You think he isn't up to it?"

"He's a reserved boy, Alison. He's moody. I worry about that."

"He's quite keen at school. Although, I guess I make up for his quietness."

"I'm not sure you could handle him full time. But go ahead and send me that information."

"Absolutely. Then we can go over all your questions. I do have one for you, though. In his term paper, I'm curious why Dante was drawn to the last verse of Bob Dylan's song 'Mr. Tambourine Man.' He illustrated the lyrics beautifully with Egyptian hieroglyphs, but he's a bit young for hits of the sixties." Dante's illustrations had been lovely: a carefree dance, a star-filled sky, the sea, the moving sands. Though, at the song's lines about memory and fate, he had drawn a single hieroglyph of a stone block.

"Dante's father would sometimes write down the lyrics of songs he heard, and I kept some of them around. Dante just liked that one, I guess." She sounded uncomfortable, and Alison decided not to pry, but after a moment she spoke again.

"Alison, I worry about him. Not because he's trouble. He's not. He's a serious boy. Too serious, I think, the way he keeps things inside."

Alison waited, sensing that Emma needed to collect herself before saying more.

"He lost his mother. My daughter Serena. He would have heard it. . . . And then his father left him. No child should have to go through something like that." Her voice was shaking now. "I don't know to this day if he remembers it. He doesn't talk about it."

Alison wondered about Dante's father's unexplained absence. She wondered, too, why Emma had said, "He would have heard it," when she referred to Dante's mother's death. Dante had told her his mother died in a car accident by herself.

"Emma, if this is too difficult—"

"No, let me get through it. My husband and I took him and Nora. Dante was already a little withdrawn. The trauma probably made it worse. I thought he'd grow out of it. I'm not sure he will. And he told me once that he can see things in his head. Pictures, he calls them. He said they foretell things. It's nonsense, of course. It's some dream world he's invented."

"Okay."

"He'll just sit for hours and read or draw. He can be distant, but impulsive, too. It wouldn't be easy for you on the cruise."

"I understand. But I also enjoy the challenge of drawing my students out. Given everything, shouldn't we encourage Dante to engage? Feed his curiosity?"

"I'm not trying to restrict him, Alison, or deny him this opportunity. But you need to know these things about him."

"I'm grateful that you've trusted me with it. We don't have to decide anything now. I'll send the materials, and we can discuss it again when you've had a chance to see the details."

· ✦ ·

ON A SATURDAY TWO weeks later, Dante, Nora, and Grandma climbed into a Fine Discoveries Foundation van to meet Alison for dinner at her condo on Lake Shore Drive. Dante smiled when he saw the foundation's logo on the van's door: a compass rose with

Alison's bassoon and calamander stick crossed to form the points north, south, east, and west.

Earlier in the day, when Grandma announced that they had been invited to dinner at Alison's home, he had guessed that she might be considering him for a trip. Grandma would give nothing away, but Nora had given him a wink and told him she would set up a blog so he could write about it.

It was dark now as they drove into the city. Dante sat quietly, looking out his window and guessing which lights would come on or be turned off next in the labyrinth of tall buildings.

"What are you thinking?" Nora asked with a sigh.

"Nothing."

"It's your seventeenth birthday and there's nothing?"

"Okay, I got a picture of something," he allowed. "In Alison's apartment."

"Of what?"

"It's a carved bird. It has a curved beak. It's old looking."

"So that's bothering you?"

"No, you're bothering me," he answered.

"Don't be so touchy. You better snap out of it or Alison will think you're a psycho and won't consider taking you anywhere."

"Okay, enough," said Grandma. "Clear your head." She was echoing his grandfather's words when he saw Dante stuck in a day-dream or a mood. "Clear your head."

The driver pulled the van up to Alison's building and escorted them to the concierge, who walked them to an elevator.

"But which floor?" Grandma asked anxiously as the doors closed.

"This is a private elevator," Nora said in an awed whisper.

When the doors opened to the foyer of the twenty-second-floor penthouse, Alison called, "Come in," and then hugged Grandma and told Dante and Nora to explore. They went first to the balcony that overlooked Lake Michigan to the east, then walked back across the living room—past a music nook, a table crowded with orchids,

and a bookcase that displayed mementos from Alison's travels—toward a second balcony that looked west to the Chicago skyline.

Alison stepped up next to them. "This is where I watch over my buildings," she said. "I love their stories. No pun intended."

Dante turned around to take in the living room again. His eyes rested on a carved bird on the bookcase and then on the music nook.

"That's my old bassoon," Alison said, gesturing at the instrument resting upright in its stand. "I had it made in France. They told me calamander wasn't the most suitable wood, but I told them to do it anyway. So the sound it makes is, let's say, distinctive. My own. It inspires me to compose. Or it used to, anyway. I haven't composed in, well, a number of years. I guess I'm a little blocked."

She pointed to an array of precision tools and explained that she made her own reeds for the bassoon, then held up a big double reed that had been soaking.

"Can you play us something?" Nora asked.

Alison demurred, but then she shrugged, inserted the reed into the instrument's bocal, and took a long breath.

She struggled with her first notes, but soon the hulking wood-wind was producing a sound that was now lyrical and droll, now plaintive and low. She had chosen a passage from a classical piece that evoked early Italian music, and her eyebrows danced as she played with a spirituality that connected the four of them to the vast lake, the glowing skyscrapers, and the dome of the night sky.

"What about this?" she said, and somehow gave the same piece a flavor of jazz, then country, then hip-hop, and finally salsa, improvising effortlessly. She added a riff from "Mr. Tambourine Man," to which Dante mouthed the words quietly. She ended with something he didn't recognize but thought must have been her own, and he was moved by it.

"Anyway, that was from *Ancient Airs and Dances* by Respighi, with some variations." She laughed. "Plus a little Dylan. And some other stuff, which I hope didn't ruin your appetites. Let's sit."

After dinner, she rose to bring in Dante's cake, but Emma held up a hand.

"First, a little business," she said, reaching for her bag and pulling out a large envelope.

"What's that?" Dante asked, observing Alison's logo on the envelope.

"Just some paperwork I'm going to sign for a cruise Alison's invited you to go on next June."

"A cruise?" he cried. "I'm going?"

"Looks like it," said Alison.

"It's to the Seven Wonders," said his grandmother, handing him a brochure.

"Sweet," said Nora. "Now we can have cake."

"Can we have it on the balcony?" Dante asked. "The one that looks over the lake?"

"Certainly," Alison confirmed. She slipped into the kitchen and returned with a cake decorated with a map of the Eastern Mediterranean. A lit candle marked each of the Seven Wonders, and ten more bordered the edge of the map. Their golden light illuminated Dante's earnest face as she placed the cake in front of him.

As they sang, he saw that the candle for the Pharos of Alexandria was larger and flamed brighter than the others. He oriented the cake so that its map faced north, then lowered his head and peered eastward through the candles—across Lake Michigan, the Atlantic, and the Mediterranean—imagining each candle an Ancient Wonder.

"What are you doing?" muttered Grandma. "Make a wish and blow them out, son."

Dante smiled at Grandma's impatience, but the night's celebration had not wiped away the detachment that was always with him. So, as in previous years, he took a breath and wished to have a happy life, despite the unsettling feeling that if he did, it would not be as everyone else defined it.

He blew out the candles, and when the trick candle representing the ancient lighthouse relit itself, he assented to their calls to make a second wish.

To understand why my father left, he said to himself. *Why everything broke. Just to know why.*

He blew out the Pharos candle again, and as it flamed once more, he wondered if it was affirming his wishes or mocking him.

· ✦ ·

LATER, DANTE RETREATED TO the music nook and began to sketch in one of Alison's composition books. His grandmother started to object, but Alison said it was fine.

After pouring coffee for Emma, Alison stepped over to Nora. "Are you really okay with your brother going away?" she asked.

"I am," said Nora. "But he'll need you."

"How so?"

"He'll need you to believe him. For when he gets the pictures in his head."

"Yes, your grandmother told me about that."

"At first, he told only me. Then, when some of the pictures worried him, he told Grandma. He didn't really want to, because he thought she wouldn't believe him, and I guess he was right, because she doesn't. But I know they're real. I'm with him sometimes when he gets them."

"Go on."

"Well, one time, while we were out shopping, he knew that someone dinged our fender before we got back to the car. Another time, he told us what the costumes would look like in a play before it started. And he once described the mural in a restaurant we'd never been to before. And just today, in the car—well, you know that wooden bird in your bookcase?"

"Yes, I got it in Copenhagen. It's a museum reproduction of a carved ibis from ancient Egypt. I noticed Dante looking at it."

"That's because he knew it was there. He saw it in his head. He told us on the way over."

"But he couldn't have known. I've never mentioned it to him. Okay, wow . . . you know, he did the same thing at the Tribune Tower a couple of weeks ago."

"You'll get used to it," said Nora.

"Anything else?"

"Well, no. I'm just telling you so you'll understand if he gets weird or something."

"I do appreciate that, Nora." She paused. "Your grandmother tells me he has moods . . ."

"Well, I think his mind is just on other things usually. So he can get prickly. If he doesn't always say much . . . he's just in his bubble."

"Okay."

"That's when he might do something you don't expect."

· ✦ ·

AFTER HER GUESTS HAD left, Alison fell onto her sofa and flipped through the sketches Dante had made in her music composition book—her foundation's logo, her carved ibis, and the Hillwood Stone.

He had rendered the brick from two angles, including the bottom, where he had drawn what looked like a stamped letter *I*. She was puzzled as much by its meaning as by how he could have known it was there—*Does he really know what it looks like underneath without seeing it?* She leaned her head back, marveling at the unexplained, and felt touched that he had written, in his irregular hand, *For Alison.*

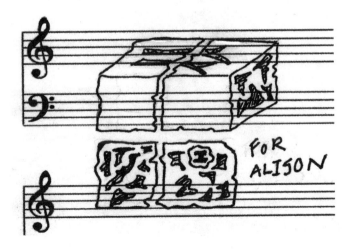

THOTH

2

In Air

It was early June, the eve of the Ancient Wonders cruise, and the moon outside Dante's bedroom window was as bright as he had ever seen it. He lay still, watching the tree shadows tap like fingers over his outstretched form as if to relay a message from the radiant disk.

A picture came to him: a low and ancient rectangular wall just two bricks high . . . and on each of the top bricks, a little mosaic . . . and set inside the wall, a tiled floor, a terrace, with a mosaic depicting a large white-and-black bird that soared above a marsh of reeds and water lilies—and a snake.

He asked himself where this place could be, but now the shadows shook and swayed as if to usher the picture away, as if to say he had seen enough.

· ✦ ·

To allow Dante to savor his first takeoff, Alison didn't speak as their plane taxied, nor through the roar, rattle, and thrust of its ascent from O'Hare into the cloudless sky.

"Your thoughts?" she asked when the plane leveled off.

"Just thinking that a bird can take in everything from up here. The good and the bad. And just the quiet . . ."

"That will change when we get to Cairo. It's a bustling city, more so than Chicago even. I know you'll fall under the spell of Egypt. What am I saying? You already have. But remember, you must always follow my lead on this trip. You've graduated, but you're still a few months shy of eighteen, so you'll need to follow my orders, if I have to give any."

"Okay."

"Otherwise, your job is just to discover. And to let me know if anything's bothering you."

He nodded.

"Before I forget, do you have my cell number in your phone?"

"I didn't bring a phone. I just have my laptop. Nora's expecting me to write. To start a blog."

"Good, you should. Now, you'll be around journalists the whole time this week. It's a working cruise for all of us."

"Okay."

"It won't be all work, though. And that's what I love most about traveling. The unexpected. Like this one time, years ago, I was walking around the French Quarter in New Orleans and heard this music—like nothing I'd ever heard before. I followed it and found a woman on the street playing a contrabass flute, this enormous instrument comprised of nearly ten feet of tubing. Well, it must have been in the upper nineties that day, and just as humid, but she seemed above it, making this gorgeous music. Her playing made me look at my instrument and its possibilities in a new way. And inspired me to do a little composing, too. To experiment with a freer style."

"Like what you played at your condo, after you played 'Mr. Tambourine Man'?"

"You noticed that, did you? Well, I once made an ambitious attempt to score an opera. But the librettist and I had creative differences, as they say. His libretto turned out to be, well, turgid." She laughed. "But I'm fond of a lot of the newer operas out there.

There's *Moby-Dick*. There's *Ainadamar*, about the poet Federico García Lorca. We did *Doctor Atomic* a while back at the Lyric. All such imaginative works. Their staging and set designs, too. I'm hoping we'll do a Philip Glass one of these days."

"He did one about Egypt. About Pharaoh Akhenaten."

"Yes. You know it?"

"I've seen clips. It's pretty cool."

"Well, I love that opera is a dynamic form, evolving—"

"There's *Hamilton* now . . ."

"You see? Anyway, that's the magic of traveling. To just drop into a new world and let it hit you—its sights and sounds, its people. And maybe discover something unexpected about yourself, too. . . . Right?" she prompted, hoping he trusted her enough to open up, even a little.

"I hope so," he answered, willing himself to smile.

When she saw his eyes begin to well up, she decided not to press him. She reached for a magazine in the seat pocket.

"I guess you talked with Grandma," he said. "About the pictures I get. And that she thinks something's wrong with me."

"She wanted me to know a little bit about you because, well, you're away from home for the first time. But your sister told me you're a thinker, and that's good, and that's why you're on this trip. The pictures—well, there are things in life we don't understand. But if you want to talk about them, or about anything, it's okay."

He nodded, but she sensed that it might not be the pictures that troubled him as much as the loss of his mother and father. Or perhaps it was both. Seeing his reticence turn to embarrassment, she opened the magazine.

"Grandma probably told you I'm not sure about going to college this fall, too."

"She did. She said you were accepted at some good schools."

"I guess I don't see the point in going if I don't know what I want to study. What you said about New Orleans—that makes me think that waiting is the right thing to do."

"I guess you have a couple more weeks before you have to notify the schools," she said. "I like to tell my students to try to imagine who they'd like to be, if that helps. It will come. Anyway, I'd just like you to have confidence in yourself."

"I'm confident about the things I see."

He wanted to say more, to tell her at least about the puzzling archaeological images he had been seeing, hoping she might know what they meant or explain why he even got them. But how could she? Would she think he was making things up? Or that he was broken somehow? He decided to reveal an innocuous picture that had come to him earlier.

"On the way to the airport, I got a picture of a man in a gray sweatshirt that said *Columbia University* in blue letters. And it had a coat of arms and some words in Latin. We'll see him. That's how it works."

"Okay." She was relieved that it wasn't something disturbing. *It's a start*, she thought. "Your sister told me you saw the carved bird in my apartment, too."

"Yes, I did."

"Having premonitions may be out of the ordinary, but I wouldn't look at it as something wrong with you. Ah, here come the beverages," she announced, grateful for a moment to ponder his prediction about the man in the sweatshirt and the concept of foretelling in general. She recalled that his grandmother had dismissed his stories. *Are he and his sister acting out an elaborate game, perhaps to compensate somehow for the loss of their parents? No matter,* she concluded, *I like their spirit.*

As she began a toast to the start of their trip, a man several rows ahead stood up and removed his jacket, revealing a gray sweatshirt. She craned her neck to see the front of it, then whipped her head around to Dante, who looked back with a wry smile.

"How often does this happen, for heaven's sake?"

"It depends. Mostly the pictures don't mean much. I mean, they don't change anything. Nora says we should play the lottery. But I don't see numbers, so I guess whatever I have is pretty useless."

"Well, I think it's probably not useless. We all seem to have the ability to sense things, I suppose. And feel one another's emotions. But what you can do is . . . so vivid. Well, I'm speechless." She shook her head and joked, "Maybe you're just wired more efficiently."

"Or, maybe it's something in the air," he offered. "Something I pick up."

"Some say it's the heart that has the most to do with it," she mused. "Anyway, I've been thinking again about your school paper, that part where you translated Dylan's verse into hieroglyphs. Your grandmother told me your father liked the words, but what do they mean to you?"

"I like that it's about getting away. I like the images in it."

"Right. Of dancing under a starry sky. And of the sea and the sands. But, that hieroglyph you drew of the heavy-looking stone . . . ?"

He didn't respond.

"Well, it was next to Dylan's verse about memory and fate," she prompted. She saw that the question troubled him. "Just one more question, okay? Do you ever feel down, or lonely?"

"No. Grandma says I should be more outgoing—she's always telling me to go outside and do something. But I am doing things. Just not what she thinks they should be. . . . I've been thinking about all the relics at the Tribune Tower."

"Okay."

"Each one got there through a different path, and each one had to have passed through a lot of different hands, over a long time."

"You've reminded me of that poor man who tried to sell that brick from Hillwood."

"I got a picture of it, Alison. I got it that morning I went on the

First Lady with you last year, before we saw it in the display case. It has a mark on the bottom, a roman numeral one, or a capital *I*. I didn't mention that part to you."

"I noticed it on the drawing you made for me. I did wonder how you could've seen the bottom. Are you saying you saw the brick in, like, three-sixty?"

"Yes. It's there. As plain as the footprint Robinson Crusoe saw in the sand."

"Right. Any idea what it means?"

"Sometimes I wish the pictures came with captions," he said after a moment. "Anyway, I guess even things that aren't alive can communicate."

"Indeed."

Someday, I'll check with Dyllis about that mark, she told herself, though she had no doubt now that Dante was right.

"I want to collect something from each wonder on this trip," he said.

"Well, whether it's in the form of a souvenir or a memory, something will speak to you."

"Something already has. That brick." He turned to look out his window at the daytime moon, imagining it becoming the moon-disk crown of Thoth, who the ancient Egyptians believed accompanied Ra across the night sky. He recalled the teasing city moon that had messaged him earlier through the trees' shadows. He hoped it would offer more where he was going.

Thoth might communicate in a different way, he thought. *And if he does, he will do it forthrightly, not with shadows.*

· ✦ ·

Dante felt the plane turn and begin its descent to New York's Kennedy Airport for their connecting flight to Cairo. He pointed to the Statue of Liberty just below Manhattan's southern tip, telling Alison that it resembled the Colossus of Rhodes, which people had visited for hundreds of years even after an earthquake toppled it.

"It's hard to believe there's nothing left of it anymore," he said later as they taxied to their gate.

"Nothing left of what?" she asked.

"The Colossus."

"Oh, right," she said. She had been watching the man with the Columbia sweatshirt, admiring his thoughtful demeanor as he retrieved his bag. And when he glanced back before he walked toward the exit, she couldn't help but wonder, *Was he looking at me?*

· ✦ ·

After takeoff on their EgyptAir connecting flight, Alison pulled a bulky binder from her bag. "My lecture notes," she told Dante. "Aah, nothing concentrates the mind like having to lead a high-profile tour in a few hours." She flipped to her notes on the Great Pyramid. "I'd love to hear your thoughts on what I should highlight about the wonders."

"The ancient Greeks considered them to be sights that every traveler should see," he said. "You could start out by telling the guests that."

"True, they popularized the wonders way back in the third or fourth century BC, in the time of Alexander the Great. So I guess I'm not the first Seven Wonders tour guide. That takes some pressure off. All right, our first stop will be Giza, outside of Cairo. The Great Pyramid."

"Pyramid of Khufu. Or Cheops, as the Greeks called him."

"Good. The oldest of the Seven Wonders by far, and the largest. And the only one still standing. It's said that the stone cutting was so precise that a matchstick could scarcely fit between its massive blocks."

He suggested that she talk about the polished limestone casing stones that had once covered the pyramid but were later stripped off for building work in Cairo. And that a pyramid is the most stable architectural design, helping to explain why the tallest wonder had outlasted all the others.

"And Khufu's sarcophagus is inside," he said. "In the King's Chamber. Looters took everything else out, but it's still there, deep inside. A tomb with hundreds of tons of stone around it."

"You must go up and experience it. Are you claustrophobic?"

The question brought back his dim memory of the night he had heard his mother's screams and of a darkened space. He looked away.

"We can do this later if you want," she told him. "Unless you want to go over any of the others."

"The Hanging Gardens of Babylon," he said. "I like that it's the only wonder that's undiscovered. And that it was different from the other wonders—a huge private garden that King Nebuchadnezzar built for his wife, who was homesick for Persia."

"Princess Amytis," she said. "Imagine the beauty of the place, with its lush vegetation and water features, all towering above the Euphrates River. We'll have a Babylon expert coming aboard to talk to us about it. A Doctor Ali . . . something."

"He should know if the Hillwood Stone is from there, right?"

"You're persistent about that brick," she said. "You'll have an opportunity to ask him. Now, I forgot to tell you, when we get to the Mausoleum—*Mau-so-le-um*," she repeated, voicing the syllables in a playfully foreboding tone. "We may meet my reporter friend Dyllis there for lunch. It's not that far from where she works for CNN, in Istanbul. She wrote the story in the Trib about the Hillwood Stone, remember?"

"I can't stop thinking about that."

"Go on."

"There's more to it. More than what I saw at the Tribune Tower. That brick is connected to something bigger."

"Want to tell me?"

"I have to. Because it's going to be part of this trip somehow. A picture of a bird came to me last night, Alison. I want to call it a mosaic. The bird was white, with a black head, neck, beak, and feet, and black at the tips of its wings. And the mosaic was set into a walled, tiled terrace. The wall was made of bricks like the Hillwood Stone. And the bird's the same as the carving in your apartment, except that the one in my picture was in flight, over a marsh. From its markings, it has to be an ibis, the African sacred ibis."

"Well, that's a lot," she said. "But yes, the ibis is a marsh bird. Common in ancient Egypt. Not anymore, though."

"Do you think they were common in ancient Babylon, too?"

"I suppose they must have been, along the Euphrates and definitely in the marshes to the south."

"Alison, the ancient Egyptians had a major deity who was depicted with the head of an African sacred ibis. Thoth."

"Not to correct you, but I believe it's pronounced 'thohth,' not 'thawth.' Rhymes with oath."

"Oh."

"That's what the Greeks called him. I don't know what the Egyptians called him."

"It was something like Djehuty."

"You never cease to amaze me."

"He was the god who invented hieroglyphs and writing. You didn't see where I wrote about him in my term paper?"

"Of course I did. So where are we going with this?" she asked.

"I don't know, but like I said, there's a little wall around the mosaic. And it's made of bricks just like the Hillwood Stone."

"I see."

"So, is it Egyptian or Babylonian?"

"Well, neither culture is supposed to have had mosaics like that . . ."

"So, what does it mean? What am I seeing? And where?"

Alison pressed her fingers to her temples as she tried to recall a passage from a book she had read years earlier. She spoke haltingly, remembering only the broad themes of the passage: "The seasons come and pass . . . and ibises foretell the coming of storms . . . of gales. Men live and die."

She began brightly, but by the end her tone had darkened, though she tried to mask it.

"What's that from?" he asked.

"It's by a favorite author of mine. Bruce Chatwin. I guess he's talking about signs . . . the foretelling of things. As a young man in England, he felt an urge to go to Patagonia. He was intrigued by his grandmother's stories about a cousin who had lived there—a ship captain. He wrote about it in his first book. I was lucky enough to hear him give a talk way back. He was so wonderfully attuned to things. And, well, you remind me of him."

3

CAIRO AND THE GREAT PYRAMID

ROM HIS WINDOW, DANTE took in the great fertile fan of the Nile Delta until it faded into the horizon behind the aircraft's wing. *The African sacred ibis would have been plentiful there*, he told himself. *Papyrus plants, too, that the Egyptians made paper from and wrote on in hieroglyphs invented by Thoth. And somewhere there, maybe, the ibis mosaic.*

He dozed, and then awoke to see the broad blue stripe of a great river and the green stripes of farmland hugging its banks—three bands of color brushed across a canvas of desert tan.

"The Nile," he whispered.

As the plane banked, a sprawling beige and white city began to fill his window.

"We're above Cairo," he told Alison. He pressed his face to the window, trying to locate the Giza Plateau. "There they are. Nine pyramids. We're going there." He fixed his eyes on the largest and noblest of them all, the Great Pyramid. The Pyramid of Khufu.

"And now you're feeling . . . ?"

"Closer," he told her.

· ✦ ·

THE TAXI TOOK THEM into the city center, and although it was midday, it struck Dante that Cairo must have a permanent rush hour. When they reached Tahrir Square, Alison pointed to a domed, coral-colored building with a great arched entrance.

"The Egyptian Museum," she said. "Wait until you see what's packed inside that place."

"There's our Hilton across the square," said Dante.

"The hotel is a landmark," she told him as they walked through the lobby's alluring arcade of shops. "And it has this famous gathering place for Cairo visitors." She gestured at the Sherlock Holmes Pub. "Let's go in. We're meeting someone."

Seconds later, she was waving to a stylishly dressed man in his early thirties.

"Dante, meet Marshall Reyes. He's going to be on the cruise with us as tour director. He grew up in Chicago, too, and went to your high school, in fact. He was a hotel concierge and event planner before he moved to DC."

"I did weddings, parades, you name it," Marshall told Dante. "Including the Puerto Rican People's Day Parade. Chicago Pride Fest, too. In DC I'm still a concierge, when I'm not helping Alison plan her foundation's tours."

"We've been all over the world together," she said. "Anyway, Marshall was hired to help plan our wonders tour. He recommended me to do the lectures."

"Glad I could return the favor," he said.

"He's been working with the organizers for a couple of months, getting things ready for us."

"Well, I can't say I've had much input. I'll explain, but here's where we are right now. Our seven guests have arrived."

"From . . . let's see if I can remember," said Alison. "*Travel + Leisure, Condé Nast Traveler*, the Travel Channel. *The Travel Show* from the BBC. And one of the London papers—the *Independent*?"

"Right. Plus the *New York Times*, and a freelancer for those airline in-flight magazines. Two others are on their way from Germany."

"The big shots behind this tour," Alison told Dante.

"Right," said Marshall. "One's a baroness. She's an older lady, one of the tour's investors. Haven't met her, but she sounds cool. The other one, well—"

"Monica Deuss. We've spoken a few times on the phone. Do you find her, shall we say, difficult?"

"Difficult, yes. Also haughty, autocratic, miserable . . . I could go on."

Miss Deuss, he explained, had called him earlier to say she and the baroness would be arriving late, and she had threatened to fire him if the wonders shows and excursions didn't go without a hitch, even though he hadn't been in on the planning for most of them.

"I can get along with almost anyone, Alison, but this one's a piece of work. And it didn't help when I told her that most of the guests are skeptical about the cruise's viability. There's not much left of the wonders, after all."

"What did Miss Deuss say to that?"

"She was dismissive. She said something like, 'You can hardly be expected to understand the long view.' Then she told me to just do my job and not second-guess her."

"Sounds like you'll have your hands full."

"So will you, Al. You're considered staff too, remember. She mentioned you on the call this morning."

"How so?"

"Said you better deliver."

"Charming!" Alison laughed. "But what do you think she meant by the long view?"

"I know exactly what she meant. She wants to build a Seven Wonders resort. And it would have actual objects from the wonders, although it seems to be a work in progress. So, we can expect her to lobby the guests shamelessly to write positive reviews as free advertising for her cruise and her almost-resort. Are you ready for this?" he asked Dante. "Ever been on a cruise?"

"Just on the Chicago River," he said.

"On the *First Lady*, then, with Alison?"

"Yes."

"Then you know she'll make the wonders interesting. I will take care of the people part. They can be even more interesting."

"I told Dante's grandmother you'd help me look after him, Marsh."

"Got it. Then we'll be a team on this little adventure."

"What do I need to do?" asked Dante.

"Whatever the situation requires, bro," he said with a laugh.

"Okay, we're going to check in now," said Alison.

"See you tomorrow, then, at the reception."

"He speaks five or six languages," Alison told Dante as they walked. "He makes it his business to know things. Years ago I told him he'd make a good spy if he ever got tired of concierge work."

"What did he say to that?"

"'Too dull, I would think.'"

"I like him," said Dante as they passed under the Sherlock Holmes Pub sign.

"I knew you would," she said, tapping the detective's walking stick with her own.

· ✦ ·

AT THE RECEPTION FOR the guests the next afternoon, Dante tapped Alison's shoulder and said, "That's the guy we saw on the plane. The one you liked, with the sweatshirt."

"I believe it is," she said, suppressing a smile. He was wearing a blue blazer now, and with freshly cut salt-and-pepper hair, he looked younger. A boyish fifty-five, she decided. And now he was walking toward them.

"Didn't I see you guys on a flight yesterday? I'm Jasper James, from New York."

"Professor James?" said Alison, almost giddily. "You're giving the kickoff talk. I'm supposed to introduce you."

"Then you must be Alison Fine."

"Yes, and this is Dante, my student. And yes, I guess we might have seen you on the plane." Dante rolled his eyes. "What brought you to Chicago, Professor?"

"Just an archaeological seminar I didn't really dig," he quipped, taking a sip of his wine.

Alison smiled. "Sorry to hear that. So . . . would that be a *shard*-onnay you're drinking?"

"Why, yes," he groaned. "I guess that would explain its earthy notes. A pleasure to meet you both."

"The tour organizers sent me your résumé," she said, taking it from her bag. "Let's see, doctorate from Rutgers, professor of cultural anthropology now at Columbia—"

"Professor," Dante broke in, "have you heard of the Hillwood Stone?"

"Of course, although I gather its owner has never stepped forward to claim it. It's still in its case at the Tribune Tower, no?"

Dante nodded.

"Funny how objects like that turn up . . . objects of mysterious provenance." The professor surveyed the room. "Not uncommon. But that guy who tried to sell it—a Mister Mishky, as I recall— wasn't smart to take it to museums."

"Why?" asked Dante.

"Well, he would've had better luck selling it to a private collector or a dealer. Hah! They don't necessarily ask questions, do they?" he enthused, his voice rising. "Nope."

Dante smiled at Alison as the professor warmed to the topic, but then he noticed a man who was edging closer to them. He was struck by the man's reptilian features—the small, cold eyes and the sharp-tipped tongue that cut through his calculating lips. As he watched, the man brushed off two other guests as he tried to listen in.

"Do you happen to know if there's a mark on the bottom of that brick?" Alison asked the professor. "Like a capital letter *I*?"

Dante watched the eavesdropper move closer.

"Did you say an *I*?" the professor asked keenly.

"Yes, Dante thinks he's seen . . . no, he knows, there's a mark on the bottom of it."

"I didn't know that," said the professor. "If there is, that would be the mark of an organization called Ibis."

Alison and Dante looked at each other.

"What, you've heard of them?" the professor asked.

"No," she answered.

"Right, you couldn't have."

Dante tapped Professor James's arm to alert him to the eavesdropper, but he didn't react, seemingly lost in thought.

"Well," he said finally, "I don't know how you've come to believe that the Hillwood Stone has that mark, young man, but . . . Ibis," he repeated, shaking his head. "They acquired that, too? Remarkable. Are you sure about that mark?"

The professor didn't wait for an answer. "I've done casual research into Ibis over the years. They emerged during the Renaissance, a time of great collectors and collecting. They've been somewhat quiet in recent decades, but they're most certainly still active, still ruthless, still eager to acquire."

The eavesdropper gave him a disapproving look and began to walk away, then turned suddenly and approached.

"I see the professor is entertaining you with tall stories," he snapped in his British accent. "You speak recklessly, sir," he hissed. "Most indiscreet." His mouth settled into a steely smile. "I need to speak to you privately, Professor."

Professor James looked unfazed, if not delighted, by what he had sparked.

"Meet me over there," the man demanded, and walked off.

"Uh-oh," said the professor. "Ibis is a taboo subject, you see. They dislike publicity intensely. Anyway, it's interesting to see Doctor Peter Sackville here. I suppose he's advising the tour organizers in some way. He's an Egyptologist. From Cambridge. Also, my employer this summer. We're doing some research together at the university here."

They heard Sackville call.

"You better go," said Alison.

"Yes, to get my knuckles rapped."

"What just happened, Alison?" Dante asked, as Professor James left.

"Ibis," murmured Alison. "The beginning of a gale, maybe. I'm sure it's nothing."

And men living and dying, thought Dante, remembering Alison's words from Chatwin. He tried to make sense of it all: the orphaned Hillwood Stone, marked and broken; his picture of the ancient mosaic of an ibis; Professor James's revelations about a secret and ruthless organization of the same name; and now, the menacing Sackville, who had become unhinged at the professor's mere mention of it. He observed Alison's expression, one he hadn't seen before, one of apprehension, as if she, too, was trying to understand the unsettling exchange that had just occurred.

But he also saw her resolve. He knew she would try to shield him from any further brushes with the covert world that Professor James had described and that Sackville so chillingly embodied. *Yes*, he told himself, *Alison will act fiercely to protect me*.

He wished she wouldn't. If a gale was coming, and if it would bring answers, he wanted it to begin.

· ✦ ·

AS THE GUESTS MINGLED, a man wearing a white uniform and

holding a cap with gold braid "scrambled eggs" on its visor tapped a glass for attention. He looked to be forty years old and solidly built, and he was flashing a gleaming smile.

"Good afternoon, everyone! I am Captain Nikkos Nicolaides of the Greek cruise ship *Modestine*," he announced, "and I'd like to say a few words about our upcoming trip." After outlining the Seven Wonders itinerary, he apologized that the ship would not be calling at ancient Babylon.

"The Hanging Gardens have not been found among the ruins in Iraq," he said. "Also, it would be impractical to take *Modestine* across the desert."

He called on Professor James to give an overview of the wonders, which the professor was obliged to extend because the next speaker, Miss Deuss, had yet to appear.

She did not materialize, so after the professor concluded, the guests' chatter resumed.

"Marshall," said Alison, "would you introduce Dante and me to the guests? But let's just do a speed-greet. I'm a little tired."

Within minutes, they had met each of the seven journalists joining them for the tour. The last, and Dante's favorite, was the blunt, wry David Dickenson of the *New York Times*, who complained that he was on the tour only at the insistence of his editor.

"I'm going to try to give it substance, Mister Dickenson," said Alison.

"I don't doubt you on that," he told her. "I know your work. It's the marketing hype the organizers are throwing at us." He held up the tour's brochure and quoted a line from it. "'We're giving the wonders a *wow factor* they haven't had in more than *two millennia!*' All this 'wonders wow factor' nonsense, whatever that means." He looked around the room. "I suppose I could do a profile on the shadowy Monica Deuss. So where is she? Late for her own party," he scoffed.

"Let's pray that he never feels the need to skewer us," Alison said to Marshall as Dickenson walked away. "Listen, after that, I should probably go and polish my talk for tomorrow. We're going to excuse ourselves."

"You have to hang on for a few more minutes," Marshall said as he looked out to the lobby. "The baroness has just checked in. Miss Deuss shouldn't be far behind. Ah, it looks like the baroness is coming straight in."

Baroness Renate von Weber was in her mideighties. The willowy aristocrat wore a tailored navy suit with a pyramid-shaped brooch that featured a pharaonic head in gold and enamel. Her face was lined but handsome, her eyes intelligent, her silver hair worn up. Alison marveled at her gracious smile and effortless poise as she navigated her way through the room toward Captain Nikkos.

"Formidable," Alison intoned in her passable French.

"Beeindruckend," agreed Marshall in his perfect German.

"Take us to meet this woman, Marsh."

The baroness immediately pulled them into her conversation with Captain Nikkos, proclaiming the guests' good fortune to have such accomplished professionals as Marshall and Alison guiding the tour.

"So I believe that this tour must educate, enlighten, and inspire," she told them. "And that is why I have invested in it."

She turned her attention to Dante and began quizzing him about the wonders. He had the feeling she knew the answers, but he enjoyed the challenge. His answers impressed her, he assumed, because after each one she rewarded him with a robust pinch of his ear.

"Ach, I am enjoying this moment," she declared, as she seized a glass of champagne from the tray of a passing waiter. "Alison, I trust you will dazzle us with your knowledge in the week ahead. Dante, I see you are carrying a laptop. You must record your observations. And Marshall," she added with a sympathetic sigh, "do have patience with my companion, Monica Deuss." And with that, she bid everyone goodnight.

"Oh, she was marvelous," Alison said to Dante and Marshall as they walked to the elevators. "She must have descended from the pharaohs."

"Did you see her pin?" remarked Dante. "A pyramid, with a pharaoh's head."

"Fabergé," said Marshall. "Like the rest of her jewelry . . . which will soon be taken up to the ship by armed escort."

"Thanks for your help tonight, Marsh," said Alison, as she steered Dante to the elevator.

"Sorry, but you have one more obligation. I'm afraid the delicious baroness comes with a side of cold sauerkraut. That's her over there, at the desk. Monica Deuss."

"All right," sighed Alison.

"Excuse me, Miss Deuss," Marshall called to the tour organizer.

She turned and acknowledged Marshall with a distracted, "Yes?"

"I just wanted to introduce you to Alison and her student—"

"Oh, the tour guide," she said, forcing a smile as she inspected her duty-free handbags, scarves, and perfumes. The bell captain waited nearby with her array of Louis Vuitton suitcases.

Alison guessed that Miss Deuss was in her midthirties and was struck by her resemblance to the baroness, except that she seemed to have none of that grand lady's grace or wit.

"I want to review your notes with you tonight," she told Alison without looking at her. "Starting with that big pyramid."

"Can't we just meet in the morning?"

"No. We're doing the pyramid tour first thing tomorrow instead of in the evening. Come to my room tonight at eight o'clock." She nodded to the bell captain and was gone.

"If it's any consolation," said Marshall, "she's like that to all of her subjects."

"But why the change of schedule, Marsh?"

"Because I couldn't get tickets to the sound and light show for tomorrow night at the pyramids. By the time she authorized me to purchase them yesterday, it was too late. Sold out."

Alison shook her head and dismissed the encounter with Miss Deuss with a sweep of her stick. "Come to my room at seven and we'll order room service. Let's enjoy ourselves. It's on her."

· ✦ ·

ALISON HEARD A KNOCK on her door and hoped it wasn't Miss Deuss. She was relieved to see Professor James.

"I've come to apologize for earlier," he told her.

"Oh? Well, come on in. Dante and Marshall and I are about to enjoy some Egyptian fare. Join us."

"I couldn't help but overhear your conversation with Alison and Dante, Professor," said Marshall.

"Yes, I was pretty loud, wasn't I? That's what I want to talk about."

"About Sackville?" said Alison. "About how you pushed that odd little man's buttons?"

"Sorry. I hope it didn't upset you."

"Why did he take you aside?"

"To warn me that I should refrain from talking to you about Ibis, and that it would be unwise for me to mention them in my presentation. You could say it was just some friendly advice to not stir anything up, or you could put it down to professional jealousy. He doesn't like anyone knowing more than he does. But when he started pumping me for information . . ."

"So, you think he's connected with them?" asked Alison.

"Well, first let me give you some background." He explained that Ibis's collection of antiquities was thought to surpass anything in the world, but that no one knew for sure which area or period they specialized in. They had formed in Prussia under a different name, but had come to be known as Ibis when they shifted to a new base.

"Probably here," he said. "Roughly a hundred years ago. But not Cairo. Alexandria. That's my hunch."

"Where the ancient lighthouse was," said Dante.

"But who do you think they are, exactly?" asked Alison.

"Guessing their identities has been a parlor game for a long time. A Medici here, a Rockefeller there? I mentioned earlier that they've been quiet for quite a while. Frankly, there doesn't seem to be much left of them. Anyway, it's just a hobby for me. Most leads I've followed have gone nowhere."

"Why do you think they're dying out?" asked Marshall.

"Because when antiquities are discovered now, they can't just be carted away brazenly like in the old days. Think of how much was taken from Egypt and Greece and other countries by the old colonial powers. Countries now guard their national treasures. So I suppose Ibis just isn't a club anyone wants to join anymore. Well, I wanted to tell you all this because—to answer your question, Alison—I suspect there's more than meets the eye with Sackville."

"Wonderful."

"I'll be frank. I've suspected that he's one of their agents. Well, a buyer maybe, or a consultant. That's why I was baiting him earlier."

"Are we talking about black-market trading here? Antiquities smugglers?"

"Not necessarily, but they do have a history."

"You're not saying we're in danger, are you?" pressed Alison. "Because . . ." She looked at Dante. "You know, you've been cooped up all day with us. Why don't you and Marshall go down to the lobby and explore for a while."

Okay, they want to talk, Dante told himself as he put on his Chicago White Sox cap and walked to the door. But the professor's words had taken root. Already he felt drawn to Alexandria.

· ✦ ·

ALISON WAITED FOR THE door to close before finishing her thought. "Because I'm responsible for him."

"If I've overdramatized this thing, I'm sorry," said Professor James. "But it's too much to ignore now."

"What do you mean?"

"That mark you told me Dante imagined he saw on the Hillwood Stone—the letter *I*? Well, I've known Sackville for a decade and he's never objected to me speculating about Ibis. But now that we know the brick is from their collection, they won't want that to get out. Especially if one of their agents was involved in Mishky's death."

"Good grief," said Alison. "Well, I certainly don't plan on talking about it. But how do you think that brick fell out of the hands of the mighty Ibis and into the lowly Mister Mishky's?"

"Beats me. But I suppose Sackville will be keeping an eye on me now."

"I don't like where this is going. That would mean he's interested in us, too, Dante and me."

"I don't think you need to worry. But, tell me, what's the deal with Dante? He seems very deep . . . I mean, the way he seems to know things."

"You're right, Jasper. And I'm learning more about him exponentially since we left Chicago. Sometimes he can, well . . . foretell stuff. Don't look at me like that. He doesn't understand it either."

"I'm skeptical."

She told him that Dante had foretold that they would see him on the plane and that he had pictured the Hillwood Stone in the Tribune Tower lobby, where he'd never been before. And that he had also pictured a mosaic depicting an ibis and believed the brick was connected to it.

"So, precognition," said the professor. "Impressive. I'd like to ask him about that mosaic, and the mark he imagined on the Hillwood Stone."

"Only if you don't ever discuss him with Sackville. And by the way, he doesn't *imagine* he saw the mark. He knows it's there. He's dealing with some things, Jasper, and keeping a lot to himself. So I don't want you to push him."

"Right. You know, if I didn't have this consulting job with the university, it would be fun to tag along with you guys on your cruise. Here's my card. If you want to stay in touch, I'd like that."

"I would, too."

· ✦ ·

IN THE LOBBY, MARSHALL noticed that an Egyptian boy had struck up a conversation with Dante. The boy, a year or two younger than Dante, was wearing a cap with the logo of a Cairo soccer team. A moment later, the two had traded hats and were walking toward him.

"He knows about Chicago," said Dante.

"White Sox, Bulls, Obama," said the boy, with an engaging grin. "Salaam alekim. I am Medhat. Please call me Med."

"Ahlan wa saalan, Med. I'm Marshall."

"Med's father has a shop in the old city," said Dante. "He wants us to visit."

Med handed Marshall an embossed card printed in Arabic on one side and English on the other. "Giza-Saqqara Trading Company," he declared. "Gifts and Antiquities."

"We'll see if we have time tomorrow," said Marshall.

"I will come to the hotel at three o'clock and take you," said Med. He wrote on another card and handed it to Dante. "This cell phone number is mine. I always have my phone for business."

· ✦ ·

IF THAT HILLWOOD STONE belongs to Ibis, thought Alison, *Dante is going to drill into the whole thing. I need to stay ahead of him. If I only can.*

She called her friend Dyllis Kirby in Istanbul.

"I'm so glad you answered, Dyl."

"A good reporter is always accessible. Has your tour started yet?"

"Just. I'm in Cairo with one of my students, and I won't sleep until you verify something. Do you remember the story you did years ago in Chicago, about the Hillwood Stone and the death of the guy who tried to sell it to the Trib?"

"My first byline."

"Do you remember if it had any markings on it?"

"Well, yes, it had a glob of some sort, on the bottom. Resin, or wax."

"With a mark? A letter *I*?"

"That's right. Why?" She heard nothing for several seconds. "Alison?"

"Oh, Dyl, I'm just a little stunned. My student told me he saw it. And I've just learned that there's a secret organization that marks their acquisitions with it. And there's a creepy guy here named Sackville who may belong to them, and I'm with a kid who sees things that other people don't, and I'm already not lovin' my boss much. Otherwise, everything's just wonderful—"

"Hey, slow down. What's going on?"

After filling Dyllis in, Alison concluded, "So my student is drawn to that brick. And he was captivated by what the professor told us about this Ibis organization. . . . I'm fearing the worst about this, Dyl. Sackville knows we know the brick belongs to Ibis, and they don't want anyone to know that. I just think my student might open up a can of worms."

"Well, that's what you get for mentoring precocious kids," said Dyllis. "Seriously though, that's the first I've heard of Ibis. Their existence isn't far-fetched, I suppose. But your student seeing the mark? That's weird, Alison. The Hillwood Stone went straight into a display case after Mishky's death, when this kid would have been, what, three or four years old? How could he have seen that mark?"

"Long story. Let's just say Dante's no ordinary precocious kid. But this Ibis really concerns me."

"Is someone threatening you?"

"Nothing like that. But Mishky died under suspicious circumstances, you remember. I think the professor suspects that his fall from his motel balcony wasn't an accident. I can't imagine what may be in play here."

"Listen, get some sleep. I'll do some checking into Ibis."

"Okay, but I'm counting on your discretion."

Alison took comfort in having Dyllis as an ally, but worried that her probing might stir things up every bit as much as Dante's. *What have we gotten into?* she wondered.

It was past time to heed Miss Deuss's summons to go over the notes for her talk, so she decided to have the pages delivered to the woman's room instead. That done, she checked in on Dante, turned off her phone, and fell into a fitful sleep.

· ✦ ·

IN THE MORNING, ALISON met Dante, Marshall, and the guests in front of the hotel for the bus that would take them to the Giza Plateau and the Great Pyramid. As Alison approached the bus, Miss Deuss took her aside.

"I read your notes," she told her. "I need you to punch it up."

"Can you be more specific?" said Alison. "The content? My delivery? What sort of punch are you looking for?"

"Just make it interesting," she snapped. "And the next time I tell you to meet with me, show up."

Once the guests were seated on the bus, Miss Deuss picked up a microphone. "So we begin our journey to the pyramid this morning," she bellowed over some ear-piercing audio feedback. "So we go, into the very dawn of civilization." She pointed east, to the rising sun. "Right into the dawn," she declared with a flourish, even though they would be driving south, then west.

The baroness, looking pained, stared out her window.

"Oh, and an entertainment will greet us at each site," Miss Deuss continued. "A stunning visual display or reenactment that will bring each wonder to life."

This was met with mild interest, but when she made a blatant pitch for favorable reviews, the guests became so visibly turned off that even she sensed it. When David Dickenson barked, "Foul," she handed the microphone to Alison with a petulant, "Here, you talk to them."

"Thank you, Monica," Alison whispered, "I won't need the mic."

She smiled at Dante and began.

"Who was Pharaoh Khufu, this man who reigned for more than two decades in the Fourth Dynasty, forty-five hundred years ago?" She noted the irony that the sole likeness of the man, whose monument is the largest pyramid, is a carved ivory statuette just three inches tall, the smallest of any Egyptian royal.

"Well, this little seated Khufu," she continued, "was not found in his pyramid, but at a temple necropolis at Abydos to the south of here. In nineteen hundred and three. And it's said that it was discovered headless, and that the archaeologists sieved through debris for several weeks until they found his tiny head."

"I hate to admit it," said David Dickenson to Michael Scott of *Condé Nast Traveler*, "but I think I learned something."

"Anyway," said Alison, "the statuette is now in the Egyptian Museum here. It begs the question: Where are his tomb treasures? They must have far surpassed those found in the tiny tomb of the boy pharaoh Tutankhamun."

Dante wondered what Ibis might possess of them.

As the bus pulled into the lot at Mena House, a luxury hotel at the edge of the Giza Plateau, Alison concluded, "We're going to stop here for refreshments and let you contemplate that view of the pyramids. Just imagine how the Great Pyramid would have looked out there by itself, with the highly polished white limestone casing stones that once covered it. Imagine it gleaming in the sun. Imagine it in the moonlight . . . and those casing stones would have made it another thirty-five feet or so taller. Over the centuries, most of them were removed and used for building work around Cairo."

Alison had insisted on the stop at Mena House to set the mood. Earlier in the year, on a call, she had objected to Miss Deuss's gaudy ideas for "an entertainment" at the Great Pyramid, arguing that the guests would be better served if they saw the pyramids' renowned sound and light show instead. She had prevailed, but now there would be no show and she would have to try to compensate for it.

Her narration flowed on as the bus left Mena House, but Dante heard little of it. His eyes were fixed on the Great Pyramid's massive, sloping sides. The one facing the morning sun was brilliant, almost buoyant. The one facing north was in shadow, ominous and heavy. The great monument seemed to him at once welcoming and foreboding. Either way, he reckoned, he was in the heart of ancient Egypt, and this would surely bring him closer to understanding the beguiling pictures he had been seeing.

But directly before him as the bus parked was the Great Sphinx, whose expression made him wonder if anything would be revealed here at all. Still, Alison's words about encountering the unexpected gave him hope that something like what had happened to her in New Orleans might also happen to him.

He cast his eyes back to the bright eastern face of the Great Pyramid, where the three smaller Queens' Pyramids stood in a row. The tallest of them was one hundred feet high. *Impressive*, he thought, *but tiny next to Khufu's, which rises five times higher.*

In the visitors' lounge, Miss Deuss announced that she was in talks to produce a line of "upscale" wonders souvenirs that her guests and all of their readers would be "eager to own." He heard them snicker, then dismiss her calls to climb up inside the pyramid to Khufu's burial chamber.

"Done that," said one.

"When I was a lot younger," added another.

"My legs still ache from it," joked another.

A worried look came over Miss Deuss's face as she watched them open their notepads and laptops, or simply stare off.

Alison filled the silence with the story of Aida, the captured Ethiopian princess who fell in love with the Egyptian captain Radamès. "Verdi's opera premiered in Cairo in eighteen seventy-one," she said. "It was enthusiastically received. The costumes and sets were astonishing. It was a triumph—"

"Then, let's do a camel ride," Miss Deuss broke in. "I'm afraid tickets were sold out for the sound and light show tonight. Marshall dropped the ball," she lied. "So, I guess I should tell you we'll be leaving for Alexandria tonight instead of in the morning."

"Nice planning," mumbled a guest. "If all you have for us here is a camel ride, I'd rather get some work done."

"Or return to Mena House," said another. "And not by camel."

Miss Deuss made a beeline to Alison, but Alison held up her hand before she could speak.

"We need to write this one off, Monica. Let them do their jobs. Don't make things worse."

"As long as we're here," Dickenson barked, "someone should take Dante inside that pyramid."

"I'll do it," said Marshall. "To make up for dropping the ball."

Dante and Marshall were first in the group behind the weathered Egyptian guide who would lead them through the pyramid's passages to Khufu's tomb. Dante took in the graffiti left by tourists of centuries past as he duplicated the guide's deft footsteps up the ancient steps and timbers of the Grand Gallery. When they reached the entrance to the King's Chamber, the guide invited Dante to go in first.

For a moment he was alone with it, the empty sarcophagus that once held the coffin of Pharaoh Khufu. It was as he had seen in photographs—a stark, unlidded trough carved from solid black granite. And even as it stood before him, empty and solitary in this chamber once filled with treasures, he could imagine the voices of the ancient workers who carved it there, and the chants of priests and sobs of royal mourners as Khufu's coffin was carried in.

But now, as the rest of the visitors entered, screams and shouts suddenly penetrated the chamber from the Grand Gallery below. "Just some boorish tourists," Marshall told him, but it intensified his childhood memory of helplessness and dread. He gasped for air. He felt himself fall against Marshall . . . then being carried down the cramped tunnel past the tourists, and being unable to block their chilling screams from his ears.

Outside at last, he opened his eyes and took the water Marshall offered.

"What happened to you in there? Are you okay?"

"Yes."

"I guess it was the closeness, then. Too many people?"

But he was too absorbed by the faces of the men and camels around him to reply. And as he watched the camels' hooves move in soundless pats that imprinted the sand and sent up puffs of dust into the air, he imagined the men and camels that must have borne treasures away from this and the other pyramids on the plateau, and from Babylon, too, long ago.

"Do you know the names of those?" he asked Marshall, pointing to the Queens' Pyramids as they walked back.

"I'm rusty, but that one, the most damaged one, I think is Queen Heteph—"

"No, the middle one."

"Oh, I'm thinking Queen Meritites," said Marshall. "That third one, the tall one, I can't remember." But he saw that Dante was taking a photo of the middle one, and that his eyes remained fixed on it even after they had passed.

Queen Meritites, Dante repeated to himself.

Back in the visitor's lounge, Marshall took Alison aside to tell her that Dante had fainted inside the pyramid. "Something got to him. He wouldn't tell me."

"Poor kid," said Alison. "I'm glad you were with him." She walked over to Dante. "You okay?"

"Yes."

"Claustrophobia . . .?"

"Partly, I guess," he answered, and headed to the bus.

· ✦ ·

"THAT'S ONE DOWN," SAID Alison as she walked with Dante and Marshall through the lobby of the Hilton.

"Six root canals to go," said Marshall acidly, his eyes following Miss Deuss as she marched past them alone to the elevator.

"Well, our train doesn't leave until seven thirty, so let's regroup here in the lobby later and explore the city a bit—just us. Maybe check out your friend's shop, Dante."

"Med said he'll be here at three."

· ✦ ·

ALISON POINTED TO THE Egyptian Museum across from the Hilton, telling Med, "We'd like to pop in there first."

Inside, she ushered the other three through the great wide halls lined with statues of pharaohs, priests, and scribes and through rooms filled with glass cases packed with jewelry, scarabs, and amulets. A mummified crocodile reminded her of Sackville, but she kept it to herself. After showing them the Tutankhamun rooms, she led them to a case that held the little statuette of Khufu.

"There he is," she said. "All three inches of him. Still, he has quite a presence."

"You can feel his power," said Dante. "Look at his expression."

"Right," said Alison. "Very austere. Pharaohs were depicted that way."

"I wonder what he was like, though, as a person, as a father."

"I'm guessing he liked kids," said Marshall. "He had twenty-four of them."

"Okay, guys, we're done here," said Alison. "Take us to your shop, Med."

The Giza-Saqqara Trading Company was on an antiques row of sorts. Carved deities, papyrus paintings, and books filled its front window. Inside, Med led them through the space, pulling on one ceiling-bulb chain at a time to light the way through the maze of tall cabinets. Upon reaching a large desk near the back, he asked them to wait, then disappeared behind a curtain into the family's living quarters. Soon, he emerged with his father, a compact man in his late thirties.

"I am Saad," said the man. "Welcome." He invited them to take a seat on the cushioned benches near his desk.

"Mister Saad," said Alison, "may I see some of your older pieces? Or some good-quality reproductions? Nothing too big to carry, though."

"That's specific," said Marshall. "I guess we're going to be here a while."

As Saad led Alison and Marshall to a bank of cabinets with packed shelves, Dante asked Med to take him around the shop. The boys disappeared into the semidarkness, where more bulbs waited to be switched on to illuminate the contents of still more cabinets.

Alison looked at Marshall, at once excited and overwhelmed by the number and variety of objects before her. She was relieved when Dante returned with Med. His expression told her he had seen something.

"That little statuette of Khufu?" he began. "I just saw its pair, I mean, companion. In my head . . . a picture. It's a woman, and she's in the same pose."

"So you think it's here?" Alison asked. "In this shop?"

"I think it must be."

"The real thing?"

"I don't know. But it looks like ivory. And it has a little inscription like the one on the Khufu statuette. It's chipped."

She turned to Saad. "Would you have a small statuette of a seated figure? A queen, maybe? It would be about three inches high."

Saad made his way to another part of the shop.

"What's going on?" asked Marshall.

"Patience," said Alison. "You'll see."

Saad returned with four seated figures of varying size, age, and quality and placed them on the Oriental rug that covered his desk.

"This one," said Dante immediately, pointing to the smallest figure.

"This one is very old," said Saad. "It is very good. It is maybe three thousand, in dollars."

Marshall cleared his throat. "A thou an inch."

"Oh, Mister Saad," said Alison, "I wasn't thinking of spending that much."

"Miss Alison, we would like you to have her. Two thousand five hundred."

Dante saw that she looked encouraged. He smiled, knowing she must have it.

"Well, I'm shaking," she said. "I will treasure her. She's extraordinary."

· ✦ ·

"JASPER," ALISON CALLED TO Professor James, as she swept into the Hilton lobby with Dante and Marshall. "I'm glad you're here."

"Just popped in to say goodbye."

"Well, wait until you see our little purchase."

The professor unwrapped the statuette, turned it over in his hands several times, and measured it with his pocket tape.

"Well?" she asked.

"I see some script in the same area as on the Khufu statuette that was discovered—"

"Yes, we know—" She turned, sensing someone over her shoulder.

"You've been shopping," said Miss Deuss. "Nice piece."

"Thank you," said Alison, as she took the statuette from Professor James and rewrapped it. "We were just heading up to my room. Excuse us."

"Where did you find this?" the professor asked as they rode the elevator up.

"In a shop in the old city. Dante found it. Well, pictured it."

"How much did you pay?"

"Twenty-five hundred."

Professor James shook his head.

"What?" she asked. "Too much?"

"If it's authentic, it's worth at least several hundred times that."

In Alison's room, the professor produced a big magnifying glass from his pocket. "You laugh, but it comes in handy," he said, and began to examine the piece. "Well, it's too bad that some of the hieroglyphs are missing from this chipped area. But the workmanship is fine. I'd need to study it, but from those three little remaining hieroglyphs, I'd say this is Queen Meritites. She was Khufu's first wife and was, of course, entombed in one of the little Queens' Pyramids."

Marshall and Dante looked at each other.

"The middle one," said Marshall. "Dante and I passed it this morning."

"How can you tell from those hieroglyphs it's her?" asked Dante.

Professor James explained that her name was represented by a grouping of hieroglyphs, including the three that were still visible on the statuette. Together, they meant "Beloved of Her Father."

"The warmth and intelligence of her expression seems modern," he said, "in contrast to the stylized expression of Khufu. So she doesn't seem to be from the same period. Still, she's very old," he concluded. "It's intriguing to speculate that Meritites wanted to break with tradition and possibly even designed it herself. Wouldn't that be remarkable? May I keep her for a while? I'd love to study her, to see if she's authentic."

"Well, I guess so," said Alison.

"Thanks. Out of curiosity, Dante, how did this statuette appear to you? And how did you come to see the mosaic, and the mark on the Hillwood Stone? Can you control this? Channel it at will? Do you think you can discern more about Ibis?"

Dante waited for the barrage of questions to end before answering. "The pictures just come, Professor. I can't turn them on and off." He walked to Alison's table and began a sketch of the statuette, unable to get the words *beloved of her father* out of his head.

After completing his sketch, Dante walked back and took several photos of the statuette with his camera. "Are you going to tell Doctor Sackville about her, Professor?" he asked.

"Why, yes, I think so. He's an expert."

"Good. But you need to keep her safe."

"All right then, boss."

"I don't know if it's such a good idea to tell Sackville," said Alison, "since you think he's with that Ibis outfit. Sackville," she repeated, making a face.

"Let's wrap her up," said Professor James. "Now, don't worry. I'll keep her safe. You guys just enjoy the cruise. I'm jealous," he added as he left.

"Fellas," said Alison, "we have a train to catch."

· ✦ ·

Dante finished packing and then checked his email. Med had written to say that he would be visiting his uncle's farm in the Nile Delta, and would Dante like to meet up in Alexandria if he had time? Intrigued, Dante googled the train route they would be taking through the Delta, then clicked through various articles about Egyptian culture. Remembering Alison's talk earlier, he paused to read about Verdi's opera *Aida* and its Ethiopian princess taken prisoner during a war with Egypt. A line from the libretto struck him:

> *The fatal stone now closes over me.*

He closed his laptop, recalling the terror he'd felt in the pyramid's dark chamber—how it brought back the night at home long ago that he could remember only faintly.

He walked to Alison's room with his suitcase and caught the end of a call between her and Professor James.

"You mentioned the statuette to Sackville, Jasper?" she chided.

"Yes, and I could feel him drooling over the phone. Could this get the great Ibis stirring?"

"You shouldn't have done that."

"I couldn't resist a little mischief. Don't worry. I played the old snake like a fiddle."

"Be careful what you wish for, Jasper. Nile asps bite, and fiddle strings can break. No, you shouldn't have done that."

Listening, Dante felt recharged by what Professor James had put in motion—and relieved that it took his mind off the dark memory that still gripped him.

4

—

Night Train to *Modestine*

"IT'S A THREE-HOUR RIDE to Alexandria," Marshall announced to the guests as they boarded their train at Cairo's Ramses Railway Station. "And with the full moon, we'll get some nice views of the Delta."

"And be on the ship before eleven," said Captain Nikkos.

"You seem distracted," Marshall told Alison after taking a seat with her and Dante.

"I can't take my mind off what Professor James told that Sackville."

"And off Professor James in general?" he teased. "I'm picking up vibes between you two. What do you think, Dante?"

Dante smiled gamely but didn't answer.

"What's wrong?" Alison asked. "You feel okay?"

He nodded, then shrugged.

"I didn't think so," she said. "Were you sick earlier?"

"Kind of. But now, it's just . . . I'm a little woozy."

"Mild dysentery, maybe. You should be okay by the time we get to the ship."

The train pulled out of the station smoothly, and through its thick, pitted windows Dante watched the city glide past as if in a dream. He curled into his seat and dozed. But soon the train began to move erratically, as it would continue to do over the next long hours. He cursed the engineer under his breath. He wanted to sit up, but feeling queasy still, he gave up the thought and wedged himself even tighter into his seat.

In his restless malaise, thoughts emerged when the train ran smoothly, but were bumped away when it braked or bucked. A smooth stretch brought thoughts of Cairo . . . *Queen Meritites . . . beloved of her father . . . reptile Sackville—*

A sudden stop. But in time the train was moving rhythmically again . . . *Khufu's dark chamber . . . Princess Aida . . . the fatal stone . . . a figure in camouflage . . . a marble doorstop—*

A thunderous blast buffeted his window as a speeding train passed in the other direction. He covered his ears and curled deeper into his seat.

"Stop," he murmured later in his sleep. "Mama, don't scream."

"Easy," he heard Marshall say as the train coasted again . . . *the camels' quiet hooves . . . an ibis in flight . . . a constellation sky—*

A long locomotive whistle. *An all-clear or a warning?* he wondered. He lifted his head and looked out at the glimmering expanse of marshland, then fell into a wary half-sleep . . . *the Delta's tall reeds at dawn . . . an ibis watching, determining . . . a sudden potent energy—*

The vivid scenes of the Delta jolted him. Unlike the thoughts and impressions that had come to him earlier, these were pictures. He grew anxious, but the train quieted and he fell into an undisturbed sleep at last.

"Are we in Alexandria?" he asked when he awoke.

"We're close," said Alison, "but still in the Delta. We're more than an hour behind schedule."

"Why are we stopped?"

"This time? Who knows? We've had engine problems the whole way. And maybe a crazy man driving this thing. We've been stuck here for more than half an hour."

He pushed up his window. The air smelled of the marshes and the sea—rich, briny, and complex. He breathed in slowly, feeling embraced by the Delta. And although he could make little sense of the rush of thoughts and images that had come, he had never felt so attuned. *Was Professor James right?* he wondered. *Can I be in command of this?*

"Arriving Alexandria in thirty minutes," a conductor called as the train began to move.

"You were pretty restless," said Alison. "What was going on in there, inside your head?"

"Just a mix of stuff. Just everything coming in and out. I don't know . . . I can't explain." He drew a deep breath and stretched. "I'm supposed to email Nora and Grandma. And start a blog."

"We can call when we get in. Now, try not to worry about all the things in your head."

The three sat quietly as the train moved slowly past a fenced area of the marshes, where Dante spotted a group of large birds wading. When one began to taxi, he smiled at its ungainliness, but his amusement turned to awe when the bird's enormous white wings powered it into the air. The bright moon revealed its distinctive markings—its black wingtips, tail feathers, head, neck, and legs, and its long, black crescent beak.

"It flies just like in the mosaic I've seen," he said. "Those are African sacred ibises."

"So they are," said Alison. "What are you thinking?"

"That I'm glad the train is behind schedule, or I might not have seen them."

"What else?"

"That the one that flew up . . . It's almost like it knew I was looking at it."

· ✦ ·

IT WAS PAST MIDNIGHT when the train arrived in Alexandria.

"My dear," the baroness said to Alison, "Dante looks fragile. Ride with Monica and me to the ship."

"But, we have the bus—"

"And I have this," she said, pointing to a black limousine. "Otto," she said to the uniformed chauffeur who had approached. "This is Alison Fine and Dante, from our tour. And Marshall. Is there room for all of us?"

"Of course, ma'am," said Otto, a tall Egyptian man in his thirties.

"But I should help load the luggage," said Marshall.

"The bus driver has a man doing that," said the baroness. "Come."

"All right," said Marshall, "I'll just let the captain know."

But when he returned to the limousine, Miss Deuss thrust out an elbow, blocking him from getting in. "Not you," she told him. "VIPs only."

Inside, the baroness, who had not seen the slight, looked at Alison and Dante. "Why do you suppose Marshall changed his mind?" she asked.

"He preferred the bus," Miss Deuss sniffed as she got in. "And I should think Miss Fine and the boy would have as well."

Captain Nikkos, who had been watching, shook his head and waved Marshall over. "Never mind her. Jump on the bus with us."

When they arrived at the pier where *Modestine* was docked, Marshall gave the guests their cabin assignments.

"Bring my bags aboard first," Miss Deuss demanded of him as she walked up the gangway.

A grinning Captain Nikkos overheard. "Belay what you're thinking," he told Marshall, who had been looking at Miss Deuss's luggage and then to the water.

· ✦ ·

AFTER HELPING THE GUESTS settle in, Marshall found Captain Nikkos and made his report, including an account of Dante's tribulations on the train.

"He is okay?" Nikkos asked.

"I'm not sure, sir. He's still up. Out on deck somewhere."

"Very well. Now, you turn in. I'll muster him up."

Dante had been pacing off the length of *Modestine*'s main deck. At two hundred thirty feet, she was more a superyacht than a cruise ship, but she was still far bigger than *Chicago's First Lady*. He leaned over the railing and followed the sweeping white curve of her bow up from the waterline to his feet, then gazed at the colorful pennants waving from lines that rose up from her second deck to her superstructure. Belowdecks, her auxiliary engines vibrated expectantly.

"This living ship," he said aloud.

"You find her agreeable?" Captain Nikkos asked.

"Yes, sir. But why *Modestine*? Because she's small?"

He told Dante that she was named for a literary creature—one he called noble and intelligent.

"An elephant," Dante guessed.

"A donkey!" Nikkos proclaimed. "Modestine, you see, was Robert Louis Stevenson's companion when he was a young man hiking in the mountainous Cévennes in France. He became very attached to that donkey. I insisted on the name when I was offered this command. Come with me."

He led Dante up to the second deck and through a passageway close to the bridge.

"Officers' quarters," he said. "But since we didn't need a full complement of officers for this little cruise, this cabin is yours. There's a copy of Stevenson's *Travels with a Donkey in the Cévennes* there on the shelf, if you're interested. We'll see you at breakfast."

Dante decided to visit Alison before turning in. Her door was open.

"And if Monica the VIP ever jabs me with her elbow like that again," he heard Marshall tell her, "she'll get something a lot sharper back."

"He's referring to his serrated tongue, Dante," said Alison. "Come in."

Marshall told them he had thought hard on the pier about having some or all of Miss Deuss's Louis Vuittons fall quietly into the harbor.

"I can't believe the baroness has a chauffeur and limo here," said Dante. "Just to drive her a couple of miles to the ship."

"I asked her about that when I was showing her to her cabin," said Marshall. "She told me she has a winter cottage here. Must be nice."

"Otto seemed more like a peer of hers than a chauffeur, somehow," said Alison.

"I agree," said Marshall. "He seemed a little too polished. Anyway, I'm going to bed. Remember to call Chicago. It would be late afternoon there now."

Nora answered on the first ring. "Why haven't you emailed?" she scolded Dante. "We had a deal. What are you doing over there? Nothing, I guess."

"What's the latest on my blog site?"

"Grandma and I got it registered for you. I'll email you the details."

"Okay. Let me speak to her."

She told him that Grandma had gone out, and then paused, knowing she needed to put her next words to him carefully.

"Once you start your blog, maybe Papa might see it."

"I told you, you need to let that go. I don't care about him."

"Well, I do. . . . So, do you want me to research anything for you?"

He asked her to find out if any statues of Queen Meritites existed, and where the African sacred ibis lives.

"I'll work on those," she told him. "Now, do your end. Bye."

He said goodnight to Alison and headed back up to his cabin, hoping that the stream of impressions that had come to him on the train would begin to make sense.

Now, as he surveyed the broad harbor, he thought of Alexander the Great, of Anthony and Cleopatra, and of Napoleon. *They all stood here, too*, he thought. *They observed, and planned, and acted.* Looking to the east, to where the ancient lighthouse once directed its beacon out to sea, he marked the moment.

"I will look at the vague things, and the dark ones, too. I will aim myself at them. . . . It's the key, somehow, this business of Ibis."

He hoped his writing, if he could begin, might organize his thinking. He had a hunch it might illuminate the way.

As he approached the door to the officers' quarters, a vertical steel ladder attached to the bulkhead caught his eye. He stepped back and saw that it led to the ship's radars and antenna masts on the topmost deck. It rose up nearly three times his height.

Do it, he told himself.

He grasped the ladder and climbed the first few steps, then five more. Then another five, slowly, until his head was even with the top rung. He willed himself to take another step, not looking down, then pulled himself up and through the arched ladder top onto the deck.

They're still, he told himself, looking up at *Modestine*'s moonlit radars and antennas. *Their powers are dormant just now, but they'll soon awake, like mine.* He lay down, watching them, until a Delta zephyr and the predawn chatter of unfamiliar birds lulled him to sleep.

· ✦ ·

DANTE AWOKE FEELING THE sun against his eyes and *Modestine*'s steel deck against his bones. Above him, the radars and antenna masts loomed. From somewhere below, loud voices and laughter pelted his ears.

He raised his head and looked down to the breakfast buffet that had been set up near the pool. All of the guests were there with Alison, whose head was tilted back, her eyes closed, enjoying the sun. But when she opened her eyes, her blissful smile turned into a horrified gasp.

"What the—?" she hollered, pointing. "Help him!" she called to a passing officer.

In seconds, the officer's ruddy face appeared before Dante at the top of the ladder. It was framed by ginger hair and whiskers and supported by broad shoulders that displayed two gold bars each.

"You're not supposed to be up here," the officer told him in his Irish accent. "Only I am supposed to be up here. You see the sign? What does it say?"

"Restricted Area, Mister—"

"Lieutenant Regan."

"I didn't see it. It was dark."

"You've been up here all night?"

"Yes, sir."

"Why?"

"I fell asleep."

"I'm asking why you went up, not why you didn't come down."

"To see if I could make it to the top," he answered earnestly.

"Oh, a comedian."

"No—I didn't mess with anything."

"Well, come on, then, come to the ladder."

"What on earth, Dante?" Alison gasped after they descended, her eyes darting between the two.

"Lieutenant Regan, ma'am. Ship's communications officer. The young man did some exploring last night. Best if we disperse now. Captain will be taking breakfast soon. You're lucky he didn't see this."

"I went up to test myself," Dante told her. "And to see the antennas and stuff."

"Those radars could have fried you alive if they were on!" she cried.

"Sorry."

"Okay, just come and have breakfast."

"I want to check my email," he told her. He was thinking about his own radars and antennas, thinking that he might have something to say, and that he would begin.

· ✦ ·

DANTE FOUND THREE EMAILS from Nora in his inbox. In the first—subject line "Meritites"—she wrote that the queen was Khufu's first wife, but that there were no known statues or images of her.

In her second email—subject line "African Sacred Ibis"—she wrote that the bird ranged throughout Africa below the Sahara and was also present in the marshes of southeastern Iraq. And she confirmed what Alison had said, that there had been no reported sightings in Egypt for more than a century.

"But I saw them from the train," he said aloud. "One looked back at me like Thoth himself. Why were they there?"

Nora's last email provided a link and a password to the site that she and Grandma had registered for his blog. Its subject line read, "Now Begin."

Now I have to, he told himself when he opened the link and saw that she had set up his home page. He stood and paced, unsure of what to say first.

The book Captain Nikkos had mentioned caught his eye. He read the first pages, then began.

> I am on a Seven Wonders cruise aboard *Modestine*, a ship named by our captain for a donkey that Robert Louis Stevenson traveled with as a young man. Stevenson wrote, "But we are all travellers in . . . the wilderness of this world—all, too, travellers with a donkey; and the best that we find in our travels is an honest friend. He is a fortunate voyager who finds many."

> Already, I have found seven honest friends.

He named Alison, Marshall, Captain Nikkos, Professor James, Med, and David Dickenson of the *Times*. He wrote that *Modestine* was the seventh.

Next, he described his exploration of the ship the night before and his admiration of her, even though they had not yet been to sea.

> *Modestine* is like Stevenson's donkey—beautiful and strong, comfortable and brave. Her radars and antennas are alert, keen, and knowing—like a donkey's splendid ears.

He added the tour itinerary and then, under the heading *What Struck Me in Giza*, began to describe his episode in Khufu's chamber. But his sentences wrapped around themselves, leading nowhere and answering nothing about what had struck him inside the chamber, inside himself. He knew only that the screams had triggered the dark memory again.

He deleted the paragraph and began to sketch the pyramid instead. This came easily. He drew it serene and vibrant, dark and bright, ancient and eternal. He added a kinetic sky. He added the north face portal—*an access and an outlet,* he told himself, *an experience.* In the foreground he drew the Khufu statuette at actual size and, to recognize Meritites, added the three Queens' Pyramids. He labeled the drawing *Pyramid of Khufu,* the name he preferred.

Now I introduce her, he decided.

> In Med's father's shop in Old Cairo, we found a statuette. I saw it in my head first, which sometimes happens. It was Khufu's queen, Meritites, and she resembles the ivory figure of Khufu in the Egyptian Museum. She is made of ivory, too, and is the same size as Khufu. Alison bought her. We have hopes that she is authentic.

He decided not to post the drawing of the statuette he had made in Cairo, or his photos of it, thinking Alison would object. Instead, he moved on to describe the train ride through the Delta.

> I had to tell myself I would survive it. I tried to think ahead to Alexandria and the Pharos—a light in the darkness and the storms for a thousand years—and that calmed me.

As we passed through the Delta, I saw birds that looked wise, and when one took flight it was powerful and graceful. They were African sacred ibises. In ancient Egypt, they were honored as reincarnations of a god called Thoth, who wears a crown with the lunar disk. He was the god of the moon and the night sky. He regulated the movement of the stars and planets and knew all the secrets of the skies. He was the god of wisdom and magic and mathematics, and he balanced the forces of good and evil. He was the tongue of Ra and the heart of Ra. And he invented hieroglyphs and writing. I think he may guide me on this voyage.

He posted his words, along with his drawing of the Pyramid of Khufu, and then emailed Nora, Alison, and Professor James that he had begun.

Because he had mentioned the statuette, he knew he would have another audience as well. Professor James would tell Doctor Sackville, and then someone in Ibis would surely read it. And while he had been careful not to refer to the organization by its name, he wondered how much the mere mention of the African sacred ibis might unnerve them.

At least I didn't mention the Hillwood Stone, he thought, *or my picture of the ibis mosaic and the wall the Hillwood Stone must have been part of.*

Still, he felt a tingling of anticipation that made his head light and his palms begin to sweat.

PHAROS
OF ALEXANDRIA

5

ALEXANDRIA AND THE PHAROS

"**M**AYBE THIS WHOLE THING was doomed from the start," opined Deirdre Rao, reporter for the *Independent*, to Torrie Benet of the BBC's *The Travel Show*.

The guests had gathered in the ship's lounge after lunch to hear Alison and Marshall outline the afternoon's schedule in Alexandria.

"I mean, how do you construct a tour around seven monuments, six of which aren't even there? And with the one that is, she blows it. I speak of Monica Deuss, Alison, not you."

"Well," said Torrie, "a couple of the other sites should be interesting. But the rest, not so much. I don't see this having broad appeal."

"You have to wonder if she could even find Egypt on a map," said Michelle Reinhart of the Travel Channel.

"I'm still waiting for the wow factor the brochure promised," said David Dickenson.

"Well, I'm beginning to look at it as an opportunity to work on my taxes," said Donna Miranda, the in-flight magazines freelancer.

"You have your job cut out for you, Alison," teased Deirdre.

Alison tried to smile. "You're going to be the judges," she told them. "Now, everyone, you have a couple of hours to yourselves. Please be at the gangway by three for our bus to the Pharos."

"Or the place it used to be," said Condé Nast's Michael Scott under his breath.

"Three o'clock," muttered Dick Stewart of *Travel + Leisure Magazine*. "Really? In this heat wave?"

Marshall noticed Miss Deuss hovering at the door, holding her cell phone to her ear.

"Fake call," he whispered to Alison as Miss Deuss left. "She was listening. This is a tougher crowd than she expected."

"Well, let's talk about something else," said Alison, turning to Dante. "I just read it. Your first post. Proud of you. And glad we're among the 'honest friends' you've met. But not the baroness?"

"I don't know yet. She's with Miss Deuss, right?"

"You have a reporter's healthy skepticism," said David Dickenson.

"I want whatever I write about to be fresh."

"The stories are out there," said Dickenson. "If you listen to your instincts, you might find that they come rather easily."

"I want that. Alison, I want to go into the city for a while. On my own. I need to, for my next post."

"No, of course. Not on your own. And Marshall and I have to prepare for the Pharos excursion."

"I'll take him," said Dickenson.

· ✦ ·

THE TAXI TOOK DANTE and Dickenson eastward, then up a narrow strip of land between the Western and Eastern Harbours to the Citadel of Qaitbay, an old fortress close to where the Pharos once stood. Next, it took them along Alexandria's waterfront Corniche, past the historic Cecil Hotel, out to the Bibliotheca Alexandrina, then back to a row of cafés and shops near the citadel and the harbor.

"We will take tea now," said Ahmed, their driver. "This café is very good. We can sit outside. But first, take this." He handed

Dante a cap with an Alexandria soccer team logo. "You must wear it here instead of your Cairo cap."

It warmed Dante that the people at the café greeted him with smiles, except for two men who took a table after parking behind Ahmed's taxi. He assumed they were tourists, perhaps from Europe.

"I'm heating up already," said Dickenson. "Go and look around, but stay close."

Dante walked along the row of shops to the end and then turned left, down an inviting side street lined with palm trees and privacy walls. He imagined himself an antenna attuned to the neighborhood's vibe.

I'll return soon, he mentally assured Dickenson as he continued down the seductive street.

Above the walls and through the tall palms, he could make out the tile roofs and top-floor windows of the handsome old villas. He turned left again, into a narrower street behind and parallel to the row of cafés and shops. The walls here were taller and, behind them, the villas larger.

He walked on until he reached the street's walled dead end, where several guards stood at the gate of the neighborhood's most imposing villa. It boasted a tower that shot up over the nearby shops, with windows that would have offered views of the citadel and the harbor. On the wall, a small cobalt-blue sign with white lettering read ANCIENT LIGHTS.

He had turned back, hearing only the sound of his footsteps, when a picture came: the mosaic again, but with a detail he had not seen before—a bright area, perhaps of glass. The ibis's eye.

He returned to peer into the villa's courtyard, where he felt the mosaic had to be, but a low hedge and the guards' admonishments prevented him from getting a clear view. His pulse quickened as he watched a car roll into the courtyard and its driver walk into the villa. It was Otto. He was sure of it.

He ran back to the café.

"Mister Dickenson is angry with you," Ahmed told him. "We could not find you."

"Where is he?"

"Over here," Dickenson called from the taxi.

"He was dizzy from the heat," said Ahmed as they walked to the car.

"Where were you?" barked Dickenson. "You have a nose for news, apparently, because you look like you've discovered something."

"I saw—"

"Don't tell me, or I'll write it first. If it's worth reporting, you'll write it and I'll read it."

"Do you know who lives in the big villa at the end of the street behind us?" Dante asked Ahmed.

"No. But on that street, a rich man."

Dante stared, unable to shake the fresh image of the mosaic and frustrated that he had failed to verify with his eyes that it was there. He found it intriguing that the villa, which was just blocks from the site of the ancient Pharos, had a tower that so resembled it and a name that echoed it.

"Get into the car, Mister Dante," said Ahmed. "I will take you back now. Are you listening?"

Dante was watching the two European strangers. Their shifty glances rattled him. Not having seen the mosaic upset him more.

"I have to use the bathroom first, Ahmed." He ran into the café and then out a back door into a walled garden, where he climbed onto a table and pulled himself up to the top of the wall. Across the street was the villa.

If I move forward about six feet, he thought, *I'll see past the palms into the courtyard. I'll see the white-and-black bird and its bright eye. And find out if it's a bas-relief, like those at Nebuchadnezzar's palace at Babylon, or a true mosaic. I'll see it set into a tiled terrace and sur-*

rounded by the low wall of bricks like the Hillwood Stone. I'll see it, real and whole at last.

"No!" he grunted as two SUVs pulled into the courtyard, obstructing his view of the terrace. He stood up, but the guards noticed and began running toward him. He saw only a spark of light from the terrace area between the parked SUVs before jumping down from the wall and running back to the taxi.

"Sorry, Mister Dickenson," he panted. "Sorry, Ahmed. Let's go."

During the ride back, he wrestled with what had happened. He had glimpsed the courtyard and sensed the presence of the masterwork it must contain. But the bright eye in the picture seemed to him out of character for an ancient work of art—and it was not that way in the picture of the mosaic that had come to him on the eve of the trip in Chicago.

Was my picture here warped somehow? he asked himself. *Will all of them be flawed instead of clearer here? No, I didn't imagine that spark of light.*

Either way, he decided, there was something there that honored the African sacred ibis, and someone inside the villa who did the same, someone probably more important than Otto.

· ✦ ·

FROM HIS QUARTERS IN the villa's guest house, Otto called Doctor Peter Sackville in Cairo.

"Do you have anything more on the ivory statuette the boy has blogged about?" he asked.

"The American professor has told me nothing more than what he has written," replied Sackville. "But it is intriguing."

"Obviously," said Otto, "or you would not be assigned to investigate."

"My two men followed him to a café near your villa today."

"Your men know about the villa?" Otto snapped.

"Of course not," Sackville assured him. "They just report on movements. They have no knowledge—"

"Keep it that way," Otto ordered. "Is there anything else they reported about him? Anything we can use?"

"No. Well, he may be interested in soccer. He wore an Alexandria team cap."

"All right," said Otto.

He ended the call and made another to his superior inside the villa.

· ✦ ·

THERE WAS A MESSAGE from "Gamaltiques" when Dante returned to the ship and checked his blog.

Mrs. Sara Gamal, a local dealer in antiquities, had written, "May I meet with you and Miss Fine before your departure from Alexandria? I would like to inspect your statuette. I represent an interested buyer."

"Well, I'm not interested," Alison told Dante when he showed her the message. "Anyway, we have the excursion to the Pharos now, if anyone can be bothered to come. And I want Professor James's opinion on the statuette first." She took out her cell phone. "And whether he knows anything about this Gamal person. Well . . . he's not answering."

"It wouldn't hurt just to show her my photos and hear her thoughts about it, though, right?"

"I suppose not."

She replied to Mrs. Gamal, agreeing to a meeting on the ship after the Pharos tour, and then emailed Professor James, asking him to call.

As she typed, Dante weighed whether to tell her about the villa, and that he had seen, or nearly seen, the mosaic terrace. *Not yet,* he decided. *She'll say I was out of bounds. And she's preoccupied. And not in a good mood.*

"Message sent," she said brusquely. "Meet me on the pier in ten."

· ✦ ·

"That fortress ahead is the Citadel of Qaitbay," Alison told the guests as their bus took them up the narrow peninsula toward the site of the ancient lighthouse. "It is six hundred years old and a wonderful example of Islamic architecture. It's a maritime museum now. We'll get out here," she told the driver.

Miss Deuss looked on anxiously as Alison spoke, no doubt fearing, as did Alison, that the guests would dismiss the outing as a waste of time.

"So imagine yourselves at sea, oh, say, two thousand years ago. Your destination: this port, which has no significant elevation. At last you see, reassuringly, a light, and then the structure itself, the immense Pharos of Alexandria soaring up some three hundred fifty feet, maybe more." She paused, observing that no one was looking up at the imaginary lighthouse. "Picture thirty-five stories high," she entreated the guests. "Big!" she said, gesturing. "Okay, stay with me. It's thought to have been designed by a Greek architect named Sostratus. 'On behalf of those who sail the seas,' he's said to have written."

"So why aren't we sailing the seas?" someone muttered.

She heard others grumbling about the heat but pushed on. "What did the ancient lighthouse look like? It probably had three tiers. The bottom tier would have been square, with a statue of Triton blowing a conch shell or horn at each corner. Triton was the herald of Poseidon, and he has the body of a man and a fish's tail. A merman!" she said with a laugh, trying to engage the guests. "Okay, then, the middle tier was octagonal, and the top cylindrical.

A statue of Zeus or Poseidon crowned the roof. So, at night, a great fire was kept at the top. What did they use for fuel . . . ?"

"The brochures from this cruise?" she heard Dickenson mumble.

Do not look at Marshall, she commanded herself. *If I look at Marshall I will lose it.*

"Well, they may have used dung," she said brightly. "According to the experts, yes. And roots from papyrus plants, too, from the Delta. Okay, so during the day, a mirror of some sort in the top tier would have caught the sun and reflected it out to sea. And maybe a fire was also kept burning so mariners could see its smoke. Any questions so far?" There were none. "Well, then, the Pharos was damaged by earthquakes in the tenth century AD. Two more, about seven hundred years ago, did it in. Massive stone structures don't fare well in earthquakes, as we'll see throughout this tour."

There was still no engagement from the guests.

"I'm bombing," she murmured to Marshall, who had walked up next to her.

"It's just way too hot out here today, Alison. Wrap it up."

"Okay, everyone, let me just say that the fortress here was built using some of the great blocks of stone from the lighthouse . . . the fallen lighthouse," she concluded with a sigh.

On the way back to *Modestine,* the bus took a turn that allowed Dante a clearer view of the villa's cylindrical tower. He saw that it was in fact modeled after the ancient Pharos, and he vowed to discover why.

· ✦ ·

"What happened?" Marshall called to Alison and Dante as he entered the ship's lounge. "I saw a very unhappy woman leaving just now."

Alison told him they had met with a Mrs. Gamal, who represented an anonymous buyer interested in the statuette.

"When Dante showed her his photos, she protested too much. 'Oh, it can't be ivory. It's modern, just a curiosity.' Then she offers fifteen thousand dollars."

"So we're up to five thou an inch now," said Marshall.

"She knew it was real," said Dante. "She knew it was Queen Meritites. She zoomed right in on the hieroglyphs."

"Imagine making an offer without even seeing it," said Alison. "Why on earth did you tell her it was in the ship's safe, Dante?"

"To throw her off. And to cover Professor James. But did you catch her comment about my cap? She called it an Alexandria team cap. But this is my *Cairo* team cap I have on—the one Med gave me. So why did she say she was a fan of Alexandria's team and invite us to a game? Because I was wearing an Alexandria cap the taxi driver gave me this afternoon when we were at a café and I was walking around by myself—"

"Wait a minute. You walked around by yourself where?"

"Behind the café our driver took us to."

"Why wasn't Mister Dickenson with you?"

"Well, the heat got to him. I just stepped away to look around, then I couldn't stop once I saw this old street, and then a big villa." He paused. "You're right to be suspicious of Mrs. Gamal. Someone had to have told her about me—the boy with the Alexandria cap. Someone sent her. They probably told her to soften us up by inviting us to a game." He caught his breath. "I saw Otto there at that villa, Alison."

"The baroness's chauffeur?"

"He's more than that. You were right. He wasn't wearing a uniform this time, and he walked straight in the front door."

"Did he see you?"

"No."

"Well, you've said a mouthful. All I know is that the statuette must be worth a lot more than she offered. And that you ought to say no more about it in your blog." She shook her head and held up a hand, signaling she wanted no more discussion.

"I think we're onto something," he said.

"More like in the middle of. And I don't like it. Why hasn't Professor James called me back?"

She reached for her phone and called.

"Hello, Jasper? I'm with Dante and Marshall. I'm putting you on speaker. Okay, so there's big interest in the statuette here."

Professor James admitted he had steered Sackville to Dante's blog. He told her he didn't know Gamal but suspected that she was probably acting for Ibis.

"I thought we agreed this Sackville is trouble, Jasper." Now she glared at Dante. "Your last post said a lot about the statuette. And ibises."

"I was careful not to mention Ibis itself, though, Alison. But this is a good thing, isn't it? To get a peek at them?"

"I think you're right, Doctor Dante," said the professor.

"That's not our job here, gentlemen! I didn't want anything more to do with this Sackville, this Ibis."

"But what if they want the statuette because Meritites was Khufu's wife?" Dante proposed. "She's tied to the Great Pyramid. She's another relic tied to an Ancient Wonder. Like the Hillwood Stone is probably tied to the Hanging Gardens. . . . What if Ibis collects *only* Seven Wonders stuff? And wouldn't that explain why there's so little of them left?"

"Videbimus lumen," said the professor.

"'We shall see the light,'" Marshall translated.

"Because the wonders were huge," said Dante. "All of them. I can see how the blocks of marble and stone could be taken and re-used, but what about the detailed pieces from them? The best stuff must have been saved. Even more than what's in the museums now, I mean. Ibis must have it."

"I believe Dante's right," said the professor. "I've been coming around to the same view. When I first talked with you about Ibis in Cairo, I didn't fully appreciate their Renaissance connection. That was a time when the ancient world was being rediscovered. It was a popular pastime back then to name its greatest monuments. Although, lists made even earlier named most of the wonders."

"Almost two thousand years earlier," said Dante. "By the Greeks."

"That's right. Anyway, think of the opportunities there must have been to scoop up relics from them."

"So where is Ibis keeping it all?" asked Marshall.

"That's a mystery," said the professor.

"And why the secrecy?" asked Alison.

"Because a lot of it may have been acquired illicitly? Or maybe they just like their privacy. But I think Dante's idea is a breakthrough—"

"We don't need to be getting any deeper into their business," said Alison.

"Fair enough. But I'd shake your hand, Dante, if I was with you now."

"It wasn't that hard," he said.

"Think about it, though," said the professor. "What we could learn about them now. Ever lift up a flat rock and see what's under it?" He laughed.

This was too much for Alison. "You're both so cavalier. These people were already all over us, Jasper. In Cairo you made sure Sackville heard us discussing the Hillwood Stone and the mark Dante saw on it. They might suspect we know something about that whole thing with Mishky, too . . . and now they want the statuette. It's us they're focused on now. Isn't that great? The Ibis syndicate versus Alison and Dante. And you're both itching for more."

"Sorry, Alison," they said together.

"Just so you know, Jasper, we've told Mrs. Gamal that the

statuette is here on the ship. To throw them off. And to protect you, by the way."

"I appreciate that."

"Okay, enough about this. I'm supposed to be working, in case everyone's forgotten. Don't we have to be on deck, Marshall?"

"Yes, soon."

"I have something to say first," said Dante.

"Can't it wait, Dante?"

"Never mind, then," he said, looking away.

"Okay, but hurry, please."

He recounted how he had been drawn to the villa and that he had seen Otto there. "I didn't tell you this yet, Alison, but I climbed the café's wall to get a better look at the courtyard. And I'm sure the mosaic is there."

"The same mosaic you told me about on the plane?" said Alison.

"Yes, but before I could see it, some SUVs drove in and blocked my view. Who lives there?"

There was a long silence before Alison spoke.

"Dante, don't even think about blogging about who or what you think is at that villa. I want you to stick to writing about the tour and the wonders. I want no taunting of Ibis."

"I have to second that," said Professor James. "If you've indeed found the nest of Ibis, you don't mention it. You drop it."

Dante agreed, but his mind was on the two strangers at the café, whom he had yet to tell Alison about. He realized it was they who must have reported him to Ibis. *They followed us all through the city to the café. They saw my cap. They must be working for Sackville.*

He knew they wouldn't drop it, and he felt his stomach tighten.

· ✦ ·

MODESTINE PULSED WITH ACTIVITY as the crew made ready to sail from Alexandria. At the baroness's request, Marshall checked in with the ship's office.

"Anything for the baroness?" he asked Lieutenant Regan.

"A fax came in a few minutes ago," he said, placing it in an envelope and sealing it. "It must be important. She's waiting for it."

Marshall brought it to her cabin and stood by as she moved to her window to read.

> Dearest Baroness: We are advised by S. Gamal that object ref. πK-QM-Stte-i-01 is of acquisition rating deemed 8-plus. Offer rejected by owner. Your assistance, please.

> My condition is as before. "The shipwreck of old age" applies. But to you, a bon voyage. I shall wave.

Marshall detected a wistful resignation in her demeanor as she finished reading.

"Yes?" she asked, looking up, having forgotten that he was there.

"Will you need to send a reply, my lady? I'll wait."

"That will not be necessary."

"Good night, then, ma'am."

"Old friend," she said aloud after Marshall had left, "you cling to old habits. But what of my petitions to you to disengage? You resist." She tapped her fingers against her brooch. It was another Fabergé creation—a gold Triton blowing into a seashell of blue sapphires. "Ach, enough. I will assist you, old tyrant, this one last time."

She wrote her reply and took it to Lieutenant Regan herself.

· ✦ ·

CAPTAIN NIKKOS ANNOUNCED THAT *Modestine* was repositioning to a spot closer to the Pharos site before heading to sea for Rhodes. He asked that everyone assemble on the main deck at the bow.

Moments later, an immense scrim some fifty feet across and one hundred fifty feet long unfurled from a blimp hovering above the Citadel of Qaitbay. Onto the scrim, a projected image appeared—a Renaissance-period drawing of the ancient lighthouse.

The guests moved to the railings as one image appeared and dissolved into the next: an ancient mosaic from Saint Mark's Basilica in Venice depicting the Pharos and a sailing ship; a series of bronze coins struck in Alexandria in the second century AD showing the lighthouse with its many windows and tiers; a series of speculative drawings from centuries past.

"Clever," pronounced Dickenson. "I much prefer to see it this way."

"This sort of revives things, at least for now," said Torrie.

"A nice end to the day, Alison, all things considered," Deirdre added.

And nice, thought Alison, *to soon be putting some distance between us and Sackville and Mrs. Gamal . . . and Otto, and that villa, and who knows what else.*

As the images displayed, Dante looked across the harbor to the buildings that rose up against the darkening sky. The villa's prominent tower was easy to spot now, and a soft light glowed inside. He saw a figure shadowed against it. *Otto?* he wondered. No, the figure was portly and somewhat stooped. Now it made a motion. *A wave?* He wondered if anyone else had noticed, but they were all focusing on the images on the scrim. All save the baroness, who gave a furtive wave back before walking to her cabin.

When the projections ended, *Modestine* made her way out of the harbor slowly, but as she passed Alexandria's outermost buoy Dante felt her powerful engines kick in. He lingered on deck, watching the city's lights fade and the tower of the Ancient Lights villa blend into the horizon.

So much revealed here in Egypt, he mused. *So much left unanswered*. He longed to stay, but above him he saw *Modestine*'s radars whirring alongside her bristling antennas. And beyond them, the stars, dazzling in their number and brightness, just as Alison had said.

So we'll go, he told himself. *To sea, with* Modestine *and the sky.*

6

AT SEA: BABYLON AND THE HANGING GARDENS

DANTE MARVELED AT HOW easily *Modestine* sliced through the long, rolling swells of the open Mediterranean. *Easier than I can walk through this wind*, he thought as he made his way aft.

He found Alison and Marshall on the stern, looking up to the darkened pool deck and the wall of tarpaulins buffeting in the gusts.

"Miss Deuss had the tarps put up earlier," Marshall told him. "She wouldn't tell anyone what's behind them or what she's planning. Gotten any pictures?"

"Nothing."

"She must've enabled a pop-up blocker in you."

"I'm supposed to introduce our lecturer on the Hanging Gardens up there," said Alison. "But, Marsh, those projections of the Pharos tonight were wonderful. I know that wasn't her idea."

"I could've helped her with this one, too, if she'd asked."

Suddenly the tarpaulins began to come down and Captain Nikkos's voice blasted from the ship's speakers.

"I, Nebuchadnezzar, King of Babylon, invite all to a feast in my Hanging Gardens."

"Here we go," said Alison.

They made their way up to the pool deck, where dozens of paper lanterns had been hung, their light shimmering off the pool's water and the oiled torsos of four uneasy crewmen dressed only in gold pantaloons.

"Maybe Cher will perform," said Marshall.

"Behold my verdant gardens," Nebuchadnezzar's voice sounded again as spotlights panned across the plastic greenery that covered nearly everything.

"That's the most fake foliage I've seen in my entire life," said Marshall.

At the sound of a gong, more crewmen appeared, dressed as soldiers from a culture no one recognized. Next, a line of servers carrying great trays of food filed in to the bludgeoning music of *Carmina Burana*.

"Such a contemplative garden," observed Alison.

Another gong, and Captain Nikkos appeared, dressed as the king. There was no mistaking his displeasure as he surveyed what Miss Deuss had done to his ship.

"Welcome to the Hanging Gardens of Babylon," he read from his script as the bombast subsided. "I have created them for my wife, who was homesick for her native land. Oh, Princess Amytis of Media, come and join me."

"I wonder who gets to play the delicate princess?" said Alison.

Dante laughed as Miss Deuss, wearing a flowing silk gown and a conical hat with a veil, twirled onto the deck between four feather-fanning maidens. She acknowledged the applause she had ordered the crew to deliver and then, as a dark chord sounded, signaled her soldiers to poke at a tied-up prisoner with their rubber-tipped spears.

"She seems to be enjoying that," said Alison.

Captain Nikkos read again from his script, "Ladies and gentlemen, our host Monica Deuss is deeply committed to rekindling interest in the Seven Wonders of the Ancient World and to making them accessible to new audiences everywhere."

He frowned at the clumps of vines she had taped sloppily to the bulkhead next to him, then scowled when a strong gust ripped them off, damaging the bulkhead's pristine finish.

"I have the pleasure," he said with difficulty, "of introducing Monica Deuss."

"After tonight, let there be no doubt that we will bring the wonders to life again!" she enthused, clapping and jabbing her hands in turn at the oddly costumed crew, the lifeless foliage, and the buffet.

Only the buffet was applauded by the guests.

"Well, then," she said, "I have an announcement before we bring up our Babylon scholar. I am in partnership with a group that will develop a world-class resort and historical park that will boast a large-scale replica of each wonder. It will also include a museum with dozens of never-before-seen objects from the wonders themselves."

"Who are your business partners?" shouted Dickenson. "Where are you getting the objects from?"

Behind him, the baroness approached a man who stood by himself. He looked surprised to see her and greeted her coolly.

"The resort is a sound venture, Mister Dickenson," Miss Deuss responded. "I can assure you." She called on Alison to introduce the speaker, who had come aboard in Alexandria.

"Oh, great," said Alison, "I haven't even met the man." She was relieved to see him approach with the baroness, but had to ask herself which of the two looked grimmer. She thought the man handsome, despite his scowl, and guessed his age to be about fifty.

"Alison," said the baroness, "this is Doctor Ali Khalil from the University of Baghdad. Miss Deuss's spectacle has offended him. Will you reassure him that we are not all lunatics here?"

"I'm appalled by this, too, Doctor," said Alison. She was struck by the intensity of his eyes, one of which appeared to focus in a different direction, and by their color—a deep lapis lazuli blue. "Fortunately, you have the floor now and—"

"No," he snapped, "I won't be part of this. And this news of a theme park?" He threw up his hands.

"But the guests will appreciate your expert perspective, Doctor. Please do it. You can reset the tone. You don't have to endorse any of this."

The baroness was more direct. "Sir, Miss Deuss will sue you for breach of contract if you do not speak. She is quite cold-blooded."

"Smash this vulgarity!" urged Alison, as she jabbed the deck with her stick.

Doctor Ali's defiant expression gave way to a faint smile. "All right. I'll do it. For you, miss."

From her throne, the princess stared at them.

"We better get over there," said Alison. "Is there anything you'd like me to highlight when I introduce you? Maybe something about your family?"

"I have none," he said, looking away.

The baroness shook her head to signal that Alison shouldn't inquire further. "You might mention Doctor Ali's efforts to revitalize the marshlands of Iraq," she suggested as they escorted him to the lectern. Alison did so, and his lecture began.

"Imagine here," he said, pointing to an aerial image of the Euphrates projected onto a screen, "a little town that grew to become the greatest city in the world, so that by about six hundred

BC, under King Nebuchadnezzar the Second, the city is fortified by a miles-long system of walls, some more than eighty feet thick."

Next, he showed a photo of an arid landscape dotted with sand mounds and broken mud-brick buildings. "Why has so much of the ancient city been lost? Floods and the changing course of the river. Great sandstorms. Earthquakes. Inept excavations at times. Wars," he added, almost to himself. "We don't know what the Hanging Gardens looked like. We have only imaginative drawings and educated guesses about its location. Some insist that it did not exist at all, or that it did, but in a place other than Babylon. No, it was here, just to the south of Baghdad."

He then showed a photo of people among their boats and houses in the marshes of southeastern Iraq.

"The vegetation would have been wonderfully varied in the Hanging Gardens. But perhaps the core plantings were from these vast wetlands, the Mesopotamian Marshes. We would have seen reeds, of course, and plants like papyrus, eel grass, and water lilies. For centuries, the inhabitants of these wetlands, the Marsh Arabs, or Ma'dan, have used the reeds to weave mats and to build their wonderful arched dwellings."

During Doctor Ali's presentation, Miss Deuss had been circulating among the guests, lobbying them to write favorably about her ventures. But when Doctor Ali went on to pronounce her production "cartoonishly inaccurate" and "ignorant," she stormed over to Captain Nikkos.

"The fair princess is going to order the king to shut him down," Alison whispered to Marshall.

"Now let me give you a sense of what the Hanging Gardens was really like," Doctor Ali continued. "Let us conjure an image of Princess Amytis, who, I believe, oversaw its landscape design and botanical collection, which may have been even more impressive than its architecture and engineering."

Captain Nikkos pointed to his watch and gave Doctor Ali an apologetic shrug.

"That's so rude," said Dante, as Captain Nikkos called for music and Miss Deuss clawed her way down a vine-choked stairway to her cabin. "Nikkos shouldn't have interrupted."

"Alas," sighed Alison. "Buffet, anyone?"

"You don't want to stick around for Tarzan to swing down from the vines?" said Marshall.

"I need to tell you something, Alison," said Dante as they walked. "When we were watching the images of the Pharos tonight, I saw the villa's tower. There was someone watching us. The light went out when I looked. They're following my blog all right. And the baroness—"

"Alison!" boomed Captain Nikkos, who set his drink down and took Alison's hand theatrically. "As the fair Princess Amytis is indisposed with a malady of the spirit, perhaps you would consent to be my concubine?"

Alison had to laugh. "Can you give me a couple of centuries to think about it, Your Majesty?"

Dante left.

· ✦ ·

LET THEM HAVE THEIR *drinks and jokes*, Dante thought as he walked to the stern. The wind and the sea had picked up, and *Modestine* was straining now. To the west, lightning strikes revealed an ominous, clouded sky.

He pulled his camera from his pocket to take a photo, but lost his balance and fumbled it. He could only watch as it fell to the deck and bounced over the side into *Modestine's* roiling white wake. He gripped the railing with both hands, upset with himself and resentful of Miss Deuss and Captain Nikkos, and Alison as well.

Why did Nikkos have to interrupt? he fumed. *Twice! First, cutting off Doctor Ali, then cutting in just now, when I wanted to tell Alison and Marshall so much. And what about all the others? Otto, Sackville, Mrs. Gamal, the men at the café . . . and the man in the tower who waved, and the baroness, who waved back. All of them shadowy, all of them circling.*

Clear your head, his grandfather's voice told him.

He went to his cabin to write.

I wrote in my first post that I saw the statuette of Khufu's queen in the Cairo shop. Already, a dealer wants to buy it. For an anonymous client, she said, but I know of a secret organization that collects.

I also saw a picture in my head, last year, of an ancient brick that's in the Tribune Tower in Chicago. I believe it's from the Hanging Gardens of Babylon. It has a mark on it, the letter *I*.

And in Alexandria today, near the site of the Pharos, I saw for the second time a picture in my head of a great ibis work of art. I cannot say more.

He dared not. It was enough that he had mentioned "a secret organization," violating the boundary Alison and Professor James had set. He had also alluded to the Hillwood Stone, even if he hadn't named it. And he had all but revealed what had come to him in Alexandria, even if he had avoided using the words *mosaic* and *villa*.

He asked himself if he was saying too much or too little, and decided to wait before posting his words. Instead, he emailed Nora, asking her to research antique maps of the Eastern Mediterranean over to the Euphrates River. He told her how inspiring Doctor Ali was and how intimidating he had seemed at first, with his lazy eye and his brusqueness, but that now he knew him to be kind.

Lucky him, he told himself. *Lucky to know the marshes and the ruins of Babylon.*

"What's threading through me from so long ago?" he asked aloud.

He went to the ship's library on a hunch that Doctor Ali was there, and he was right.

"I saw you at the luau tonight," Doctor Ali cracked. "What did you think of my talk?"

"It made me think."

"About what?"

"Ancient Babylon would have had ibises, right? I mean African sacred ibises."

"What's your name?"

"Dante."

Doctor Ali crossed his arms and looked up as if he were imagining that time and place. "Well, Dante, yes, ibises were there, and I like to think that Princess Amytis would have delighted in having them roaming freely in her gardens."

"You were going to say more about her when Captain Nikkos cut you off."

"Ah, yes. I have a wonderful mental picture of her as a bright and capable woman. I often think of myself there, conversing with her about all manner of things. I guess we archaeologists do that," he said with a laugh. He then spoke of the richness of the Iraqi marshes before a series of government policies in the nineties had dealt them a nearly fatal blow.

"They once covered an area twice the size of your Florida Everglades. And though they will never be the same, I give my energies to their restoration. When I'm not teaching at the university in Baghdad, that is, or working at the Babylon ruins. But yes, the ibis is present there now and was in ancient times."

"Are you familiar with the Tribune Tower's collection in Chicago?"

"Ah, yes, the building with the artifacts embedded in its façade. I visited once. A curious but quite wonderful attraction."

"I'm from Chicago," said Dante, speaking rapidly now, "and there's a glazed brick there with a little mosaic on top. It's called the Hillwood Stone, but no one knows for sure where it's from. Do you know it?"

"Only from photographs."

"I think it could be from the Hanging Gardens. Is that possible?"

"Well, I suppose it could be, but the existence of a Hanging Gardens artifact in Chicago is maybe less possible. But, why not?" he allowed.

"So the Hanging Gardens could have had bigger mosaics, too, like floor-size?"

Doctor Ali explained that mosaics made from pebbles and shells had been found in ancient Mesopotamia, from well before Babylonian times, but none from the Hanging Gardens period with the Hillwood Stone's refined quality.

"If there were mosaics at the Hanging Gardens," he added, in a less convincing tone, "they would likely show the same Babylonian gods as their bas-reliefs—the lion, the bull, the dragon."

"But not more natural scenes?" asked Dante. "Because I'm sure there's a big mosaic related to the Hillwood Stone. I've seen it. Or almost did—"

"Is that so?"

"I mean, in my head. It's an ibis flying over a marsh, and it's flat, not a bas-relief. So if there's a little mosaic embedded in the Hillwood Stone, why not a big floor mosaic from the same time and place?"

Doctor Ali listened intently but did not respond.

"The Hillwood Stone was probably stolen," Dante continued, "and no one's ever claimed it. But I think I know who owned it. Alison doesn't want me talking about this, but it has a mark stamped on the bottom of it. The letter *I*."

Doctor Ali's expression darkened.

"Can you tell me more about it?" Dante asked.

Doctor Ali looked uncomfortable, but he answered that there had been an undocumented dig centuries earlier at the ruins of Babylon. "A surreptitious dig by a powerful organization," he stated directly, and with a hint of contempt. He now seemed relieved to be speaking of it. "An organization known by few and mentioned by others only under their breath."

"Then it *is* Ibis," Dante declared.

Doctor Ali looked surprised, but he would not confirm it.

"Okay, I want to post this tonight," said Dante, as he opened his laptop and brought up the blog entry he had saved.

Doctor Ali's mouth tightened as he read it. "So I've told you little that you didn't already know or suspect. You all but name them. But I must caution you. Ibis does not tolerate intrusions. You must not irritate this group. They will smash you like a gourd and think nothing of it. Do not mention them in this blog, even obliquely. Delete your reference to an ibis work of art in Alexandria, and especially your speculation about the Hillwood Stone."

"Then I would have nothing to post. I'm going to send this as is. I don't care if it upsets them."

"I'm not your guardian, but I have a responsibility to tell you that you're playing a dangerous game. I will say no more, except that you must never write or speak about what I've told you."

"I thought I'd find you two bookworms here," called Alison. "May a fellow nerd join you?"

Dante pulled his laptop toward him and posted his words.

"Hello, anybody home?" she asked.

Dante looked up defiantly.

"Look," she told him, "I know I've been wrapped up with the tour. I owe you some time."

The two looked at her silently.

"What's going on?" she asked. "You look like you've just blown up a bridge. Both of you."

Still, neither spoke.

"Okay. Fine. So, Doctor, I just came to thank you for doing your talk. It was well received by our otherwise disgruntled guests."

"Thank you."

"I noticed you were chatting with the baroness just before we were introduced. How do you know each other?"

"We don't," he answered.

Dante looked at him, believing it was untrue. He decided not to question him, imagining instead the Mesopotamian Marshes and the gardens of ancient Babylon that Doctor Ali had evoked earlier, because that did feel true. So, too, did his passage through the Nile Delta, where he had seen the ibises. True, too, the pull of the Pharos-like villa in Alexandria, where he felt the ibis mosaic had to be.

He told himself there were other truths as well, ones yet to be revealed, including the baroness's connection to the man in the tower. And as *Modestine* carried him to the next wonder, he began to understand who, and where, he had to be.

· ✦ ·

It had been the man's habit to climb the stairs from his library to the tower each evening before meeting with his aide. He would look out first from the south window to view the mosaic terrace in his courtyard, then out the north window to the harbor, where he would imagine the ancient Pharos standing.

But he had seldom gone up in recent years. For a man in his late eighties, the climb was difficult, and he had recognized that the views now brought nostalgia more often than purpose.

On this night, however, he had needed to reconnect with these touchstones, and to wave to his friend the Baroness von Weber as she sailed from the harbor.

"Excuse me, sir," he heard his aide call.

"Yes, Otto."

"Did you want to meet tonight?"

"Yes," he answered. "What time is it?"

"Past nine, sir. Were you sleeping?"

"I suppose so. I am coming."

In the library, he took his customary seat behind his desk opposite Otto. At one end of it was a granite obelisk nearly two feet high and etched with hieroglyphs. At the other were framed photos of him as a young man, posing with colleagues at the ruins of ancient buildings.

"There is another communication from the American boy, sir," Otto reported.

"From his . . . what is it?"

"Blog, sir."

"What does he tell us this time?"

"You're correct that he's talking to us, sir, even if he doesn't know who we are. The issue now is that he's doing it very publicly. Here is his latest posting, from a moment ago." He handed the man his phone.

"Ah, yes, your smart telephone. Smart because it owns those who think they own it." He handed it back.

Otto summarized, "So the boy says that there is a secret organization that collects. He mentions the brick in Chicago, and that it bears the letter *I*. And teases that he has somehow seen an ibis work of art, here, in Alexandria. Someone must be leaking information to him, sir."

"Nonsense."

"How else, then, can someone—a youth, and in just two days—uncover so much? Things that no others have discerned."

"A young mind is uncluttered, Otto. I begin to appreciate the gift he writes of, be it intuition or something like it. And it appears that he is testing himself as much as us. You do not see it?"

"I saw a frail and aloof boy when I drove him from the train station to the ship. I saw nothing special about him."

"Then you are blind. Here is a young man who is interested in antiquities. He has had the serendipity to have lived in Chicago, where he has seen the so-called Hillwood Stone. He has sensed our mark on it, and is intrigued by the story of Ibis told to him by the American professor, whom Sackville has failed to muzzle. He goes shopping with his guardian, only to find a pharaonic treasure." Now his eyes bored into Otto's. "A priceless statuette of Queen Meritites that was staring us in the face in Cairo. How did we not know of it?"

He rose and began to move about the room.

"Listen to him, Otto. His first blog yesterday shows us he is an imaginative thinker. He appreciates the ibis. He ruminates about Thoth. His posting tonight tells us much more—that he is not afraid to probe. Finally, his obsession with the Hillwood Stone. He implies that the mark refers to Ibis. It is a taunt, really."

"His guardian must be enabling him," said Otto. "And their American professor friend."

"We are enabling him more," the man roared. "The clumsy Mrs. Gamal has not served us well in this."

Otto apologized, but reminded the man that the larger question was Dante's reference to an "ibis work of art" near the site of the Pharos. How would Dante have been able to perceive it?

"You told me that Sackville's men followed him to a café near us," said the man.

"Yes, but he could not have known about this villa."

"Respect him, Otto. Perhaps he was here. For now, he has

merely said that he knows of a secret organization that collects. But if he speculates any further about the mosaic here, or about Chicago . . ."

He dismissed Otto with an order to review the security camera video. Returning to his chair, he rested his eyes on a fifties-era pirate lamp made from plaster, a kitschy piece that was out of place in the room. He had acquired it on a lark with his late wife to decorate the bedroom of their newborn son. He had liked how the pirate stood, arms akimbo. He had liked his grin and swagger, his black floppy hat and trousers, his open white shirt and red sash, and his gold belt buckle and sword. He rose, walked to the library table where it sat, and switched it on. The red shade cast a warm glow onto a framed photo, taken nearly forty years earlier, of a serious boy whose eyes looked away.

Focus on the present, he reminded himself, *on this boy named Dante.*

In past years, in times of crisis, he had found strength and clarity at a secluded monastery in Greece. It had been fourteen years since his last visit there. He poured a glass of water from a crystal carafe and contemplated going back, then offered a toast. "To young Dante, and our connection. You test us, as you must. The issue has been joined."

Otto's return startled him. Had he been speaking aloud?

"You have viewed the video?"

"Yes, sir. The boy was here, as you suspected. I recognize him. And he wears the cap that Sackville's men reported. He passed by our gates and soon after climbed a wall across the street. He may have seen the mosaic. I've transferred some images of him to my phone."

"Let me see him."

It was as he expected. He saw Dante's intensity, but also his vulnerability. He turned to look again at the photo next to the pirate lamp.

"All right," he said softly.

"And now?" asked Otto.

"We act."

Otto observed a transformation in the old man, a reemergence of the warrior who would respond to this latest threat with the same cold precision that he had employed against adversaries in decades past.

"We must shut down the young man's talk of the brick. Send a comment to his blog that the mark he sees is clearly an *H*—for Hillwood. Or Harvard. The Hermitage. Anything. Say it is someone else's mark."

"Yes, sir."

"Next, call Sackville. He must determine the location of the statuette. Is it on the ship or not? Gamal has failed. Tell her to stay away. I have asked the baroness to assist."

"There is one other concern," said Otto. "Do you have confidence that the baroness can manage Monica Deuss?"

"Her Ancient Wonders resort," scoffed the old man. "I have given the baroness my word that I will not intercede unless she asks. I will respect that, for now."

· ✦ ·

In the ship's library, Alison tried again to engage Dante.

"Not speaking to me, then?" she asked.

"You can read this." He turned his laptop toward her and waited for her reaction.

"Dante, this is going too far. The speculation . . . I told you—"

"It's my fault, Miss Fine," said Doctor Ali.

"No, I'm responsible," said Dante. "Doctor Ali warned me not to post it. But Ibis doesn't scare me. They've probably read it already. At least they're listening."

"And I'm not?" said Alison.

"Not lately . . . and it isn't speculation."

"I'm not saying you're incorrect, Dante. I'm saying you're provoking—"

"Didn't you notice that the baroness didn't wear a brooch tonight for the Hanging Gardens show?"

"What?" she said, shaking her head. "It's late, Dante. I don't want to debate this. Computer off, please. We'll talk in the morning. The sea is kicking up, so be careful walking to your cabin."

"What's done is done," said Alison to Doctor Ali after Dante had left. "He's acting out. I don't know. . . . It beats silence, I guess. He said you tried to talk him out of posting it. What do you know about them?"

Doctor Ali revealed that he had sufficient knowledge of Ibis to know that what Dante had written would irritate them, and that they would not ignore it. He told her that she should be aware that they had long tentacles and should keep Dante close, at least in Rhodes, until she could determine how they would react.

"You should inform the captain what is happening," he added. "Please do that."

"How on earth am I supposed to know how they'll react?" said Alison. "What exactly do you know?"

"Two kinds of people are drawn to archaeology, Miss Fine: those who seek to discover, learn, and preserve, and those who are selfish and want only to acquire. Ibis is in the second category," he said coolly. "I have said enough. I will see you in the morning when we arrive in Rhodes. To say goodbye."

"Before you go, Doctor . . ."

"Yes?"

"Well, your briefcase," she said, stifling a grin. "There's stuff sticking out of it. Straw or something?"

"Ah, my marsh reeds. I didn't have the chance to talk about them. I was cut off, you remember." He opened his case and looked for a wastebasket.

"Wait," said Alison. "May I have a few? Just as a memento, for Dante."

"Of course. Good night."

Alison stayed on, watching the sea spray whirling past the library's windows, how it danced, hung suspended, and shuddered before slapping back down into the sea. She wondered how she could reach Dante, how to understand what troubled, tossed, and drove him. How to support him and at the same time protect him.

One of us has to figure this out, she told herself.

From the ship's speakers, she heard Lieutenant Regan announce that, for their safety, passengers were prohibited from going out on deck in the storm. "Especially the pool deck," he added, "as we clear away the garden that no longer hangs there, but instead blows about perilously."

Next is Rhodes harbor and another daffy entertainment, she mused. *And another clash with Miss Deuss, no doubt.* She stood and gripped the ends of her stick as if to wring some strength from it, then walked to her cabin. *Deal with it*, she told herself. *All of it.*

· ✦ ·

DANTE STEWED AS HE walked the passageway back to his cabin, wishing he had written more in his blog, wishing he had confronted the two men at the café. The ship's tossing only worsened his mood.

"Damn this storm, and your donkey kicks, too," he cursed as he was thrown against the bulkhead a second time. "Sorry, *Modestine*. Just get us through this. Get us to the harbor."

He imagined the vulnerability of wooden ships of ancient times, how easily they must have broken up in storms. And how the sailors must have searched the horizon for the reassuring Colossus or the light of the Pharos before being tossed into the cold sea. In the darkness. To drown.

"Sorry, again, *Modestine*."

The day's events filled his head, but it was the thought of the mosaic that gripped him most. He thought back to the luminous sky before the storm moved in. It brought an idea.

He began a new post.

> At sea now in a storm. Before the sky clouded over, I saw it alive with stars. I imagined Thoth guiding them. Doesn't the African sacred ibis deserve a constellation like Cygnus the Swan and Aquila the Eagle?

It had always struck him that the geographic locations of the wonders made a pattern of a bird in flight. But which stars would line up to match that pattern? After the day's frustrations, it was a welcome diversion. He thought it through as he wrote.

> The African sacred ibis constellation would have seven stars matching the pattern made by the locations of the Seven Wonders. The three stars in Orion's belt could be its body and upper wing. Those stars would represent the Colossus, the Mausoleum, and the Temple of Artemis. It would have two stars for its lower wing, representing the Pyramid of Khufu and the Pharos of Alexandria. A sixth star, to the left, would be its tail, for the Statue of Zeus. The seventh star, far to the right, would be the eye, representing the Hanging Gardens of Babylon, where the ibis thrives.

An odd feeling came over him as he wrote "where the ibis thrives,"

What connection does Ibis have to that wonder where the ibis thrives, in Iraq? he asked himself.

Now, as he wondered if someone in Ibis could have imagined the Seven Wonders captured as a constellation as well, he opened his laptop and brought up a map of the Eastern Mediterranean. He placed a piece of writing paper over it and drew a heavy dot at each Ancient Wonder site. Around the pattern of dots, he loosely sketched an ibis in flight. The drawing pleased him—and it echoed the shape of the ibis in his pictures of the mosaic. Next, he brought up a star map and placed the paper over it, lining up the dots for Rhodes and Halicarnassus and Ephesus with the three stars in Orion's belt first. Would the four other sites line up with any bright stars?

They did not. At least not exactly. And worse, there was no bright star at all to represent Babylon, the ibis's eye. It was not enough to make the constellation work.

"What am I doing?" he mumbled. He pushed his drawing aside, telling himself he would imagine a star there and leave it at that.

He noticed an email that had arrived from Nora with the subject line "Maps," and opened it.

You weren't very specific, but here are some links to old maps.

You're meeting interesting people. I googled Doctor Ali Khalil. He's a big scholar and environmentalist, and I could see the lazy eye you mentioned. It's called amblyopia.

He sounded out "Am-blee-OH-pee-ah" as he began to explore the maps in Nora's links. None seemed suitable until he came across an elaborate, if inaccurate, map of the Mediterranean and the Levant drawn in the sixteenth century by a Dutch cartographer named Vander Hoof. He enlarged it on his screen, placed a fresh piece of writing paper over it, drew a dot over each wonder's site, and then positioned the paper over the star map.

"Close," he whispered. "Rhodes, Halicarnassus, and Ephesus align with the three stars in Orion's belt. Alexandria pretty much aligns with Sirius, and Giza with Muliphen. And Olympia is near Alhena. Six stars to six wonders."

And while the dot for Babylon still aligned with no bright star in the heavens, he realized that was appropriate. After all, he told himself, it was the most elusive wonder, the wonder that was lost.

He nodded, certain that someone in Ibis would have conceived the same constellation and imagined a star to represent the Hanging Gardens, just as he had. He sensed that it was esteemed by Ibis above all the other wonders, even if he didn't yet appreciate why.

He was now fighting sleep, but he looked again at the image of the Vander Hoof map, hoping to see a credit for the person or museum that possessed it. There was none, save the words *Private collection.*

Ibis's private collection, he thought. *It belongs to you, the figure in the tower. And when we sailed from Alexandria, did you spot me when you waved to the baroness? I've been warned about you. But we are joined somehow. We are connected.*

He had to put a name to the man. He knew from the way he'd moved in the tower that he was old. And that he must be the head of Ibis—so, like the Pharos, he was a light. He remembered the sign outside his villa.

"I will call you Ancient Light."

He felt the shadowy organization coming into focus at last— their obsession with the Seven Wonders, their Pharos-like villa, the African sacred ibis mosaic that had to be from the Hanging

Gardens. And now the map and the ibis constellation that so artfully connected the wonders.

He added to his post.

> Just now, I discovered an old map by Vander Hoof that shows the position of six of the Seven Wonders sites aligning with six bright stars on the celestial map. If I place a seventh star at the position of the seventh wonder—the Hanging Gardens of Babylon—the stars make a pattern of an ibis in flight. The map makes my constellation real.

He could not stop himself from writing more.

> I believe the map was important to another person before me. Someone in Ibis. And that the land that was Babylon means more to them than I am able to understand.

> I have to thank my sister Nora for her research that helped me find the Vander Hoof map.

He posted it. He had named them. He had said Ibis, and knew they must now come after him.

· ✦ ·

Over the next two hours, Dante stayed awake to watch for comments to his blog, sketching views of the Hanging Gardens to pass

the time. When a comment appeared from "Ra," he dropped his
pen.

> You are misreading the letter *I* you claim to have
> seen on an "ancient brick." Turn it 90 degrees and
> you will see that it is an *H*, the mark of any number
> of museums or institutions or people, and nothing
> more. Your assertions are foolish inventions, and
> your readers should know this. You should retract
> them, and, in future, cease.

"Of all the things I've written tonight," he said aloud, "you react
only to the Hillwood Stone." He viewed the comment as more
than an attempt to discredit him—the sender had chosen the name
Ra, the supreme Egyptian deity, to intimidate him.

Angered by the rebuke, he posted more to his blog.

> I know of an ibis mosaic terrace that sits in the
> courtyard of a guarded villa in Alexandria. The
> owners have put in its eye a bright object that
> would represent Babylon, where the mosaic must
> have been found. And the symbol stamped on the
> ancient brick—on the Hillwood Stone—is an *I*,
> one hundred percent. And it's probably stamped
> on the Vander Hoof map and on everything else
> Ibis owns.

> And to Ra, I say: You are not hidden. I recognize
> you, Ancient Light.

Who will be more furious with me now, he wondered, *Ibis or Alison?*

It was nearly four o'clock, and outside he could see the sky brightening over the island of Rhodes to the northeast. He pressed his hands and forehead to the window and thanked *Modestine* for carrying him through the storm, then made his way to the main deck, directing his thoughts to the powerful man in the tower: *I am coming in. So good morning, Private Collector, Ancient Light. I will know you.*

7

RHODES AND THE COLOSSUS

DANTE BEGAN TO MAKE out something odd through the fog as *Modestine* neared the harbor jetty at Rhodes.

"Good morning, guests, and welcome to 'Breakfast with the Colossus,'" he heard Marshall recite from the pool deck above him.

Moments later, as *Modestine* slowed to a stop, he understood why Marshall's voice had sounded flat. Coming into view was a storm-battered, thirty-foot-high replica of the Colossus commissioned by Miss Deuss. The headless hulk was grotesquely twisted. Its right arm, which she had insisted should hold a beaming torch aloft, dangled at its side. The battery-powered torch sat in a puddle on the jetty, its bare bulb emitting only a feeble glow.

He heard Alison begin her narrative, her voice strained.

"The Colossus of Rhodes . . . Oh, dear . . . a ten-story-high bronze statue of the sun god Helios. Fifteen storics with its pedestal. Now, about that torch . . . He likely didn't hold one, but rather held up his arm with his hand opened in a hailing gesture."

"It was a torch!" Miss Deuss shouted.

"Okay, let's go with a torch," Alison obliged, "but it wouldn't have flamed."

As if on cue, the torch bulb popped, prompting titters from the guests and cheers from the crowd of locals on the jetty.

"Just cut to the earthquake," Miss Deuss growled.

"Okay, so an earthquake toppled him, just fifty-six years after he was built."

The Colossus creaked and Miss Deuss screamed, "Pull!" to the men yanking on lines attached to the teetering eyesore, until at last it crashed to the ground and became a heap of plywood and chunks of Styrofoam, some of which began to skip across the jetty and into the harbor in the breeze. Recorded rumblings emerged, belatedly, from the ship's speakers and from the jetty.

"Well, that was a colossal something," Dickenson cracked.

Dante waved to a pilot boat zigzagging through the floating debris toward *Modestine*. The harbor pilot waved back, then hailed Captain Nikkos, who shouted, "Come aboard, sir. Take us in. If you'll have us."

"That was a proper storm last night," the pilot told Dante on his way to the bridge. "Today I retire," he said, handing him a hefty metal coin struck with Helios on one side and a sailing ship and sea serpent on the other. "You seem a worthy lad, a sailor. Keep the coin well, for courage and hope. But tell me, who is Modestine?"

"An honest friend," Dante answered.

He stared at the Colossus wreckage and wondered about his own fate after his challenges to Ancient Light and to Alison. He gripped the coin hard, grateful at least for *Modestine* and the pilot's blessing.

· ✦ ·

DOCTOR ALI HAD NEARLY reached the gangway when he heard a call from Miss Deuss.

"You can't leave yet."

"Excuse me?"

"You need to help me fix this," she told him, as she positioned herself between him and the gangway. "That writer from Condé

Nast—Croft or something—he just told me he's leaving. He said some of the others may, too."

"It's Scott," Doctor Ali corrected her. "Don't you even know their names?"

"I need you to talk to them. I need you to convince them to stay on."

"I can't do anything about that. And why didn't you tell me the baroness would be here?"

"Well, you wouldn't have come, would you?"

"You concealed your partnership with the baroness when you pitched this to me. I thought I could trust her, in spite of her . . . allegiances."

"Yes, allegiances," she snapped. "How you scoff at them. How superior you are. Suppose I reveal what I know about your past? I've picked up plenty about you—"

"What do you want?" he demanded.

"An ally. I believe you have leverage with Ibis. You can help me realize my vision. I want my resort to be extraordinary, something you could be proud of, too."

"Say what you have to say, then."

"That's better," she purred. "Okay, I want the little statuette the Americans have. They like you. You should have no trouble convincing them to part with it. Once I have it, I gain Ibis's respect." Lowering her voice, she added, "And I want you to have an . . . encounter . . . with that boy. Something to frighten him into silence. His blogging is exposing Ibis. If they're incapable of stopping him, I will. And they'll thank me for it, in the form of a generous gift of objects for my resort. You see?"

"You underestimate Ibis," said Doctor Ali.

"I know that they're fading and vulnerable. If they can't stop the boy, there will be countless claims on the collection. There will be nothing left of it."

"So be it," said Doctor Ali. "You will not have my help."

"Oh, I will, or I'll expose you. I can get you arrested with a single phone call."

"I've done nothing—"

"Really? Could you prove that, Ali?"

"Look, I have no influence over him. I mean, them. Ibis."

"Yes, you do. And influence right at the top. With *him*, as you just let slip."

Doctor Ali stiffened.

"You seem angry," she told him. "Have I touched a nerve? You, the so-called preserver of antiquities, protector of the environment—a criminal? You'll do as I say. Contact the big man that you claim to have no influence with. Tell him I want more than the baroness's paltry offer of a few loaned objects. Tell him that you and I will not only deal with Dante but also acquire the statuette, which I will, of course, share with him."

When he asked what she meant by an *encounter*, she cracked open a tote bag containing a mask and headdress of Thoth, part of a costume for the show she had planned to put on in Cairo before Alison talked her out of it.

"Get Dante to go to the afterdeck tonight," she said. "You appear, wearing this mask, and tell him he mustn't mention Ibis or the Hillwood Stone again in his blog. Thoth is very real to him. He'll listen."

"You're mad."

"Think through the dialogue, Ali. Make it convincing. Here—" She thrust the bag at him. "There's a stun gun in there, too—frighten him into obedience by whatever means. Then later we'll discuss how to get the statuette from his hippie governess."

"You think I would do this?" he snapped.

"Isn't it a fair trade, if it keeps you out of prison?"

He turned and walked back to his cabin, weighing whether to cooperate or threaten her back; whether to alert Alison or leave the ship.

"Doctor Ali," he heard Dante call as he reached his cabin. "I came to say goodbye. Are you leaving or staying?"

"Deciding."

"Are you okay? I guess this didn't turn out the way you wanted."

"No," he answered with a grim smile. "Miss Deuss's idea of honoring the wonders is not what I expected. I just want to return to my quiet life in Iraq."

"Quiet? But you said you have a lot of responsibilities there."

"I suppose I do. But I turned away from much bigger ones. More was expected of me, you see." He stopped himself, then reached into the tote bag and took out the mask. "In your blog, you mentioned Thoth. You may have this."

"Whoa!" Dante laughed. "It's really authentic looking."

"It was a gift to me from Miss Deuss, but I cannot use it."

"Thanks. Here, I wrote down my name and address for you."

"Okay, then, Dante Rivera."

Rivera, he repeated to himself, studying Dante's face.

· ✦ ·

AT MISS DEUSS'S DIRECTION, Marshall announced the cancellation of the excursion to the Colossus site.

"That may be the first good decision she's made," Alison told him. "I suppose most of the guests will opt to stay on the ship. And pen some damning reviews. Such a shame."

Marshall reported that three of the seven journalists had bailed from the cruise—Deirdre, Michael, and Torrie—but that Doctor Ali had changed his plans and would be sailing with them to Bodrum.

"Why on earth would he want to stay, Marsh?"

"Don't know, but I saw Miss Deuss talking to him earlier at the gangway. He didn't look happy."

"Well, it does look gloomy. Guests are leaving, my talks are horrible, and I'm losing Dante somehow."

"That's not you talking, Alison. Look, I'll grab Dante and we'll go ashore."

"Oh, Marsh," she said in a voice so hollow he didn't recognize it. "Perk us up."

· ✦ ·

THE MAN SWEEPING UP bits of the Colossus in front of his café invited Alison, Marshall, and Dante to take a table.

"It's on to euros now," she said as she scanned her menu. "Bloody expensive, too. I remember when you could get a coffee and a sandwich for a dollar in this part of the world."

"When was that, the Middle Ages?" said Marshall.

Dante stared at his menu.

"Well, grade school," laughed Alison. "I was here with my parents. Can you picture us in our tie-dye shirts and bell-bottoms?" She watched Dante, hoping for a reaction. "Hair's the same," she said, trying again. "Okay, I'm going to freshen up. Excuse me."

"She's trying to fix whatever's come between you, you know," Marshall told Dante. "You could meet her halfway. She doesn't understand your resentment."

"Maybe she cares more about other stuff, other people. . . . She's not listening."

"She has a lot on her mind, Dante."

"That's all right." He looked away.

"Hey, it's not true that she doesn't care. Uh-uh."

"How do you know?"

"Because I have a little more history with her than you do. Since way back when I was seventeen."

Marshall told him that he had been in Alison's first group of students after she set up her foundation.

"We went to Machu Picchu. I was troubled back then, trying to deal with coming out. I was afraid that people wouldn't accept me, or understand. Except that she did. She had my back. And proved it."

"What happened?" asked Dante.

"I got bullied by a few local guys when I was walking with her after we arrived in Peru. They started name-calling."

"Like what?"

"The kinds of slurs you can imagine. I got shoved. And then one of them put me in a headlock. Alison stepped in and handled the second one, who was starting to kick me. Her stick found its way to his feet and tripped him."

"She had the stick then, too?"

"Of course. And the guy who had me in a headlock—well, I just instinctively swung my arm up and somehow my fist connected squarely to his jaw, and he let go. And then Alison marched toward the third one and whacked a light pole with her stick, and I guess he thought better of tangling with her. They all took off. Don't ever doubt her."

As Alison returned to the table, Dante saw two men approaching from the other direction.

"I saw those guys in Alexandria, Alison. They acted suspicious. What are they doing here?"

"Battle stations?" asked Marshall.

"Nah, they look manageable," said Alison. "Let's see what they want."

"Excuse us," said the first man. "Aren't you from the ship?"

Alison stared at them impassively.

"Well, we saw you come from the pier," the man continued. "So we assumed . . ."

"Yes," said Alison, "we're from *Modestine*."

"How do you like her?" the second man asked. "We know the ship from a cruise we took four or five years ago. We loved it."

Dante knew that *Modestine* was less than a year old. He narrowed his eyes to signal Alison.

"And you are?" asked Alison.

They introduced themselves as Mister Riggio and Mister Jerrie, owners of an antiques shop in London.

"We're on a buying trip," said Riggio. "We deal in small items."

"We found a statuette," said Dante. "We bought it in Cairo."

Now Alison narrowed her eyes at him in reproof.

"We'd love to see it," said Riggio. "We can tell you if it's authentic. We might make you an offer."

"It's a statuette of the first wife of Pharaoh Khufu," said Dante. "What dynasty would Khufu be, then?"

"Kung Fu, you say?" said Jerrie. "That's the Kung Fu Dynasty, obviously, which would make it a few hundred years old."

"You're off by more than four thousand years," Alison scoffed as Dante laughed. "And I don't think *Khufu* was into martial arts."

"Jet lag," said Jerrie sheepishly. "We've just arrived."

"You didn't just fly in from London," said Dante. "You were in Alexandria yesterday. I saw you."

"You must be mistaken," said Riggio, his voice turning darker. "So, can we see the statuette?"

"Beat it," barked Alison as she took up her stick. "Who are you impostors working for?"

Too flustered now to answer, the men looked at each other and hustled away.

"The brass," huffed Alison. "And why didn't you tell me about them sooner, Dante? I've never grounded anyone, but you're coming close."

He looked at Marshall and stifled a laugh.

"What?" she said. "Are you two conspiring? Because I don't need that right now."

"Just thinking that those guys got off easy," said Dante.

"I told him about Peru," said Marshall.

"Oh." She showed Dante a dent in her stick. "I was hoping I wouldn't have to damage this thing again. I find that the best defense against a bully is your wits. Why, though? Why didn't you tell me about these idiots?"

But when Dante bugged his eyes at her playfully, she broke up.

"I may be laughing, Dante, but—"

"Sorry, Alison. They didn't bother me in Alexandria. Although I'm pretty sure they reported me to Ibis. So . . . don't we have to get to the bottom of this? Don't we have to shine a light on Ibis?"

"My instructions were, if you remember, not to provoke them."

"I posted more," he heard himself say. "Late last night."

"About what?"

He told her about the commenter who insisted he was wrong about the mark on the Hillwood Stone and demanded that he stop blogging.

"I said I was sure it was Ibis's mark. I said I knew there was an ibis mosaic at the villa, too. I had to counterpunch him, Alison."

"And who is *him*?"

"Ra. But I've named him Ancient Light. He's the man in the villa. The man Otto works for. I'm sure of it."

She closed her eyes and began to count to ten, but Dante continued, telling her about his ibis constellation, how its stars connected the wonders, how it resembled the mosaic in his pictures, and that the mosaic was revered somehow by Ibis.

"It's happening so fast . . . I can't stop it. Why me?" he asked, his eyes pleading.

"I don't have an answer, I guess. But we'll figure it out. So Marshall told you I'm not such a tyrant?"

"If I was with you guys in Peru, I would have helped."

"I know that."

· ✦ ·

WHEN SHE RETURNED TO her cabin, Alison found that an envelope had been slipped under her door. It bore the baroness's crest, as did the invitation inside.

Tea
Four o'clock
At my cabin

Such an honor, thought Alison. *Or is it? She seems to be more than just one of Miss Deuss's investors. She also has a prior connection to Doctor Ali, even if he denied it. Who is this woman?*

It was already past four. *Tea with a baroness and you're in shorts and sandals!* She threw on a pair of white slacks, wedge espadrilles, and a scarf—a vintage Hermès Cosmos—and raced to the baroness's cabin.

Her door was open. Inside, a steward was setting up the tea service.

"Now you see why I brought my chef along," said the baroness with a mischievous grin, as she gestured toward the tiered stands of sweets and small, crustless sandwiches.

"Indeed," said Alison. "This is lovely, Baroness von Weber. That, too," she said, gesturing to the baroness's brooch, which depicted the face of Helios in gold with a rayed crown of emeralds.

"Thank you. Dante and Marshall admired it earlier. Do you have children, dear?"

Alison shook her head.

"Nor I. What if I had had a child like Monica Deuss? Perhaps such a person is enough family in one's life."

"Then Miss Deuss is . . . your niece?"

The baroness nodded. "Grandniece, actually, but thank you. You suspected it?"

"Well, I saw a resemblance. Sorry, my lady. I meant a physical resemblance. I guess I'm relieved that we see eye to eye on her."

The baroness poured the tea and identified the sandwiches and desserts, including freshly made marzipan, her chef's specialty.

Alison chose a sandwich, and waited.

"Of course, my grandniece is trying to make a name for herself. I applaud her for that. But she is failing. It is painful to watch. Is this your opinion, too?"

"I'm afraid so. I have no doubt that we'll all survive this, but the experience has hit one person especially hard."

"You refer to Doctor Ali."

"Yes. I think it broke his heart to see what she's doing. I'm curious . . . he told Dante and me he didn't know you. But you introduced us . . ."

"Ali is a leading expert on Babylon and the Hanging Gardens. Of course I would know him. Professionally." She took a sip of tea. "Perhaps he forgot that he had met me previously."

Alison thought it unlikely that anyone would forget meeting her.

"Well, I have given my grandniece too much space, so all of this is my fault. But enough of her. It has been a delight to have young Dante on the tour. And his writing," she added, "so insightful."

How does she know about that? Alison wondered. *Marshall says she has no computer, no cell phone. Is this clever patrician playing me? And why her defensiveness about knowing Doctor Ali? What does she want?*

"The statuette he found in Cairo . . ."

Finally, thought Alison.

"Is it authentic, do you think?"

"Possibly," said Alison. "But if it isn't, I'll still treasure it for the memories of this trip with Dante."

"Memories, yes. May I see it?"

Alison grimaced, annoyed by this latest inquiry about the

statuette. She told the baroness about the unsettling interactions she had had with Mrs. Gamal in Alexandria, and with the men who had just grilled her when she was ashore. *I'm in no mood right now to give anything more away about that statuette*, she seethed. Her expression clearly conveyed her reluctance to discuss it.

"Forgive me, then, Miss Fine. I just thought I might have an opportunity to look at it. Just to enjoy it, really. Not another word about it. I suspect the reason for all the interest is your young man's blog. It is far-reaching, I am told. We are all reading it. The guests show it to me. Let me show you something."

She walked to her desk and pulled a photograph from a leather portfolio.

"You mentioned that you will treasure your memories of this trip with Dante," she said, handing Alison the photo. "My husband. Well, one of them. The second, I think."

Alison laughed. "He's very handsome, my lady. Was this taken at a university? It looks like Heidelberg, maybe?"

"He was the director of the Egyptian collection there. Do you see what he is holding?"

"My goodness," said Alison. "The Khufu statuette?"

The baroness nodded. "It was entrusted to him for study. So, you understand my interest in the little companion statuette you found?" She paused. "Miss Fine, if your statuette is authentic, I would very much like to purchase it. Can you see why I would like to reunite the ancient couple in memory of my husband, if only virtually, with this photograph? Would it not be wonderful and fitting?"

"Oh, my lady, I don't really know if she's authentic. I do have an expert looking at her now," she said, without naming Professor James. "But if she is authentic, maybe she should just stay in Egypt."

"Of course."

Alison realized she had implied that the statuette was not in the ship's safe, contradicting what Dante had told Mrs. Gamal. "Well,

I mean, I'd rather she just stay in the ship's safe for now. I meant that an expert is looking at *photos* of the statuette, in Egypt. Dante took the photos . . . for the expert to review. You might ask Dante to show them to you on his camera."

"Thank you. Well, I do hope you will give me an opportunity to purchase her."

"I think not."

"I understand," said the baroness. "Your appraiser is, may I ask?"

"A knowledgeable person that I've met, I mean, know."

"Very well. Now, do not trouble yourself with all the noise around this. Or with the problems with the cruise. Concentrate on your work, and I will attend to Monica Deuss."

"Thank you. And thank you for tea."

"You may thank Werner, my chef."

"How will I recognize him?"

"Well, if you can picture Hercule Poirot . . . except the mustache of Chef Werner is blond and not tidy."

"Then I'm sure I'll spot him."

"But you haven't tasted his creation," said the baroness, waving a hand at the marzipan Mausoleum on Alison's plate. "He made it in honor of the wonder we will visit next."

"I thought I might take it for Dante. May I?"

"Of course."

After Alison left, the baroness went to her desk to write a note that would be faxed to her friend in Alexandria:

> My effort to acquire Item πK-QM-Stte-i-01 un-successful. Am convinced it is not on ship. Likely in Cairo for study by owner's recent acquaintance: Prof Jasper James.

· ✦ ·

AT DINNER, ALISON BRIEFED Dante and Marshall on her visit with
the baroness.

"Maybe I'm sentimental," she told them, "but I think she was
sincere in wanting the statuette in her husband's memory."

"What if she's connected to those two men?" said Dante.

"I don't know," said Marshall. "Those guys didn't seem to be
operating with a lot of direction. But you're right, we can't rule out
the possibility that everyone who's approached you guys about this
statuette is working for the same person."

"Well, I wouldn't think the baroness takes orders from anyone,"
said Alison.

"Not so fast," said Marshall. He told her he had delivered a
sealed note to the baroness the night they left Alexandria, then he
took from his pocket a note he had found earlier in the communications room.

"I meant to show this to you at lunch. It was sent to someone
she calls 'Old friend.' I think it must be her reply to that note I
took to her."

Alison read it aloud.

You continue your pursuit, and, alas, you will have
my help. Will apprise you of progress.

"She's with Ibis," said Dante.

"Well, we don't know who she's telling she'll help to do what,"
said Alison, even as she worried whether, and to whom, the baroness might report their tea conversation. "I just don't want to believe
she's part of a conspiracy against us."

"Alison, please listen," said Dante. "That comment from Ra—
the man I'm calling Ancient Light—he's trying to direct attention

away from Ibis, and from the Hillwood Stone and what happened to Mishky in Chicago. And now I'm getting comments on my blog from all over. Everyone wants to know more about Ibis. And the villa—"

"No more about this, Dante."

"He's the head of Ibis," Dante insisted. "I told you I saw someone in the villa's tower when we sailed from Alexandria. It was him, and I saw him wave to the baroness. And she waved back. She's part of it. So is Otto."

"Okay, time out," she told him, holding up her hand. "Dialing Dyllis, here," she mumbled.

"Huh?" said Marshall.

"A friend with CNN in Istanbul," she said as she scrolled her phone contacts. "I need another opinion about what Dante's stirred up. Dyllis, it's Alison."

"Ah, so are you close to Turkey now? Can't wait to see you."

"Right, we're leaving Rhodes soon, but that lunch at the Mausoleum we planned last year will have to wait. Blame it on Ibis. I'm concerned, Dyl."

"Well, I did do some checking, as promised, after you called me from Cairo. I didn't find much about them that's credible. Could be it's all a bit blown up. A myth."

"Myth?" said Alison. She told Dyllis about Dante's discovery of the villa in Alexandria, their meeting with Mrs. Gamal, the confrontation with Riggio and Jerrie, and the comment from Ra telling Dante to cease blogging. "There's nothing mythical about Ibis, Dyl. And those two men who've been tailing us—we think they work for Sackville. If they weren't so inept I'd really worry. But maybe that makes them dangerous. And now Dante believes the baroness is connected to Ancient Light."

"Who?"

"The Ibis leader." She lowered her voice and stepped away from Dante. "His last blog is what's really unraveling me, Dyl. He wrote that he's been to that villa. He thinks it's ground zero for Ibis. He's dangerously out of bounds. I feel I ought to call his grandmother. Return home."

Dyllis advised her not to decide yet, saying she would check further into Ibis. "And I'm thinking out loud here, Alison, but, you know, sometimes the best strategy is to create more publicity. I'm looking at Dante's blog now. I'm thinking we address the *I* versus *H* ruse they've put out there and expose them for trying to discredit Dante. We shine a light on them . . . keep them honest."

"That's what Dante thinks, too. I don't like the idea of more publicity, but if someone opens this up, I want it to be you. And I brought Dante along to discover, after all. I don't like playing censor."

"Good. I'll talk to my reporters. If Dante is right—if there really is a private, and perhaps ill-gotten, Seven Wonders collection somewhere—well, that would be big. And if Dante's going to explore this, he'll need you to guide him—"

"Through the inferno?" Alison quipped. "Like Virgil with the poet Dante?"

"You're the best guide our Dante could have. Embrace it."

"Well, then, ciao."

"Trust yourself, Alison. I'll be in touch."

8

HALICARNASSUS AND THE MAUSOLEUM

T HE LONG BLAST FROM *Modestine*'s horn signaled to the harbor
at Rhodes that she was under way, her next stop, Bodrum—
known as Halicarnassus in Mausolus's time—just sixty miles
north on the Turkish coast.

Dante took his Thoth mask and laptop to the pool and opened
an article he had bookmarked about the Mausoleum.

"Unlike the pyramids of the Egyptian pharaohs," he read, "the
tomb of Mausolus was ornate and bristled with statuary and friezes.
The massive marble structure was felled by earthquakes."

The sun had set now, and as he pictured Mausolus and his sister
Artemisia riding their chariot atop the roof in the moonlight, he
had to smile.

"Another tomb, though," he said, remembering his episode inside Khufu's pyramid. He pulled the Thoth mask from his bag and
admired its moon-disk crown, crescent beak, and striped blue-and-
gold cloth. *Thoth might communicate in a different way,* he told
himself, recalling his thoughts on the airplane days earlier. *Not with
pictures or shadows.*

He stood and pulled the mask over his head, and as he closed his
eyes there came a muffled, whirring sound and vibrations so deep
that he wondered if the energy was from *Modestine*'s radars and
engines or from Thoth himself.

"What's happening?" he murmured, looking up, almost as if commanded. "Heart," he whispered, recognizing the vessel-shaped hieroglyph that was burned into the night sky. "Finally."

He remembered that the ancient Egyptians believed the heart held their soul, mind, and spirit. He remembered Alison saying it was the heart that sensed feelings and emotions.

Listen, he told himself. *Something from Doctor Ali . . . a terrible distress. And more . . . something he's carrying, keeping inside.*

He tore off the mask and ran down the stairway to the main deck, nearly colliding with Marshall.

"What are you doing?" Marshall called to him.

"What the situation requires . . . like you said."

"Okay, but where?"

"Doctor Ali," he panted. "He's still aboard?"

"Yes, he decided to stay."

"I have to stop him," he called back as he ran. "He's upset with Miss Deuss. He might do something."

Marshall looked at his watch. "Hmm. I suppose we could just let this play out. . . . Hey, I'm kidding," he shouted after Dante. "Where are they?"

"Her cabin."

Modestine's running lights lit the deck only dimly as Dante raced aft. Through the evening fog he could make out Doctor Ali pacing haltingly outside Miss Deuss's door some thirty feet ahead. But as he closed in, he felt his heart pound and his legs go leaden. A dizzying, blinding white field swirled in and around him. And against this field a man appearing in silhouette . . . his father . . . acting all at once tense, angry, frustrated, and then turning to him, his face pained . . . and now only darkness, and hearing his mother's cries, and no one hearing his own.

He called out, but no sound came. He called out again, but only a feeble, guttural "No-oo" escaped his throat, and he fell.

Hearing the plea, Doctor Ali turned away from Miss Deuss's door and ran to him. At the same time, Marshall arrived.

"There's a gash in his ear," said Marshall. "I'll get help. Don't move him."

Doctor Ali cradled Dante, calling to him, and calling again, until he opened his eyes.

"No, Papa!" he begged to the anguished face above him.

"It's me, Dante. It's Ali. You're safe."

He was shaking. "I tried to stop it."

"What did you try to stop?"

"Him . . . I don't know . . . You."

"Take a big breath," Doctor Ali told him. He drew his hand to his forehead and began a prayer for Dante, and for himself.

"Is he okay?" Alison shouted as she arrived with Marshall and the ship's nurse.

"He's frightened," Doctor Ali answered. "He spoke, but he seems confused. Please . . . take care of him." He excused himself and walked back to Miss Deuss's cabin, where she stood watching.

"What's all that about?" she complained. "Come in and close the door."

"First, I get rid of this," he told her as he pulled the stun gun from his jacket and threw it into the sea.

"Was that the boy?" she asked. "Did you do it already?"

"No," he answered, glaring at her. "He fell. I reject your plans for him."

"You're not off the hook."

"I'm done!"

He left her and went to the baroness's cabin.

"I assumed you left the ship at Rhodes, Ali. I am glad you stayed. You know I wanted that."

"And I want an explanation. Monica Deuss's invitation to me, to do the lecture—"

"It was my idea."

"It always is. But why?"

"Because I never see you. Because I knew you could add substance to this venture."

The baroness was unfazed by his news that Miss Deuss had demanded his help in acquiring objects from Ibis, and Alison's statuette as well. But when he told her Miss Deuss had threatened to expose him, she blanched.

"You must not engage with her on this, Ali." She paused to calculate her next words. "Please try not to worry."

"You think it's that easy? You're not living with my burden."

"You must keep your silence." She turned away, wishing she could say more. "And not volunteer anything to Dante."

"You know I never wanted anything to do with Ibis. I don't seek to undermine it either."

"Well, I want to believe that. Except you drink too much. And maybe you say things that are not . . . discreet."

"I've cautioned him not to speak of Ibis. Do you approve, my lady?"

"I do not approve of your sarcasm. I think you should not be talking to him at all, in fact."

"Your niece wants me to stop him from blogging. She gave me a stun gun! I went to her cabin—"

"Have you harmed her?"

"No. Dante ran to me. He fell. He's hurt."

"Mein Gott."

"I want your help in protecting him."

"Well, I am fond of him . . ."

"Answer me," he demanded. "Will you protect him and Alison from Deuss?"

"Of course."

"And from Ibis?"

"You overestimate my influence. The Ibis principal will not tolerate more revelations from Dante. But neither will he fail to appreciate what that boy did for you tonight, so I will convey that to him."

He knew she could commit to nothing more. He turned to leave, unsure of his next steps, either now or when the ship would dock in Bodrum.

"But stay, Ali, and bear with us," she told him. "Enjoy the cruise, perhaps. Find some peace, perhaps."

· ✦ ·

THE BARONESS WASTED NO time in summoning Miss Deuss to her cabin.

"We have business to discuss," she stated.

"Well, then, *let's*," said Miss Deuss, seizing the offensive. "Ibis possesses so much. Or does it? You've promised it, but it's never seen. Where is it?"

The baroness ignored the question. It was one her grandniece had asked many times. "You were offered some pieces for your resort. That is all you need to know."

"I need more than a few loaned tidbits. I want a bigger commitment to the resort, and to the cruise. To reinvigorate them."

"You mean salvage them. I see nothing coming of either now, given your decisions."

"I don't know what you mean by that."

"That is precisely the problem. You haven't a clue."

Miss Deuss remained defiant. "I deserve a little help."

"When treachery fails? I will get to the point. You have grossly misrepresented your assets to your investors. Some have told me they doubt you. And now you have misled your guests. Our offer to loan you some objects was contingent upon your successful passage through a series of gates, this cruise being one of them. And you are failing. Worse, you would harm Dante. I have just spoken with Ali."

"Ali is a coward. Useless."

"Leave him alone. And leave the Americans alone. I am going to advise the organization of your transgressions."

"Do as you like. But know that I will expose Ali unless you can deliver more items from the collection."

"Be very careful, niece. Blackmail is a crime. I will not allow you to harm Ali, or the organization."

Miss Deuss responded with a sullen stare.

"You may proceed with your project," the baroness continued, "provided you cease deceiving your backers and the guests."

"And just how will I attract visitors without more from the collection?"

"You must improvise, my dear. Have you considered reproductions? Someday, if you prove worthy, a loan of more pieces may be offered. This will be my recommendation to the leadership. Focus on improving yourself. And this chaotic cruise. Be happy that we do not shut you down completely."

Miss Deuss turned to leave.

"I have not finished, niece. Do not threaten me again. And do not threaten Ali, or mention his past again. To anyone."

MARSHALL BROUGHT DANTE'S LAPTOP to the ship's dispensary.

"He'll want this," he told Alison. "How is he?"

"Still sleeping. How did all this happen, Marsh?"

"He told me he had to stop Doctor Ali from going to Miss Deuss. Ali said he was saying, 'No, Papa,' after he fell."

"Poor guy. He relived something tonight."

"Like he did inside the pyramid. And on the train, when he called for his mother in his sleep."

"Oh, Marsh, what happened when he was a kid?"

· ✦ ·

FOUR HOURS LATER, DANTE began to wake, a rhyme pulsing through his head.

> *A marble mausoleum gone,*
> *A heavy marble doorstop strong,*
> *A memory coming at me . . .*
> *Camouflaged.*

Where am I? he wondered.

Alison stood nearby, her face drawn, as a nurse told Marshall, "So no concussion. It's less about the wound than anxiousness. We gave him a sedative."

He put his hand to his head and felt a bandage. Alison leaned over him, and he was glad that her head eclipsed the harsh fluorescent lights above. Around her shadowed face her unruly hair became a corona.

"Alison? Am I alive?"

"You are, but you had a fall. You're just a little medicated."

"Did Doctor Ali . . .?"

"Doctor Ali is fine. Everyone's fine."

"I tried to stop it."

"Stop what?"

"Something from happening. But then, something else took over."

"I guess you did stop it," she said. "Because nothing happened, except for you falling. Doctor Ali helped you. Marshall, too."

"I saw a hieroglyph before that. In the sky. A heart."

"Okay," she said, smiling to conceal her worry.

"Are we near Bodrum?"

"Still a few hours away," said Marshall. "The captain is taking his time on this leg. He wants us to arrive at dawn."

"The Mausoleum," he said softly. "Can you wake me?"

"Sure."

"My computer . . ."

"It's here," said Marshall. "You did a brave thing earlier tonight, going to Doctor Ali."

"Oh," he murmured.

Alison began to ask him again what he had tried to stop, but saw that he was asleep.

· ✦ ·

AT FIRST LIGHT, ALISON returned to the dispensary and found Dante sitting on his bed. He had drawn the Mausoleum and filled the sky around it with clouds, all of them heavy and dark.

"I've emailed Nora and Grandma," he told her. "They said you called. They said you wanted us to return home."

"I thought it best. But we don't have to decide right now. We'll play it by ear, so to speak. Does it hurt?"

"Not as much as when the baroness was pinching it."

"Let's go out on deck. So, do you want to tell me what came over you last night? You cried out."

"I just tried to help Doctor Ali, that's all."

"But you called for your father. Do you remember?"

"Why aren't we docked yet?"

"It's a small harbor, so we've anchored here," she answered, letting her question go. "The motor launch will take people ashore later."

Dante took in the hundreds of sailboats, the hundreds of white buildings that ringed Bodrum's harbor, and, looming above it, the fifteenth-century Bodrum Castle, which had been fortified with stones from the ruined Mausoleum.

"I wonder who he really was," he said.

"Who? Mausolus?"

"My father. And why he didn't want me around."

"Oh, no, Dante, you shouldn't think about him like that—"

"I'm going to get ready."

"Uh-uh," she told him.

"But I'm okay. I don't want to miss the Mausoleum."

"Afraid not. Go on to your cabin, please. I'll check in on you at noon, before I go ashore."

· ✦ ·

ALISON ADMIRED CHEF WERNER's marzipan Mausoleum as she reviewed her notes in her cabin. She was looking forward to giving it to Dante before boarding the launch for the tour. At a knock, she put her notes down to answer.

"What's the matter, Marshall? You look awful." She saw that he was clenching several rolled-up sheets of paper.

He handed one to her. "It's an email Dante printed. It's from his sister. I found it on his desk when I went to check on him."

Dante—I found these articles. There was no car accident. That's not how Mama died. Don't be angry
with Grandma, or Papa. Or me for sending this.

The note included two links, one to the *Chicago Tribune*, the other
to the *Chicago Sun-Times*.

"What was in the links?"

Marshall handed her a second sheet.

"Oh, wow, this is the story Dyllis wrote about Mishky's death."

"It says the police were looking for the person who arranged the
meeting Mishky had at the Trib to sell the Hillwood Stone."

"Yes, I remember."

"It doesn't name that person, but this article from the *Sun-Times*
a couple of days later does. Enrique Rivera. From Humboldt Park."

"Oh, no," Alison gasped.

"Dante's father?"

"Yes. I know the name from Dante's school records."

"There's this paragraph from the article," said Marshall. "'Rivera's
wife, Serena Brooks Rivera, died earlier this week at the couple's
home. The woman was pregnant, but the child, a girl, survived.
The two had been arguing, according to a neighbor.'"

Now she understood what Dante's grandmother had said
to her—that Dante would have heard his mother's death. *How,
though, did his father get mixed up with Mishky?*

"Where is he, Marsh? Can you check the lounge and I'll—"

"I've checked. Lieutenant Regan told me he went with a few of
the crew to drop mail ashore. He said they should be right back."

"No," she said, grabbing her stick. "He's not going to be
coming back with them. He's dealing with this somewhere. The
Mausoleum."

She scooped up her bag, knocking the marzipan to the floor and
breaking it in two.

"We need to go to him."

· ✦ ·

DANTE SAT ALONE AT the bow of *Modestine*'s speeding motor launch. He ignored the crew's banter as he studied a map on his computer to determine his route to the Mausoleum.

"Go back without me," he told the crew when they reached the pier. "I'm going up to the Mausoleum. I'll see Alison there later."

"No," said Eyüp, the sturdy Turk who was *Modestine*'s boatswain. "You did not tell your people this, I think. Anyway, the Mausoleum is close. I will take you, but only for a minute."

"I want to go alone, Eyüp."

"I will stay near to you. Your head is okay?"

Dante felt the bandage. He had forgotten the wound, but touching it intensified the memory that had overwhelmed him outside Miss Deuss's cabin the night before.

Eyüp followed as he made his way through the town and up a hill, then to the edge of a field strewn with ancient stones and broken columns from the ruined Mausoleum. He walked to a foundation stone and sat.

Eyüp stepped away to the edge of the field, giving him some respectful distance, and greeted a man dressed in a suit and holding an instrument. Dante could not make out the instrument until the man began to play. It was a bassoon, and its sound brought back the night six months earlier when Alison had played for his birthday. That had been a night of celebration, but the notes streaming to him now were from a work of profound sorrow.

He tried to remember his mother, anything of her, but there were only vague impressions . . . her sundress . . . her gentleness as she combed his hair . . . sometimes a song at night . . . the times he would watch her looking off, looking sad inside. And when his father was there, he remembered the tension. He remembered how he would sit off to himself, but at other times he would be too "on," too agitated, and how any loud noise would unnerve him. It began to come to him now, how upset his father had been that night, and the argument that woke him.

On the road nearby, a bus lumbered in, and when its brakes sent out a shriek, he held his hands to his ears as he did the night he heard his mother's screams.

"Papa," he whispered. "She died then. And you left."

He sat motionless, determined to see more than just glimpses of that night. Now, finally, it showed itself . . . the arguing . . . his father's pacing . . . his clothing, tan and brown. Camouflage. Then, his father moving toward him and guiding him with firm hands on his shoulders down the hallway and into the small cupboard under the stairs. The scrape of the heavy doorstop. The darkness. And again the screams, some of them his own . . . then quiet, and nothing more.

Sensing an approach from behind, he turned. It was the two men again, some forty feet away. *They must be desperate now*, he thought. *There will be no more polite games. I could run, or yell for Eyüp. No, by Mausolus, I will not be timid.*

He looked up to the sky and saw that another hieroglyph had formed, this time of an ancient Egyptian ship. Then, next to it, another, resembling feathers.

The boat's sail was unfurled, which he knew meant a voyage up-stream, against the current. But the second hieroglyphs looked only vaguely familiar. He knew they were not feathers, but that they were organic, perhaps a plant.

Reeds, he told himself, *and pens were made from them, as Alison said. All right, push against the current. Make the journey. Back to Egypt. To Alexandria, of course. To find out. Hadn't the Pharos candle relit itself? And write it out, wherever it leads, with as many pens as it takes.*

"What's he doing?" he heard Riggio say.

"He's in some kind of trance," said Jerrie.

The mournful sound of the bassoon flowed across the field again.

"I don't like it here," said Jerrie.

Dante turned and looked up. *Ignore them,* he told himself, and he would have had he not smelled Riggio's rancid breath and felt Jerrie's foot press down hard onto his own.

He looked over to Eyüp, who had begun to run toward him, and held up his hand to signal he didn't need help.

"We're going to take a walk," said Riggio. "Back to town. And you can tell us more about the statuette."

"I will not," Dante declared. "You mess with me and you'll regret it."

"Let me be clear," said Jerrie. "You're going to bring it to us. This afternoon, or life will become very difficult for you."

"It already is. So what."

"Stand up," said Jerrie, pressing his foot onto Dante's even harder.

"We don't have the statuette, you morons."

"Where is it?" demanded Jerric.

"Where do you think it is? Why don't you ask your boss?"

"It's at the university, then," declared Jerrie, pushing him away. "It's in Cairo, isn't it." He turned to Riggio. "So Sackville has it. Or soon will. I suspected it. Maybe he sent us here to make the big shots think we're tracking it. Maybe he's been playing them. And us."

"Forget this kid, then," said Riggio, and they stormed off.

Eyüp reached him just as Alison, Marshall, and Lieutenant Regan arrived from the other direction.

"Did they hurt you?" Alison cried.

"I'm okay. They're more interested in Doctor Sackville now."

"Give us a minute, guys," Alison told the others. She pointed to a broken marble column with her stick and suggested to Dante that they sit. She told him she had seen what Nora sent.

"You were only three, right?" she asked. "Do you remember them . . . your father and mother?"

"I remember them a little, but it's not just memories." He began to tremble. "I felt them here."

"Do you understand what happened between them?"

He answered haltingly. "Grandma always said my mother died in an accident. I never questioned it. But I had an old memory of being in bed, and hearing things, and being scared. And looking out from my room toward the kitchen. That's all I remembered, until last night, when I saw Doctor Ali pacing outside Miss Deuss's cabin . . . It was like seeing my father that night, arguing with my mother, and I tried to tell them to stop . . ."

"And that's when you fell?"

"Yes. I began to remember more after seeing Nora's email . . . And then more came to me here." His words trailed off, but then came back in a rush. "When I got out of bed, I must have surprised my father because he took me to the cupboard. Then I heard him push a heavy piece of marble against the door. We still have it. Grandma said he wanted to make something from it some day." He stared down at the marble column as he spoke.

"Do you want to move away from this thing?" she asked.

"No. And then I heard their voices some more, but then cries so loud I had to block my ears. I tried to push the door open, but the marble doorstop was too heavy. I don't remember anything else. Just, afterward, staying with Grandma and my grandfather. Then I remember Grandma telling me I have a new sister, and that she was a present from my mother. It was weird, because when she showed me, it was like I already knew her."

"Are you okay now?"

"I guess."

"Okay, but tell me, when you ran to Doctor Ali, you said you needed to help him. He was outside Miss Deuss's cabin. What was that about? Is there something going on between them?"

"She's trying to manipulate him."

"Why do you say that?"

"Because I can feel it."

"Okay. Is there anything else you want to talk about?"

"Just . . . What did my father do to my mother? And then the *Tribune* article said that he might have been involved in killing Mishky? He ran away. I don't understand."

She reminded him that the articles didn't say his father was a suspect in Mishky's death, only that the police wanted to talk with him.

"I'd trade seeing the future," he said, "if I could see more from the past. This one time . . ."

"I know. But I have to think your grandmother will tell you more about your parents once you get home."

"Unexpected things happen when you travel, like you said."

"This qualifies as one," she agreed, seeing the storm in his eyes begin to pass.

"More will happen, too. I'm thinking about Ibis now. I know what I've been writing has gotten us into trouble. I know what you're thinking, but I can't end my blog. Or ignore what I'm finding out about Ibis. I can't stop."

He couldn't read her face, but her hand reached for her stick, then swung its silver knob toward him. He waited for her verdict.

"And you shouldn't stop. So, we'll see this through. A step at a time, within boundaries, and with your grandmother's permission. But are you sure you're okay about your mother and father?"

He gripped the side of the marble column and pulled himself up. "There's still too much I don't know."

They heard Marshall call, "They're closing the site to set up for the entertainment. We need to leave."

They walked past a parked bus where roadies were unloading instrument cases. The man with the bassoon had walked over to it and was now greeting other people in formal dress as they stepped out. Moments later, three vans came up the hill.

"And that would be more talent," said Marshall. "The choir, I'm guessing."

"Tell me," said Alison, rolling her eyes. "What's Miss Deuss doing this time?"

"Mozart's *Requiem*. Highlights from it, anyway."

"Kyrie eleison! That's 'Lord have mercy,'" she told Dante. "So, she's doing music for a Christian requiem in a Muslim country at the tomb of a ruler who followed the traditions of the ancient Greeks. I might've gone with something else. . . . Anyway, look, Marsh, I have a favor to ask. Take a good look at the site here. Absorb it. You're going to do the Mausoleum talk for me."

"I am?"

"Yes. In a couple of hours. Best if Dante and I stay on the ship."

"Mausolus and his sister," Dante said quietly to Marshall. "The two giant statues in the chariot on the roof . . ."

"Yes? They're in the British Museum now, right?"

"Say that they survived the earthquake. Say they landed on top of all the rubble, and they weren't crushed by it."

· ✦ ·

"HOW DID IT GO?" Alison asked Marshall when he returned to *Modestine*.

"Well, I would say that my narrative complemented Mozart's masterpiece and the Mausoleum's moody majesty," he emoted. "I compared the brasses and strings to the building's dazzling sculptures and reliefs. I spoke of the penetrating woodwinds and percussion and how they evoked the depths of the ruler's ancient tomb. And how the choir galloped and soared like his airborne chariot. Okay, it was a little over the top."

"Was the baroness there?" asked Dante.

"She was, brooch and all. This time it was a small gold chariot and horse in profile above a big oval cameo of a Greek soldier battling an Amazon. Like my presentation, it was a bit much. Anyway, the *Requiem* was amazing. Everyone loved it."

Alison recalled her own performances of the *Requiem*, which she loved for its almost operatic drama and scale. She thought about the composing she longed to do. *Is it really just a mental block? Or, my own shortcomings? Have I been too harsh on Miss Deuss, who was at least in the arena and having a grand go of it?*

"Then," said Marshall, "she asked the guests for their patience. She promised a new commitment to the cruise and the resort. I think there's a chance she might pull this off."

"Well, then, I give her credit," said Alison. "But where will she get all the wonders stuff she's promising? Is that even possible?"

"Dyllis's story just got posted on CNN," said Dante. He showed it to them on his laptop. "It's short, but she got it right."

"Okay," said Alison as she read, "it looks like she's just laying out the facts. Uh-huh, including some I didn't know about. Dante, there's more here than I've been seeing in your blogs. It's almost as if she interviewed you."

"She did, by email this morning after we left the dispensary. She said she just needed to fill in some gaps. She kept her promise not to quote me."

Let's hope Dyllis is right, Alison thought. *That shining a light on them will keep them away from us.*

"Okay," she said, drawing a long breath. "In for a penny, in for a pound."

· ✦ ·

AT THE VILLA IN Alexandria, classical Egyptian music pulsed from a vintage Bakelite-cased radio in the second-floor library. Otto entered and handed a correspondence folder to the man standing on the balcony.

"I've printed a CNN story for you, sir. There are also first reviews of Monica Deuss's cruise by three of the passengers. The reviews are not positive. And a message from the baroness."

The man read Dyllis's story first.

"It appears that I will be known to the world now as Ancient Light."

He skipped over the cruise reviews and read the baroness's note, which reported Miss Deuss's new demand for at least five objects from each wonder in return for her enlistment of Doctor Ali to silence Dante and to acquire the statuette. She reported Miss Deuss's threats against Doctor Ali. She reported that Doctor Ali had nearly acted out against Miss Deuss, but that Dante had stopped him. She advised that Miss Deuss was "capable of further recklessness," that Doctor Ali's behavior was "unsteady," and that she doubted her influence over either of them. She added that Sackville's men had been "monstrously clumsy, if not criminal."

"Reply to her," Ancient Light ordered. "Say that absolutely no objects will go to Monica Deuss. None."

"The baroness makes no mention of her own efforts to acquire the statuette, sir."

"She advised me separately that she was unsuccessful. She believes it is in Cairo with Professor Jasper James." He paused, growing irritated. "What is so difficult about this?" he thundered.

"And the boy, sir? He is obviously the source of the CNN story. This article is damaging."

"What is their next stop?"

"Ephesus. The port of Kuşadası."

"Contact him. Say that I want to meet him and Miss Fine."

"Sir, are you able to travel? Surely—"

"Do it."

"I will invite them by email," said Otto. "But how shall I refer to you?"

"By the name he has given me."

"Yes, sir. And CNN? This reporter and many others will dig."

"Call Lord Cranleigh in London. Have his papers debunk the stories. Now, we will need someone to encourage Dante and his guardian to meet with me. How to accomplish that?"

"He has mentioned his sister in Chicago . . . so perhaps through her," suggested Otto. "I have an idea."

"Do it."

"And the two men Sackville employed?"

"They are not to be used again. Where did he find them? They are lower than common . . . pickpockets." He nearly spat the word out. "Leave me now."

"Sir, the baroness's note also raised a concern about Ali."

To this, Ancient Light did not give an answer.

· ✦ ·

ALISON RESOLVED TO ASK Chef Werner to create another marzipan for Dante. But not another tomb, she decided.

She went to the ship's galley but stopped at the swinging double doors marked *Galley Staff Only*. She peered through the doors' round windows into the stainless-steel hive of white-jacketed chefs, prep staff, and waiters, until her eyes met those of a portly, fastidious man with a broomy blond mustache.

"Chef Werner," she called. "Please, may I have a quick word?"

He approached reluctantly.

"I'm sorry to interrupt, Chef. I had tea with the baroness, and your creations were wonderful."

He bowed.

"I'm traveling with my student. Maybe you've seen him? He took a terrible fall, and he's been through some stuff today. Could you make a marzipan for him? Maybe a likeness of an Egyptian deity . . . Thoth? I can print an image for you."

"I am familiar with the Egyptian deities, madam. I will do this for him." He began a sketch of Thoth, then crossed it out. "I prefer to do something less conventional," he told her, before retreating back into the galley.

· ✦ ·

An email with the subject line "Invitation" appeared in Dante's inbox.

> Mr. Dante: I congratulate you on your blog. You have speculated about an organisation called Ibis and treasures from ancient civilisations. You report seeing a mosaic and finding a statuette. I offer you an opportunity to discuss these things whilst you are in Ephesus. I urge you and your guardian to meet with me. Do not reply to this email, but click on the appropriate link below to indicate whether you accept or decline.
>
> Regards, Ancient Light

"Yes!" Dante shouted. He forwarded the note to Nora, then rushed to Alison's cabin.

"Another message from Ibis," he told her. "This time, an email. Look. It's directly from Ancient Light."

"Okay," she said, reading. "So please tell me you haven't accepted."

A ping from the computer announced another email.

Dante opened it, but as he read, Alison saw his excitement turn to puzzlement and then to alarm.

"What's the matter?"

"I forwarded his email to Nora a few minutes ago. Look at her reply."

> Dante: You should accept his invitation and take advantage of the opportunity whilst you can. Our grandmother agrees. You will discover more about the ancient civilisations.

"Well, she's being encouraging, of course," Alison said.

"But Nora never says, 'our grandmother.' And she spells *civilization* with an *s* instead of a *z*. And she uses *whilst*. The same spelling mistakes Ancient Light made in his email. Nora doesn't make spelling mistakes."

"Well, they're not mistakes, exactly. They're British spellings. But you're right, Nora wouldn't—"

"They've hacked her! Oh, man, we're closing in, Alison. I can't believe they want to meet."

"I hope you don't think this Ancient Light's invitation is merely social, given everything you posted."

"I know I messed up, but—"

"Correct. And I made a promise to see this through with you. But now they want direct contact."

"Please, Alison. Dyllis—"

"Whatever Dyllis comes back with now, I'm not very interested in. You've upset these people. I'm sorry, but I have to think about your safety. . . . We need to leave the cruise. I know that now."

"But—"

"Maybe we'll fly to Greece and visit the Zeus site on our own before going back. I'm glad you at least agree that you went too far."

"I want to meet him, Alison. I want to know what he wants to say to us."

"What he wants is to strong-arm you. To shut you up, and at the same time get his hands on the statuette."

"But we can just stay on the ship when we get to Ephesus and meet him that way."

"Stay on the ship, yes. Meet with him, no. And the only way I might consider staying with the tour is if you decline the invitation. Which you will do. Now."

The broken marzipan on the floor caught his eye.

"What's that?" he asked.

"A marzipan sweet I saved for you. It's the Mausoleum. Or was, before I dropped it. I forgot it was there. Go ahead and toss it, would you?"

He picked up the two pieces and told her he would keep them. He held one in each hand, remembering his mother, remembering his father, and not abandoning hope that he and Ancient Light would meet.

"Now, the unfinished business, please," she told him.

He stared into his keyboard.

"You're stalling."

"Okay, it's done," he muttered as he declined Ancient Light's invitation, "but we could've met the head of Ibis."

"If we ever do, it will be on our terms, not his."

She watched him click through several news sites, convinced he hadn't heard her.

"Here's an article by Deirdre in the *Independent*," he said. "It's about the cruise."

"What's her headline?"

"Look." It read, "The Ancient Wonders' 'Woe' Factor."

"Ouch!"

"And look at this from London, in the *Direct News*. I can't believe it," he fumed. "'No Ancient Wonders Trove, Experts Say. Youth Makes Bogus Claims about Debunked Urban Legend.'"

"Well, that's a tabloid," she scoffed, but Dante saw that the words had angered her. Her cell phone rang.

"Alison, it's Dyllis. Where are you?"

"Still in Bodrum. We'll be under way soon for Ephesus."

"You've seen the stories?"

"Working our way through them. What's with the *Direct News*, Dyl?"

"That's a Cranleigh paper. They make things up. It's getting curious, isn't it?"

"More than curious at this point," said Alison. "They've hacked Dante's sister's email account and issued an invitation to meet in Ephesus."

"Tell Dyllis it's time to push back," Dante broke in. "I wanted to meet Ancient Light, but now they're saying I'm bogus. They're not taking me seriously. I can blog that Ibis is more than a myth. I can say they've hacked Nora. They can't do this to us."

Hearing him, Dyllis asked Alison to put her on speaker and explained that they were now up against the media empire of Lord Cranleigh, most certainly at Ibis's behest, and that they would need to respond.

"We're committed, remember, Alison. Dante needs to write, to correct the record."

He spoke the words as he typed.

Four things have happened that prove Ibis is not only real, but active:

1. The comment from Ra told me to cease writing and that the Hillwood Stone's mark is an *H*. Again, it's an *I*. For Ibis. And that brick is part of their Seven Wonders collection.
2. My sister's email account was hacked, likely by the same person.
3. *Direct News* is trying to undermine my posts. They ignore the facts.
4. And at the Mausoleum today I resisted two men who have been after our statuette. They are connected to Ibis.

I believe the source of all this is the villa in Alexandria. And I believe those two men will do more harm. In Egypt.

He had doubled down on connecting the Hillwood Stone to Ibis, and hoped Alison would allow it. It was the thing that seemed to irritate Ibis the most. *Good if it does*, he told himself, even if his father's connection to it weighed on his mind. *Good if this opens it all up.*

"Are you okay with that, Alison?" asked Dyllis.

She thought for a moment. "You know what . . . ? It's persuasive. I do not tolerate lies," she said slowly. "I do not tolerate intimidation." She looked at Dante and nodded. "Post it."

"Okay," said Dyllis, "things will move fast now, so don't go wobbly. You didn't accept their invitation to meet in Ephesus, I hope."

"No."

"Good. Stay on the ship once you arrive."

"I'm ahead of you there," said Alison.

9

EPHESUS AND THE TEMPLE OF ARTEMIS

U NABLE TO SLEEP, ALISON tossed, recalling Dante's distress at the Mausoleum. And turned, trying to chart the uncertain days ahead. And tossed, cursing at the unrelenting cold air blasting from the cabin's air-conditioning vent.

She hurled her pillow at the thermostat that wouldn't cut off and walked out into the warm sea air. Off the starboard beam, the sky glowed from the lights of the port of Kuşadası, where *Modestine* would anchor for the tour of the ruins of Ephesus and the Temple of Artemis.

"What awaits us here, Artemis?" she said aloud. "Artemis, cult goddess of Ephesus—your statues abundantly arrayed with pendants and gourds," she recited, calling up her notes. "You had three temples. . . . The first is done in by a flood. The second, torched by a pyromaniac. The third, the grandest, becomes one of the Seven Wonders. But by the Middle Ages, the ruins all but disappear into the swampy site until about one hundred fifty years ago, when an Englishman with a splendid name—John Turtle Wood—digs and digs and discovers your temple's remains. Today, just a single rebuilt column stands."

And so lonely a thing that column is, she reflected. *Sorry, Artemis, but Marshall will have to tell your temple's story today. Dante and I will be confined to the ship.*

To cheer herself up, she decided to invite the baroness to lunch.

· ✦ ·

DOCTOR PETER SACKVILLE JUMPED at the sudden pounding on the door of his Cairo apartment.

"What are you doing here?" he demanded of his errant agents.

"The kid says the statuette isn't on the ship," said Riggio.

"Maybe you have it," accused Jerrie, as he pushed his way into Sackville's foyer.

"Hold on, gentlemen, I have company. You'll have to come back."

"You'll talk to us now," said Jerrie.

"All right, but watch what you say," Sackville whispered. "The American professor is here."

With a fixed smile, and in one grand sweep, he led the men to the living room, introduced them to Professor James, walked them across the room to the bar, and walked back to Professor James, to whom he whispered, "Play along." He then turned to the men and lied, "Professor James and I have just finished examining the statuette."

He gestured toward a linen-wrapped object on the sofa next to Professor James, then picked it up.

"The professor is leaving it with me for a few days," he continued. "Professor, it's opportune that my two friends have dropped by. They have considerable expertise, so I'm anxious to get their opinion of it. But I'm so sorry you can't stay longer." He shook Professor James's hand and walked him to the door.

"You keep unsavory company, Doctor," Professor James told Sackville in the foyer. "Be careful."

"Sackville's doing our work for us," Riggio whispered to Jerrie. "Once the American leaves, we take it."

"And punish him," said Jerrie.

"Have your way," said Riggio, "but not before we get Ibis's address."

But while they were scheming, Sackville stole to a hallway étagère that displayed his collection of Egyptian figurines and deftly swapped the object—a wood fragment from the Great Pyramid barge excavations, not the Meritites statuette—with a cheap souvenir figurine of the goddess Hathor given to him by a poorly performing student.

"So, gents," he said, returning to the living room, "it was a wild goose chase for you, unhappily. But now you must make yourselves scarce. After your various confrontations with Miss Fine and her student, you are known, and so you must disappear . . . Poof! Like that. But I'll give you a few hundred euros extra for your trouble. Come to my office tomorrow."

"Very generous," sneered Jerrie.

"Best I can do. So, then, we're done. Sorry, mates."

"We'll have that statuette," demanded Riggio.

"Now you're getting greedy," said Sackville, feigning surprise. "Well, here then, take her. I don't want any trouble."

Riggio removed the cloth, inspected the souvenir goddess, and nodded to Jerrie approvingly. "How does it feel to be outsmarted, Doctor? We'll do business with Ibis directly now. Give us the address and a name."

Sackville had not expected this demand. Frightened, he reached for a pen and paper and began to write. As he finished, Jerrie gripped the top of an alabaster vase, came up behind him, and brought it down on his head. With a look of shocked amusement, Sackville fell heavily to the floor.

"Let's go," said Riggio, stuffing the worthless figurine into his jacket.

But Jerrie could not take his eyes off his victim, off the frozen smile and the eyes that would not close. He lingered, staring at Sackville as if seeing himself.

· ✦ ·

THE BARONESS EMERGED FROM her cabin and made the short walk to the ship's poolside café, her regal face set, her ample skirt billowing in the breeze, her silk scarf waving like a pennant. She was a veritable tall ship approaching Dante and Alison's table, and she seemed to recognize it.

"I would prefer to dock at a table in the shade," she deadpanned.

"Of course," said Alison. "Thank you for coming, my lady. I thought it would be nice to take a break from the trials of the tour."

"I certainly did not anticipate all the melodrama." The baroness sighed as she stroked her brooch, this one a figure of Artemis in cherry amber set between two temple columns in gold. She began to relate her "difficulties" with her grandniece and with someone she referred to as an old friend.

"One exasperates, and the other frustrates," she told them. "I had hoped for calmer seas."

"Where in Egypt does your friend live?" Dante asked.

"I do not recall saying that he is in Egypt. In any case, it frustrates me that he will not slow down. At what point does one say 'Enough' and pass one's responsibilities on?"

"For some, holding on to power is everything," Alison offered. "There's never a thought of retirement."

"It is not power that drives this person. It is scholarship. It is passion. And duty. I suppose I do understand it," she allowed. "You see—"

"Duty to hack someone?" Dante interrupted. "And passion to have the papers lie about me?"

The baroness looked at him coolly but didn't respond. Alison did not object.

Emboldened, he blurted out, "He's the head of Ibis, isn't he."

He knew that she could demolish him with a word or a look,

but he held his eyes on her even as the blood rose to his face. To his surprise, she smiled.

"You must not get beyond yourself, young man," she said evenly.

"Why am I a threat to him?"

"One's privacy is sacred," she said. "And one's honor. If these are violated, well then, one feels undermined. One's ground is shaken."

"What about my honor?"

She stared back at him, gauging his mettle, but he would not blink. "Do I have your word that this conversation will go no further?" she said. "And that you will not write of it?"

"I promise."

"Then I will say that you have gone beyond curiosity. I have just seen your latest blog post. You accuse. You predict conflict—"

"Yes, because the media's turned on me and Ibis is behind it, and I don't deserve that. But I was also warning your friend about those two men. He's in Alexandria, isn't he."

The baroness leaned toward Alison and lowered her voice so that Dante wouldn't hear. "I am prepared to pay you a considerable sum if Dante would simply turn his interest to other things. And something for him. A boat? A car . . . ? Does he drive?"

"For the record," Alison began, stunned by the woman's clumsiness, "I don't need money, okay? And I don't think Dante is motivated by material things." Now she raised her voice so he would hear. "And I'll just say that if you have any power to stop the intimidation that's being directed at us, you damn well better use it."

She gripped her stick and, like Dante, held her gaze on the baroness.

Above them, *Modestine*'s pennants snapped in the wind. A waiter who had approached deftly pivoted away, saying, "I'll give you folks some time."

"I see I am being dismissed," the baroness said to Alison.

Dante stood as she rose and walked away, but Alison remained in her chair.

"Well, I don't know if that will change anything," she told him, "but it felt good. Seems you were right about her being with Ibis."

"I should have gotten her to admit it. . . . I didn't think you'd let me question her like that."

"I didn't either, frankly. I just thought we were going to have a quiet little lunch."

They watched Lieutenant Regan greet the baroness and hand her a note before approaching their table with a small pastry box.

"Go ahead and open it," said Alison, as she kept her eyes trained on the baroness. "I commissioned it for you."

"Who made this?" he cried.

"The baroness's chef, Werner. It's marzipan. Do you like it?"

"Looks delicious," offered Lieutenant Regan.

"Alison, it's the mosaic! It's exactly like in my pictures—the ibis, the setting. I can't believe it."

"What? Let me see. . . . Oh, wow, he has to have been to that villa with her."

"Now there's no need to ask her if she's with Ibis."

He closed the box and rose again to greet the baroness as she made her way back to the table.

"Please, enough standing," she said with a wave of the hand that held the note. Her expression was grave. "I am sorry I insulted you with my offer of money, Miss Fine. I have news."

Alison invited her to sit.

"Professor James has been detained by the police in Cairo."

"What? Why?"

"Doctor Sackville has been murdered. Professor James had visited him."

"But that's impossible. He couldn't have done that."

"Of course," said the baroness.

"We need to help him," said Alison. "Lieutenant, can you find Marshall? Can you help us get back to Cairo?"

"There will be no need," the baroness declared. She assured them that her friend had influence with the authorities there, and that Professor James would be released. She asked Lieutenant Regan to leave them.

Dante anticipated her next words.

"Two other people were seen leaving Doctor Sackville's flat."

"Riggio and Jerrie," he said. "They were after the statuette. Just like that Mrs. Gamal was in Alexandria. And—"

"And I?"

"Ibis, all Ibis," he murmured, his eyes afire.

"You believe I am with Ibis, too?"

"Yes," he said, "and I think there are things that your friend Ancient Light knows that only you could have told him."

"Ancient Light," repeated the baroness. "You speak as if you know him."

Dante sensed that she would reveal no more. He tilted the pastry box toward her and opened it.

The waiter approached a second time, but turned away again when the baroness gasped.

"This was made by your chef, my lady," said Alison.

"Copied from some postcard," she retorted.

"There is no postcard of this," said Dante.

"What do you want?" she demanded.

"Only to understand. Just to put together all the pieces. The mosaic, the Hillwood Stone in Chicago, Doctor Ali's warnings to me . . . the tension between him and Miss Deuss. And why he denies knowing you, and—"

"All private matters, young man, and all none of your business. And that is all you need to understand! But I interrupted," she said, regaining her composure.

"The big man in Alexandria—he invited me to meet him. He adopted my name for him. I don't think he's a bad man, even if you're all trying to gag me. But something bad is happening, or will soon. He's in danger. Your collection, too."

After a long silence, the baroness relented. "I fear he will not be able to cope with it all. Miss Fine, your statuette may have been taken by those men. But, as I said, you need not go there, to Cairo."

Dante keyed in on her last words. *She's pointing us to Alexandria*, he realized. *Keep pressing.*

"There's another piece I need to understand—because it *is* my business. I know from a newspaper article that my father knew the guy who took your Hillwood Stone. What did my father have to do with Ibis fourteen years ago?"

"What? That is absurd," the baroness said with a dismissive wave. "Nothing, of course. How would we know him?"

"Are you sure, Baroness?"

"Categorically! And I speak for the one you call Ancient Light as well. Now, enough of this."

She assured them again that Professor James would be safe, but worried that her friend and the collection were vulnerable. And though she weighed her next words, she spoke them with uncertainty.

"If through your wits you could deflect . . . Excuse me," she whispered, bringing her scarf to her face. She rose, gripped Dante's shoulder and left them.

"Wow," said Alison, "that marzipan hit a nerve."

"Because it reminded her of her friend in Alexandria. And because the mosaic is everything to them. It's their heart."

"Right . . . You must be relieved that she only squeezed your shoulder and didn't pinch your ear," she joked, buying time as she wrestled with how she would respond to what she knew he would say next.

"We're meant to go back there, Alison. Ancient Light needs help. The baroness just gave us her blessing."

She reminded him that Ancient Light had been behind every problem they'd faced. The stalking. The deceptions. And now the meeting he had tried to arrange with them in Ephesus.

"What could possibly have gone wrong with that?" she asked.

"I think we just had a better meeting."

"Well, she wants our help. She's also conflicted. But don't assume Ancient Light is. Don't forget that Ibis has outwitted people for centuries. And that there's a good chance they were complicit in that deadly Hillwood Stone affair."

"We don't know for sure if it was a murder, though," he said.

"Okay, but I'm not going to hand them an opportunity to harm you. So we'll sit tight. You'll honor the baroness's request to not write about this meeting?"

"Yes."

"All right. Now, we need to find out if Professor James is safe." She called his cell phone but got no answer.

"The baroness will see that he's released, Alison. We need to help in *Alexandria*. If Riggio and Jerrie have your statuette, they'll try to sell it to Ancient Light. But they won't stop at that."

"I wish I had your powers. I wish I could see where this is going."

"I don't see it clearly, either, but I've been getting hieroglyphs . . ."

"More?" *I'll roll with this*, she told herself. "So, not pictures?"

"They're like the pictures, but separate. I mean, it's like they're coming from . . ."

"From where?"

"Thoth."

"You need to tell me if they're bothering you, Dante. Honestly. Are they?"

"No, they're like challenges, like getting advice. The first was a heart, like I told you. And then, at the Mausoleum, a ship. And then reeds. Pens. Make the voyage, see? To Alexandria. And I'll write, I'll put out there what needs to be said. We have the chance to do something good if we return. We won't have to get in the middle of anything. Aren't you worried about the wonders collection? It's all at risk now. . . . Don't you want your statuette back?"

"We don't know if it's missing yet, okay? And of course I care about the wonders. Look, you say you think this Ancient Light isn't a bad guy. But you're also upset that he's hacked Nora, and that he's trying to discredit you. So, if we go—and I'm not saying we will—it can't be about confrontation."

"I'm not angry with anyone now. I just think we can help. And maybe find some answers . . ."

"Answers about your father, too. I get that. And the baroness's answer? That your father wasn't involved with Ibis? Are you buying that?"

"I'm not sure, but, Alison, that man who discovered the Temple of Artemis looked for it for years. He dug and found an ancient road that he guessed would lead to it, and then he followed that road and dug some more until he found the remains of the temple, twenty feet down. He didn't give up."

"No, he didn't, Mister Wood Turtle didn't," she said.

"It's Turtle Wood, Alison, not Wood Turtle," he said, laughing.

"Right, I got distracted," she said dryly, looking up at Miss Deuss, who had swept up to their table.

"Come to my cabin," Miss Deuss told her. "I want to go over your talk—"

"I'll stop you there, Monica. I'm afraid I won't be doing it this afternoon. I'll arrange for Marshall to take my place. Dante's hurt, there are things going on—"

"I don't care about what's going on in your little lives. You'll come to my cabin, and you'll be on that launch at three o'clock for the tour. Is that clear?"

"You know what?" said Alison. "It is clear. You have my resignation."

"What?!"

When the waiter approached a third time, the enraged Miss Deuss cried, "What do *you* want?" She grabbed his menus and threw them to the deck. "And no, Miss Fine, you're not resigning. You're out! Get off my ship," she ordered, and walked away.

"Go and get Marshall, please," Alison told Dante. "And Captain Nikkos if you see him." She gave him a valiant smile. "Let me sit for a minute. Go."

· ✦ ·

DANTE'S RIGHT, ALISON TOLD herself. *We need to do what we can to protect the collection. The baroness seems to support that. It's worth keeping her close. . . . Perhaps bring Dyllis in. And Jasper. Put our heads together. Still, the risks. More prudent to return to Chicago . . .*

Her cell phone rang. *Okay*, she thought, shaking her head when she saw the caller ID. *So Grandma's clairvoyant, too?*

"Alison? It's Emma. I'm just calling about Dante. Nora said she sent him some articles. Has he seen them?"

"Yes. He's processing the news pretty well."

"Okay."

Alison waited, hoping she would share what had happened between Dante's mother and father.

"How is his ear, then?"

"Mending very well. But, Emma, a lot has happened since yesterday, when I told you I was weighing whether Dante and I should leave the cruise or stay on. I've resigned from my position here. I'd like to return to Egypt with Dante before we come home. There's some risk to going back there, but I worry that Dante will regret it forever if we don't. Let me give you some background—"

"I'm reading his blogs," Emma interrupted. "He seems to be making sense of things. So you just need to tell me if you think he's up to it. You've figured out by now that he's tougher than he looks?"

"Oh, yes, and he has a purpose about him."

"Then you might as well get back to Egypt."

"Well, okay." Alison laughed. "But first, please tell me . . . that article Nora found in the *Sun-Times* that connected Dante's father to Mishky and the Hillwood Stone. What's that about?"

"I don't know. I don't know what Dante's father did after my daughter died, or who he associated with."

"I ask because it's very much on Dante's mind. He'd like you to call the police, to see if they know anything more about his father."

"Yes, Nora told me. But they contacted me. Just last night."

"The police did? About his father?"

"They asked me whether I'd heard from him. After all this time. It must be because of all the publicity now around Ibis. But I told them the same thing I just told you."

"May I share that with Dante?"

"No. I'll tell him and Nora. But not before I know where the police are going with this. I'm not going to upset those kids. . . . Now, get yourselves back to Egypt. Bye."

· ✦ ·

"We have your grandmother's permission to go," Alison told Dante when he returned with Marshall. "So, you can continue to blog and aim your antennas around there for a while—from our hotel—until we get our statuette back. But this will be a focused operation. I want no mission creep."

"Hold on," said Marshall. "You're not leaving me alone with the Gila monster! I should have a say in this."

"We can't stay, Marsh. She's booted us off the ship. She'd fire you, too, but she'll need you to do the temple tour today. And then the Statue of Zeus in Olympia. I'm sorry. Sit down, okay? So, the temple is an easy one. Artemis was the goddess of the people, right? So Miss Deuss has set up an interactive day with the locals in Kuşadası—"

"Yes, a street fair," he said. "She told me she commissioned a statue of Artemis—hopefully not by the same people who did the Colossus."

Alison told him he would need only to let the guests enjoy the food and music, and then take them to the temple site.

"You can say it was called the most impressive of all the wonders," said Dante. "It was one and a half football fields long, and it had columns six stories high. A forest of columns, they say. Cleopatra had her rival sister murdered on its steps."

"And *so* much more," said Alison. "I'll leave you my notes, Marsh."

"Okay, I'll do it. On the condition that you'll have backup when you're in Alexandria. As in Professor James, and maybe Dyllis, too. I don't want to have to worry about you."

"Agreed. I'm calling Professor James now. Hopefully he's out of jail."

"What?"

"A misunderstanding," she said. "Nothing to worry about, I'm told. Though he's still not answering. Dante, go and pack. Couldn't you find the captain?"

"He's on the bridge," said Marshall. "I'll book your flights. Most likely you'll need to take a cab from here to the airport in Izmir and catch a short flight to Istanbul, then fly from there to Alexandria."

"Okay, let's get busy."

She picked up the menus from the deck and strode over to the waiter. "Two grilled cheese or whatever," she panted, and then headed to the bridge, calling into the air, "to go!" with a lightness she hadn't felt in days.

· ✦ ·

ALISON STEPPED ONTO THE bridge wing to take in the view of Kuşadası's harbor. "A last moment of calm between gales?" she whispered. "Dante's ibises . . . heralding change."

"Marshall told me you're leaving," she heard Nikkos call. "You don't need to. I have the say on that, not Deuss."

"I appreciate it, Captain, but Dante and I have some business to take care of in Alexandria."

"Very well. We'll be dropping anchor in the harbor, so you'll take the launch ashore."

But as she made her way down the short gangway to the launch an hour later, a sudden surge from the wake of a passing yacht threw her hard into the boat.

"Twisted my ankle," she said to Dante, grimacing. "Scraped up my hands, too. Let's get out of here," she told Eyüp through her teeth.

"We will tape your foot for you, miss," he said. "And your hands."

"Let's change Dante's bandage, too, Eyüp, while we're at it. . . . Thus we return to Egypt. Two mummies."

As the launch took them to the pier, Dante turned to take a last look at *Modestine*, fixing his eyes first on her name at the bow and then moving them slowly aft. At the stern he spotted Doctor Ali, and returned his wave.

· ✦ ·

ALISON'S PHONE RANG AS their taxi approached the airport at Izmir for their flight to Istanbul.

"There's bad news, and bad news," Marshall reported. He told her first that the street festival had been ruined by a downpour.

"Wait," said Alison, "Dante's asking about the statue of Artemis."

"I'm standing in front of her. Let's just say she wasn't waterproof. Let's just say she wasn't even Artemis. Not the one the people of Ephesus worshipped, anyway."

"Don't tell me it was the Artemis adopted later by the Greeks, or worse, the Romans . . ."

"It was. Diana—bow and arrows and all. What was Miss Deuss thinking?"

"She wasn't. That couldn't have gone over well with the locals."

"No," he said. "They booed it, in fact. That's when three of the four remaining guests asked me to book their flights home. Only David Dickenson is left. So she started flirting with him, hoping to get him to write a favorable review. It was her last card, I guess."

"How did Dickenson react to that?" she asked.

"He said, 'I've decided to do you the great favor of writing nothing, Monica. Because that's what all of this has amounted to.'"

"Then what?"

"She tore into me. Blamed me for everything, naturally. Then she got into an argument with the baroness about the resort. Said she'll do whatever's necessary to prevail."

"That's ominous."

"She's wounded and desperate, Alison. You're lucky to be away from her."

"Right. Look, break a leg in Olympia. Much like I nearly did when I fell into the boat."

"Such a graceful exit."

"Yes. Okay, we have to go. I'll be in touch."

She turned to Dante. "You heard all that?"

"Yes. What we're doing matters more."

"Well, it's a shame we couldn't finish the tour, or at least find you a souvenir of the temple."

Overhearing, the driver pulled a handful of bead necklaces and pendants from a box on his passenger seat.

"Amber," he said, holding them up. "The great mother goddess of Ephesus wore amber. Did you know?"

"Yes," said Dante. "Those giant gourds or whatever."

"Amber will bring you clarity and confidence," the driver declared. "And warriors in ancient times wore it for good luck."

"Okay, let me get those beads for you," said Alison. "The big ones."

· ✦ ·

IN THE AIRPORT LOUNGE in Istanbul, a picture came to Dante as he sat with Alison. It was Miss Deuss on her phone on *Modestine*, her body tense, her expression conspiratorial. When it was interrupted by their boarding call for their flight to Alexandria, he opened his computer.

Write it, he told himself.

He rapidly posted more to his blog, intending his words for Ancient Light.

> You are threatened more by others than by me. You can expect trouble from the two men who murdered Doctor S. And there will be treachery from an insider. I hope you will see me as not a threat but an ally.

> To others following my blog: Alison and I have left the cruise. I cannot reveal where we will go, but I will continue to write.

Alison had been on her phone, first with Dyllis, who promised to meet them in Alexandria if necessary, and then with a relieved but still shaken Professor James.

"I'm no longer a suspect," he told her. "An anonymous angel intervened."

"That would be the baroness."

"Interesting. Well, those two goons paid a visit to Sackville when I was at his flat. They must have killed him after I left."

"We figured. But, the statuette. Did they take it?"

"No, I never took it to Sackville's place. He kept pressing me to show it to him, but no."

"Good. I'll tell Dante. Okay, he's showing me a new post now. Take a look if you can."

"Okay. Where are you?"

"We've left the cruise, Jasper. We're in Istanbul for a flight back to Alexandria. I want you to meet us there. At the Cecil Hotel on the Corniche. Can you do that?"

"Of course."

"We'll be getting in late, around ten o'clock. And bring the statuette."

He told her he would be there, adding that Riggio and Jerrie hadn't been apprehended and that he feared they weren't done.

"That's what Dante thinks, too," she said. "And you should know that he's full of ideas about making contact with Ibis."

"I'm looking at what he's just posted."

"And I'm afraid we haven't heard the last of Monica Deuss, either."

"Why?"

"Her wonders tour is a bust. She's rattled the baroness, and that's not easy. She's up to something, Jasper. . . . Okay, Dante's telling me she's the insider he's referring to."

· ✦ ·

When the French Empire clock on his mantel struck seven, Ancient Light put a bookmark in his late father's diary and closed it. It was time for his evening briefing.

"Only days ago, Otto, my life had not been complicated by this high-tech headache," he complained. "This Internet."

"I must begin with the young man's most recent post, sir. My apologies."

Ancient Light listened, then asked Otto to read it again, intrigued by Dante's offer of an alliance.

"So they are on their way back here, then, Dante and his guardian?"

"Yes, the baroness believes they are. I have a fax from her, sir."

"What does she say?"

"She reports that the tour has all but collapsed, but that Miss Deuss continues to demand items from the collection. She cautions that Sackville's killers are certain to make demands as well. She poses questions to you, sir. Do you think you can manage the two men? Keep up with the ruthless Deuss? Thwart, or even imagine, the next revelations that might materialize in the media or the blogosphere? She closes with a challenge. Will you keep your pledge to do what is best for the organization and the collection, and for yourself?"

"Her concerns are warranted," said Ancient Light. "For these past days we have tracked the storm. We have maneuvered to protect Ibis. We have been ineffective." He stared into the middle distance for a long moment, then slapped his hands on the desk and rose.

"Contact Lord Cranleigh. Instruct him to continue the media campaign for one more day. This will provide cover for the plan I will execute. Tell the boy, using the moniker 'Ancient Light,' that if he intends to make contact with me here in Alexandria, he should expel that notion from his head. Offer him and Miss Fine a meeting at Olympia, in two days' time, with details to follow. And call the CNN reporter in Istanbul. Offer her an exclusive interview—also in two days, also at Olympia. Advise the baroness of these actions."

"What arrangements should I make for the meetings?" asked Otto.

"We will discuss that tomorrow."

"And the insider Dante references . . ."

"We will discuss Monica Deuss tomorrow as well. Now, get word to the monastery in Olympia that the abbot should expect us. And alert our guards here at the villa. Dante and the baroness are right about Sackville's men."

"Yes, sir. And regarding the matter in America . . . Can I do anything more?"

"No, Otto. Now leave me." He thought for a moment. "Wait."

"Sir?"

"You say the tour has all but collapsed. Will the ship continue on to Olympia?"

"Yes. The baroness said she will be aboard, along with Deuss and the remaining journalist."

"And Ali?"

"She said she is pleased that he decided to stay on."

"I see. I want to talk with her. Arrange a call—before my calls to Washington and Chicago tonight."

Otto watched him walk to the pirate lamp and look in turn at the buccaneer's confident grin and the serious boy in the framed photo beside it.

"Will there be anything else, sir?"

He waited, but when he saw the troubled look that had come over Ancient Light's face, he withdrew.

· ✦ ·

DYLLIS READ ANCIENT LIGHT'S interview offer with skepticism. *Is the email genuine,* she wondered, *or is it from a troll? Is it a setup by Ibis to embarrass CNN and further discredit Dante? And why Olympia?*

She called the Cecil Hotel in Alexandria and left a message for Alison. *If the interview invitation is a ruse,* she thought, *I'll need to be with her. If it's real, I'll need to be in Olympia.*

She packed a bag and waited for Alison's call.

· ✦ ·

IT WAS NEARLY MIDNIGHT when Alison and Dante checked into the
Cecil. She hobbled to her room with his help and fell into a chair.
A blinking light on the telephone caught her eye.

"It's from Dyllis," she told Dante as she listened to the message.
"I'll call her back in a bit. I'm a wreck. First, tell me, now that
we're here, what's your take on this Ibis? I mean, the Mishky thing
aside: pirates or protectors? Hoarders or noble stewards? Doctor Ali
thinks the worst of them."

"I don't know. But if they're in chaos now—like the way Riggio
and Jerrie have been acting, and Sackville, and Miss Deuss—I don't
think that's the real Ibis. I'm glad the statuette is safe with Professor
James, but it isn't important to them anymore. They're under at-
tack. That's what it's about now. Look at this."

On a map of Alexandria he had picked up in the lobby, he
pointed to the street where he had seen the villa. Alison looked
at the map vacantly, rubbing her ankle and second-guessing her
decision to return, as he circled the street with his pen. He then
pointed to the area in the Delta where they had seen the ibises from
the train.

"Look, it's a nature reserve. Anyway, according to this map,
there's another hotel closer to the villa. Maybe we can move over
there tomorrow and watch what's going on from our rooms."

"We're not going anywhere, sweetie. We're going to lick our
wounds here for a while until I talk further with Dyllis and
Professor James."

He saw her grimace.

"Your ankle—it's swollen to double—"

"Yes, so I'm going to bed. You're staying up, no doubt, so take
my phone, and when the professor calls, just tell him we'll meet

him in the morning for breakfast. If I'm alive. And leave your laptop with me. I want radio silence for a while. And don't leave your room. Okay? Good night."

She picked up the hotel phone and called Dyllis, who reported that she had received an invitation from Ancient Light.

"He wants an interview, Alison. In Olympia."

"Really?"

"He says he'll be inviting Dante and you, too. I'm going to accept."

"Yes, I know you have to."

"I mean, because I think you should, too. I'll have a production crew with me. It will be safe. Unless you really need me to come to Alexandria."

"No," said Alison. "I'm not comfortable being here now anyway. Professor James should be arriving soon. If he or Dante's grandmother have any reservations about our going to Olympia, I'll let you know. Otherwise, we'll see you there. And sorry we couldn't meet in Istanbul. No time between flights."

"Hey, this will be better."

10

THE VILLA AND THE DELTA

A LONE IN HIS ROOM and without his laptop, Dante fidgeted. He began a sketch of Artemis and the temple, but his amber bead necklace from Ephesus brought him little of the clarity or focus the taxi driver had advertised.

He put the sketch aside and stepped out to his balcony. His eyes were drawn first to Alexandria's darkened harbor, to where the Pharos once stood, and then to the street below, to the brightly lit Corniche and the traffic streaming by. *All going somewhere*, he told himself. *But what is my course? How do I sleep before I know?*

He took the elevator down to buy water.

It doesn't look like Professor James is coming tonight, he thought as he explored the Cecil's quiet lobby. He circled through it again, trying to anticipate what events might begin to unfold. And what he might do to shape them.

Have I shaped them too much already? Am I to blame for

Sackville's death? What else are Riggio and Jerrie capable of? And Miss Deuss . . . ?

Clear your head.

He remembered meeting Med in the lobby of the Hilton in Cairo and smiled, then stepped outside, where the face of the Egyptian moon seemed to offer an encouraging smile back.

He asked the doorman for a cab.

This will be just a quick drive past the villa, he promised himself. *To see who's coming or going. To see if they've beefed up security. To post a warning to Ancient Light if I have to.*

As his taxi left the hotel, he saw another pull in. He recognized Professor James inside, his face lit by his cell phone.

In his pocket, Alison's phone rang.

"Hi, Professor," he answered. "Alison's in bed, so she said we'll see you at breakfast. Did you bring the statuette?"

"I have it," said the professor. "You okay?"

"Yes. I'll see you at breakfast."

I can be back in fifteen minutes, he told himself.

As the taxi sped him along the Corniche, the briny air brought back the night he had spotted the ibises from the train. *No mission creep,* he heard Alison admonish. *But wouldn't there be time,* he asked himself, *to drive to the Delta after I check out the villa? To see the sacred birds again, up close, and be back before breakfast?*

He pulled Med's card from his wallet and called.

"It's Dante, Med. I'm in Alexandria."

"Oh," Med replied, half asleep. "Welcome."

"Sorry, Med. I had to tell you I'm back in Egypt. Are you still at your uncle's farm?"

"Yes."

"I want to go to the nature reserve in the Delta. It's called Qamar. Do you know it?"

"Yes. My uncle's farm is near to it."

"Can you meet me there?"

"Yes, I will ask my uncle to take me. What do you want to do there?"

"Just look around. Can you be there really early, as soon as it's light?"

"Okay."

· ✦ ·

WHEN HIS TAXI REACHED the top of the villa's street and was promptly waved off by two guards, Dante directed the driver to the café. It was closed, but he could not resist taking the alley to the rear to climb back up the wall overlooking the villa.

From the wall he watched Otto escort a group of people to their cars. They exchanged no pleasantries, only sober handshakes. When the villa's lights went out, he prepared to leave, but his eyes caught the movement of two figures in the shadows below a window.

He recognized them as Riggio and Jerrie.

Without thinking, he crawled along the café's wall, then across the street's dead-end wall, and jumped into the villa's grounds. He followed the men in through the window, then through a dark pantry, and up a staircase. At its top, they crept down a long hallway, and he followed them into a room—a library—where he crouched behind a large terrestrial floor globe, his heart pounding so loudly that he feared the men might hear it.

He took a sharp breath to shout a warning to the heavyset man seated behind a desk, reading, his back to him, but Riggio pushed the door closed, pulled a gun, and called, "Turn!"

Ancient Light swiveled around in his chair and stood, his eyes meeting Dante's for an instant. And although he was stooped, he was easily four inches taller than either Riggio or Jerrie. Looking almost amused, he stared down the men, who now seemed unsure of themselves, if not deferential.

He looked at Dante again, then moved to the end of his desk

and ran his index finger down the obelisk there, tapping an inscribed image of Thoth as if to signal that he was in charge and that Dante needed only to watch.

"Mister Riggio, Mister Jerrie," he said at last. "Do I have that right? State your reason for this intrusion."

With nervous bluster, Jerrie produced the pilfered figurine. "If you don't want to end up like Sackville, you'll pay us for this Queen Merra-, Meta-, Merrytrees, whatever."

"Of course, gentlemen," said Ancient Light, his resonant voice belying his frailty. "But you must allow me to inspect it first."

He held out his hand to accept the object, then walked to the balcony, turned toward the men, and lofted it into the air over his shoulder, sending it smashing into the courtyard below.

Startled, Dante leaned forward to watch, but his shoulder brushed against the globe. Its movement caught Jerrie's eye.

"Come here, you," Jerrie shouted, then grabbed Dante by the arm while Riggio kept his gun trained on Ancient Light.

"Now, gentlemen," said Ancient Light, "we must be calm. You see, the statuette was worthless. A cheap souvenir." He turned his massive frame toward Dante, his expression at once stern and curious. "You are Master Dante, I suppose," he thundered.

Dante nodded, too awed to speak.

"An honor," said Ancient Light. "But your head. Why bandaged?"

"I'm fine, sir."

"We could have met in Ephesus instead."

"Yes, sir," Dante heard himself say, "I'm sorry for breaking into your house—"

"Shut up, both of you," said Riggio. "We want ten thousand for that statuette anyway. In dollars or euros."

"And you'll tell us where your collection is," demanded Jerrie.

"Surely you know I cannot do that."

"I see that you like this boy," said Jerrie, giving Dante a shake.

"Don't tell them, sir," Dante shouted.

"Yes, he can be dispensed with right now," Jerrie threatened. "And you."

"Release him," demanded Ancient Light.

"Only if you cooperate," said Riggio.

"Do you suppose," said Ancient Light, "that the crash of the statuette was heard by my security?"

As he spoke, the door flew open and two armed guards charged in. But when Riggio turned his gun on Dante and ordered the guards to put their weapons on the floor, Ancient Light nodded, and the guards withdrew.

"So be it," he said, glaring at the men. "Do what you must."

"He's bluffing," said Jerrie.

"I do not bluff, sir. The Ibis collection is beyond the value of my life."

"And mine!" cried Dante.

Ancient Light looked into the courtyard at the mosaic, folded his arms, and waited.

The men were at a loss to respond, until a thought occurred to Jerrie. He turned to his accomplice, smirking. "I once overheard Sackville say that whoever finds the mosaic finds the collection. The *underground* collection, I heard him say."

"So?" said Riggio.

"So the courtyard. The old man gives himself away. He looks at it. The collection is here. The mosaic covers it."

Ancient Light shook his head with contempt.

Hoping to see the mosaic at last, Dante tried to edge closer to the balcony, but Jerrie pushed him away, picked up an automatic weapon left by one of the guards, and began to fire into the court-yard in broad sweeps, burst after burst.

"Stop it!" Dante shouted.

Ancient Light rushed toward Jerrie, but Riggio intervened and threw him against the table that held the pirate lamp and framed photograph, knocking them to the floor. Ancient Light ignored

Riggio's order to stay in place and dropped to the floor to gather the pieces of the broken lamp and frame.

As he did, the villa's guards rushed back into the room, this time led by Otto. Jerrie stopped shooting, but Dante feared that the ibis mosaic in the courtyard below was now just a pit of rubble.

"Tell your men to get shovels and picks," Jerrie ordered Otto as he aimed the gun at Ancient Light. "Tell them to dig."

"Enough, you fools!" Ancient Light shouted. "There is nothing beneath the mosaic."

He waved Dante over to help him up from the floor. "Your passport, lad," he whispered. "Do you have it?" When Dante nodded, he turned to the men. "I am going to walk now to my safe."

"Don't help them," Dante pleaded.

But Ancient Light's eyes bored into his. "Mark this well," he said. "Theirs is an empty pursuit."

"Open the safe," ordered Jerrie.

Ancient Light slid back a wall panel, opened the safe it concealed, and from it removed cash and a document. He placed them on his desk, then opened a drawer and took out a map of Peloponnesus in Greece. On it, he drew an *X*.

"You will find the Monastery of Saints Constantine and Helen in Olympia here, on this hillside. The collection is located there."

He then unfolded the document he had removed from the safe, a translucent vellum paper with a number of symbols that seemed to be randomly placed. But Dante recognized the pattern and shot his eyes around the room. On the wall above another floor globe, this one celestial, he spotted the Vander Hoof map.

But when he looked at Ancient Light, the old man shook his head, barking, "Pay attention."

"So what good is this paper?" Riggio demanded.

"The vellum is the key to the locations of the treasure rooms at the monastery—to the galleries of the wonders."

"No, don't reveal it!" Dante cried.

"Its use will become apparent when you are there, of course."

Dante grasped that Ancient Light's words were directed at him. He realized now that the men would take him away.

"So how do we get into this monastery?" Jerrie asked.

"With this vellum, you can enter without challenge. The abbot will accommodate you."

"If this is a trick—"

"How did you get here?" Ancient Light interrupted.

"Taxi."

"These men will be allowed to leave," he told Otto. "Let them take the small car to the airport. Instruct the guards to let them pass."

"We'll take the boy as insurance," declared Riggio. "He's dead if you alert the police, or if we don't get access to the collection."

"So how much money is this?" demanded Jerrie.

"Five thousand," said Ancient Light. "It's all I have here. Any of the smallest pieces you find at the monastery will be worth twenty times that. Now, go. But may I be allowed to say goodbye to the young man?"

At Jerrie's nod, Ancient Light took Dante's hands. Dante realized he was being secretly handed a small velvet pouch that Ancient Light must have taken from the safe as well. He felt a number of hard objects inside before slipping the pouch into his pocket.

"A touching farewell," sneered Jerrie.

"Let's go," said Riggio, and the men steered Dante downstairs.

"He must not be harmed," Ancient Light shouted from the balcony as they pushed him into the back seat of the car. "Only he will know the meaning of the vellum once you are at the monastery. Only he can reveal the catalog of treasures."

"What does he mean?" Jerrie snapped at Dante.

Dazed by the destruction around him, Dante didn't answer. *There's nothing left of it*, he told himself. *The mosaic's gone forever.* He looked up at Ancient Light, then eased the pouch from his pocket and glanced at the little stones inside. They, like Ancient Light's expression, told him nothing.

"I'm trying to figure it out," he told Jerrie. After a long moment, an idea came. "Wait! Drive to the Delta. The ibis birds there—"

"What are you saying?" snapped Riggio.

"There's a bird sanctuary in the Delta. We have to go there. The old man was trying to throw us off," he invented, hoping it sounded convincing. "The collection is there with the ibises. Don't you see? Not at some monastery in Greece. I'm sure of it."

Riggio revved the engine as he considered Dante's words.

"Let's go," Dante urged. "They won't expect us. It probably isn't even guarded. I know the way."

"We should go," Jerrie told Riggio. "If the boy deceives us, the Delta will be his grave."

Riggio put the car in gear and sped to the villa's gate. As they passed through, Alison's cell phone rang in Dante's pocket. It was Professor James again.

"Give me that," Jerrie ordered. He grabbed the phone and smashed it against the side of the car before throwing it into the street. "Which way?" he barked.

"It's to the south. Take the Qamar road into the Delta."

Please be there, Med, he prayed.

· ✦ ·

THINKING IT STRANGE THAT he had heard traffic noise when Dante answered his call from the hotel, Professor James tried repeatedly to reach him again. After checking Dante's room with Alison, and then learning from the doorman that he had left, he and she ordered a cab.

"Okay, this is the street he showed me—the villa should be down there at the end," Alison told the professor as she folded Dante's map. "We'll get out here," she told the driver.

She leaned on the professor's arm for support and hobbled up to the guards.

"We're here to see Mister Otto. Get him now," she demanded. "There . . . I see him, by that gate. Otto!" she cried, waving her stick.

When Otto's voice came over the senior guard's radio, they were escorted promptly to the gate.

"Where's Dante, Otto? Has he been here?"

Otto looked at the professor.

"This is Jasper James," she told him. "A friend from Cairo."

"Of course. We have been trying to contact you, Miss Fine."

"Don't fool with me," she warned, pointing to the taxi with her stick. "I'll send him for the police."

Otto waved the driver off. "We are the police here, Miss Fine. Please, come."

Alison gasped as they walked past the torn-up courtyard, but Otto said no more until they were inside the villa. There, he asked for their phones.

"Dante has mine," she told him.

"Then perhaps that explains why we couldn't reach you," he said, showing her a smashed phone he had picked up from the street.

"Oh no! Is Dante okay?" she demanded.

Otto held out his hand and waited until Professor James handed him his phone, then turned and walked up the stairs.

"Otto!" she shouted after him.

Moments later, he reappeared with a tall, elderly man. Together, they made a slow descent to the foyer. Otto began the introductions, but Alison cut him short.

"You're Ancient Light."

"Yes, Miss Fine. I had hoped to meet you under better circumstances. I see you are hurt. I hope you are not in any discomfort. But I assure you that Dante is safe."

"Where is he?"

"He was here. He followed two intruders in. Sackville's men. They confronted me. They took money. And Dante."

"Took him? Where? How is that safe?"

"You must trust—"

"Trust you? You sent those pigs after us in the first place. When did they leave? We have to catch them."

"I do not advise that. We must not provoke them or they will harm Dante. They demanded to know the location of the collection. The situation will be concluded favorably there."

"By the 'collection,'" said Professor James, "you mean Ibis's collection of Ancient Wonders."

"I do."

"And where is *there*, exactly?"

"A monastery in Olympia. I sent Dante and you an invitation, Miss Fine."

"What is your game, sir?" Professor James demanded. "If you're using Dante—"

"I did not want this to happen to him. You chose to return to Alexandria, after all. But we will keep our engagement in Olympia. You need not know the details. The young man has resources—some that I provided, and some that he already possesses."

Otto picked up a ringing telephone in the foyer.

"That would be your reporter friend, I suspect," said Ancient Light.

"Dyllis Kirby for you, sir," said Otto.

They heard Ancient Light confirm his interview with her in Olympia and state that Alison and Professor James would accompany him.

"He's miles ahead of us," the professor whispered to Alison. "In a funny way, I trust him. In any case, we have no choice."

"Why can't they just get the police on this, Jasper? Why not just alert the airport that Dante's with those men?"

"They come at things differently," he answered. "They prefer their own methods. And they're known to take great satisfaction in the way they achieve their desired outcomes. The way they administer justice. All of this is consistent with what I've learned about them."

She turned to Otto. "Who are you, anyway?"

Otto cocked his head slightly but didn't answer.

"Okay. Then would you mind losing the inscrutable smile? It comes across as smugness, and it's not helpful."

"I'm sorry, Miss Fine."

"Of course you are, Otto."

To calm herself, she fixed her eyes on a gurgling marble fountain at the center of the foyer. She counted thirty large jardinières, each potted with a different plant or tree.

"The kidnapping is unfortunate," said Otto. "But it is good that the young man has come into my superior's life."

"Well, whatever that means," she said. "Just tell your Mister Light I need to speak to Dyllis now."

Ancient Light heard, but did not yield the phone. He told Dyllis to write nothing more before the interview, then ended the call.

"Okay, you didn't tell her what happened to Dante," said Alison.

"This way, she does not write about it, Miss Fine." His voice, which had been reassuring, now turned cool. "You will travel with us to Olympia for my interview. There, you will be reunited with Dante. You will stay at the monastery."

"I will stay on the ship," Alison declared. "It will have reached Greece by then. I'll see this through with the captain and my friend Marshall."

"And with me," said Professor James.

"As you wish," said Ancient Light. "But please, be my guests tonight. We will fly to Athens in the morning. From there, we will take my helicopter to your ship."

"He's a good kid," said Alison, her voice breaking. "We can't let anything happen to him."

"An extraordinary person, yes, in the way he sees and discerns."

"And that pile of shards outside," said Professor James. "Was that the mosaic he was drawn to?"

Ancient Light didn't reply.

"You wanted a meeting with Dante, and you got it," charged the professor. "You enabled this. You're responsible for whatever happens."

"That's right," said Alison. "You were also the pursuer of our statuette, Mister . . . ? Damn it, what is your name?"

Ancient Light waved a finger, dismissing the question.

"The statuette of Queen Meritites is the next order of business. You will relinquish it. Otto will arrange the details. I will retire now."

"Excuse me?" said Alison.

"It must be sent to your ship," said Ancient Light.

"Let me guess. To your friend, the Baroness von Weber."

"Correct."

"I don't think so," she growled.

"Yes, it must be sent to the baroness immediately. Otto will explain."

"The arrogance," she fumed. "Absolutely not."

"Then you may send it to your friend Marshall."

"Oh, I may?" she mocked.

"Yes. He will then transfer it to the baroness. Consider it a loan, Miss Fine. The transaction will be properly documented."

He looked out at the torn-up courtyard and murmured something to himself.

"If only we could see the future," Alison whispered to Professor James. "Oh, Jasper, our oracle has been kidnapped. Dante is gone."

"Otto will show you to your rooms," said Ancient Light with finality.

"Good night, sir," said Otto. "And now," he said, turning to

Alison and Professor James, "the statuette. Is it in Cairo, or have you brought it here?"

Alison told him she needed a moment and took the professor aside.

"So, what do we do, Jasper?"

"First off, did you hear what Ancient Light said to himself just now?"

"It was in Arabic. What was it?"

"He said, 'One boy lost. Pray not another.' Well, he seems so connected to Dante. I think it may be okay to send the statuette."

"Whatever he meant, we have no choice. Dante is all that matters." She turned to Otto, then back again to Professor James. "Do we even know if it's worth anything?" she whispered.

"Oh, it is. And it makes you a very rich woman . . . unless, of course, they decide to keep it."

"Okay, the statuette is here," she told Otto, "in Professor James's room at the Cecil. We can collect it in the morning on the way to the airport."

Otto insisted that it be sent immediately. He told them he would pick up their bags from the hotel, settle their bill, and arrange an express delivery of the statuette to the ship.

"Now, to your rooms," he said.

They followed him up the stairs and through a long hallway lined with ancient artifacts.

"Only a few more yards," said Professor James, who had been supporting Alison with his arm and studying each piece as they went.

"Take your time," she told him as they inched along. "This is my top speed anyway."

"Well, this has to be better than any museum I've been to. None of these little relics has a label, but they must be from the wonders. Imagine what the rest of his collection is like."

At her door, she wished him good night, then watched as Otto led him to his room. And now, her confidence that Professor James was an honest friend to Dante and to herself kept her mind from being occupied solely by worry.

· ✦ ·

"TRY THAT ROAD," JERRIE told Riggio.

But as the car turned, its headlights illuminated yet another reed-lined dead end in the Delta marshes. It was now nearly four in the morning, and this was only the latest of many wrong turns. Once again, the frustrated men berated Dante and each other.

"I said we need to get over more that way," said Dante. "Closer to the railroad tracks."

Finally, the headlights hit a weathered painted sign with an ibis in profile.

"This is it. Go left."

Riggio drove to within twenty yards of a low concrete building and pulled over.

"That must be the keeper's house," he told Jerrie. "We'll wait here until it's light. Tie the kid's hand to the door."

The men fell asleep, but Dante stayed awake, watching for Med. As the sun began to light the sky over the vast marshes, he saw a car approach from another road, let a passenger out near the keeper's house, and drive off.

"That's my friend," said Dante, waking the men. "He'll help us."

Jerrie untied Dante but held him close as Med approached warily.

"These men are from the university," said Dante, hoping Med would understand they weren't, hoping he would help him create an opening for an escape. "They've come to see the treasures—you know, the ones owned by the big man in Alexandria. They're kept here." He gave Med a discreet nod. "You know the legend."

"Yes, it is said that there is much here," Med offered. He looked at Dante for approval.

"Yes, much," echoed Dante.

"Then take us to it," said Jerrie.

"Well, let me see," said Dante. "We know that the ibis is the symbol of the organization, right? So the birds must be the key to where the collection is hidden."

"In the mud under that little shack, I suppose," barked Riggio. "You waste our time!" He saw a light come on inside and pulled his gun out. "Come out!" he shouted.

When the keeper opened the door, an African sacred ibis appeared from behind the house. It walked up to the keeper's side, then raised its head, surveying each person in turn.

"So this buzzard is the key to the wonders?" said Riggio. He stomped his foot at the ibis, then pointed his gun at it.

"No!" Med shouted, reaching for the bird and picking it up. "These ibises are sacred. It is said that the ones with bands know the location of the treasures," he invented. "You see, this one has a band on her leg. You only need to follow her."

The keeper scolded the men for trespassing and ordered them to leave. "These boys are crazy. There is nothing here."

To the men, the denial only buttressed Med's story. But, as Med wrestled with how to extend it, Dante saw that the bird had fixed its eyes on Jerrie. *Something's wrong*, he told himself as Jerrie turned and stared at him. It was a questioning look at first, but it soon turned anxious, and the man began to tremble.

Now Dante remembered his premonition on the train of a strange energy in the Delta marshes. He shook his head, not wanting to look at Jerrie, not wanting to believe what he feared would happen.

"You must read the band on her leg," Med insisted, as he offered the bird to Jerrie. "And you must speak those words to her, in a kind way, and she will lead you to the treasures."

"No, wait, don't take it!" Dante cried.

Looking disoriented now, and still trembling, Jerrie ignored the warning and grabbed the bird. In an instant his face contorted and turned a dull, leaden blue. "Stop . . . stop it," he pleaded.

"Drop the bird!" Dante shouted.

The ibis gave a great shudder, but Jerrie only clutched it tighter. A feather broke loose, brushing against Jerrie's pants, and as it did, his legs buckled.

And now they all heard his moans and watched his terrified face as he fell. And watched his hands reach out, his fingers gnarled and paralyzed, as the bird broke free. They watched him writhe on the ground, gasping for breath, and then frantically crawl away from the bird until he was finally able to stand. And as he began to run, he turned and looked at the ibis and then at Dante with eyes as vacant and stunned as those of his victim, Sackville.

Riggio called after him, but Jerrie ignored him as he stumbled and thrashed his way into the tall reeds.

Through it all, Dante had been struck by the ibis's eerie composure. It had remained still as it watched Jerrie run off, but now it stepped toward him, its carriage noble, its eyes knowing.

"Have I done this?" Dante whispered.

The ibis turned and looked to the west, and as it did, Dante became aware of an intensifying warmth from the little stones in his pocket. At the same time, Riggio threw down his gun with a terrified scream, blowing on his hands as though it had burned him. The bird then thrust out its breast and pulsed its great wings with such force that Riggio was knocked to the ground.

Med cried, "Run!" but Riggio lunged at Dante and dragged him to the car, pushed him into the back seat, and tied his hands. And as the car sped him away, Dante could only watch as the figures of Med and the keeper grew ever smaller, until they were one with the marsh's vapory green haze. He searched the sky, hoping to see the bird again, hoping for a hieroglyph, but there was nothing.

"The map," he called to Riggio. "And the vellum. Did Jerrie have them?"

"I have them. Be quiet. And stay quiet when we get to the airport."

Dante sat in silence, his companions the chilling memories of the destroyed mosaic and of Jerrie's agony, but above all, of the ibis and the intensity of its eyes. *Why did the bird look toward the west?* he asked himself. *Was it affirming my journey to Olympia and the monastery? Or was it looking to the path the ancient Egyptians took to the afterlife, to where the sun sets, foretelling my death?*

He wrestled, too, with the meaning of the pouch entrusted to him by Ancient Light and ordained now in some mysterious way by the African sacred ibis. And the puzzle of its still-warm stones was the only thing that kept him from despair.

11

THE MONASTERY

"THIS WITHERING CRUISE," CAPTAIN Nikkos murmured as *Modestine* steamed away from Ephesus. "Another three passengers lighter now." He directed his gaze to the west, toward Greece and *Modestine*'s home port, Katakolon, the final stop of the voyage. Despite strong headwinds and a choppy Aegean Sea, he had given the order to proceed at full speed, as much to hasten the end of Miss Deuss's noxious tour as to kick up a spray that would cleanse his ship of it.

Hours later, Lieutenant Regan informed him that he had received a message from Otto. Alison would be returning to *Modestine* with Professor James, but Dante would not be with them.

As Nikkos tried to make sense of it, he scanned the coastline of Greece's southern Peloponnese. Sighting Katakolon, now less than ten miles off the starboard bow, he trained his binoculars on the familiar harbor where, as a boy, he had captained a small wooden boat he had named *Compass*. He thought of Dante, certain that something was very wrong, and called out "Godspeed," just as his father would call to him whenever he set out alone into the harbor.

Now he gazed at the hills above the town, at Olympia, where the tour would end, he supposed, not with toasts and celebration, nor with a whimper, but with recriminations.

"We've weathered it, brave *Modestine*, and that is all. What more should I have done for Dante and Alison?"

He put the binoculars down and wiped the sea spray from his bulky tortoiseshell sunglasses.

"Good afternoon, Captain," he heard the baroness say. "I am looking for my niece. Have you seen her?"

"I believe you'll find her in the library."

"Would you take me there? I want you to hear what I have to say."

"My pleasure. I've received a message from Otto, my lady."

"Yes, as did I. I will explain in a moment."

In the library, Marshall was enduring a practice session with Miss Deuss for the Statue of Zeus entertainment.

"The *Iliad* reading doesn't end there," Miss Deuss scolded him. "You'll read the next paragraph, too, and then introduce Zeus. The gods are clashing on the mountaintop."

"You do realize that we're going to Olympia, not Mount Olympus?" said Marshall. "Totally different parts of Greece."

"They are? Well, so what? The guests won't know the difference."

"You mean the *guest*," said Marshall. "It's just David Dickenson now. Plus Doctor Ali. And they'll know the difference."

"Whatever, just listen. So the gods are arguing. They're hungry, but no one wants to cook. So, after Zeus blows his top and says he'll make the Greek salad himself—the captain will play him— what do you say?"

Captain Nikkos shook his head as he and the baroness looked on from the doorway.

"Come on," Miss Deuss snapped. "You've had the script since this morning. What do you say?"

"I don't know what I say," Marshall sighed. "I really don't."

"Never mind. Just get it right by tomorrow. Now the statue. Come on."

"The Statue of Zeus," he began. "Four stories tall, carved from cedar, plated with gold and ivory, studded with precious gems—"

"Niece!" called the baroness. "You need not rehearse. The entertainment at Olympia is canceled."

Miss Deuss glared at her.

"I have learned that Dante has been kidnapped," the baroness told them. "Last night in Alexandria. He fell into an incident there. He is being brought to Olympia—"

"Kidnapped by who?" Marshall interrupted.

"By the same men who had been following him and Miss Fine."

"Was he harmed?" asked Captain Nikkos.

"No. He should be safe. They need him."

"What about Alison?" Marshall asked.

"She is returning to the ship with Professor James."

"I'm not clear," said Nikkos. "Why would the kidnappers bring Dante here?"

"They want to loot the Ibis collection, Captain. And they believe that Dante can lead them to it. I have this information from my associates in Alexandria. I see from your expressions that this news is unsettling. It disturbs me as well. I ask for your patience until this matter is concluded." She turned to Miss Deuss. "Given the circumstances, this cruise will be your last, and all work on your resort will cease."

"I won't allow you to blow it up!" Miss Deuss objected. "You act as if I'm the kidnapper—" She stopped there, calculating that if the collection was in fact at Olympia, there could be an opportunity to outmaneuver the baroness.

The baroness continued, "Captain, I should inform you that

two people will be visiting me when we dock. And that there will be an announcement regarding the collection."

"Who's coming?" Miss Deuss demanded. She hoped one of them would be Otto, but the baroness didn't answer. "Well, then, shouldn't I help with this?"

"Conceivably," the baroness replied with an almost imperceptible smile. "But you must do nothing on your own." To Nikkos she said, "Miss Fine and Professor James will be with my guests. You will permit them to board, I trust?"

"I require the visitors' names, my lady."

"One travels incognito. You may know him from Dante's blog as Ancient Light."

"¡Ay, mi madre!" said Marshall.

"I'm not sure I can accommodate you on that," Nikkos told her.

"I will vouch for him, Captain. Please trust me. Otto is the other," she added.

Her words satisfied Captain Nikkos, and the mention of Otto produced the effect she wanted in Miss Deuss. She saw the hunger in her eyes.

"Now, Marshall, walk with me," she said. "I am meeting Mister Dickenson on the pool deck to watch us dock. Thank you, Captain."

"And thank you for canceling the entertainment in Olympia." He turned to Miss Deuss. "You would have me play Zeus? To trivialize him? In my country? No. Furthermore, you had no authority to order Alison and Dante off my ship." He reached for his radio and barked an order of his own. "Lieutenant Regan, report to the bridge."

· ✦ ·

In her cabin, Miss Deuss had been trying to contact Otto.

"Finally," she said, after her third attempt. "Otto, the baroness has shut it all down. What are they up to? Why haven't you called?"

"We've been in the air. I'm with my boss. And Miss Fine and Professor James."

"Again, that Alison Fine. Who will rid me of her?"

"Did the baroness tell you that Dante has been abducted?"

"Yes. And she let on that the collection is here. And something about an announcement. What's going on?"

He told her that Ancient Light was coming to resolve the situation with Dante, but that he wouldn't reveal what he planned to announce.

"Are he and the baroness doing something with the collection?" she erupted. "Someone better tell me. We have to stop them."

"What do you suggest?" he asked.

"First, where are you?"

"At the airport in Athens. We're coming to Katakolon by helicopter. We'll be at the ship—"

"We're about to dock, Otto. I can't wait for you. Look, they've cut me off. There's no resort. No more cruises. It's over. And you know what? I don't even care anymore. But I won't let them deny me. I'm going to act before they do, Otto, I swear . . . This is our opportunity, if you're still with me. Confirm that the collection is here."

"Don't you want to wait for me to arrive?"

"I told you no!"

"All right, but you'll have to deal with Sackville's two men. And Dante. They're taking him to a monastery near you, in the hills of Olympia. The collection is there."

"Monastery," she said. "I've been there, Otto, when I was a child. I can't remember where it was, but I didn't see anything—"

"It's hidden there, apparently."

"Well, then, what do I do?"

"Leave the ship as soon as it docks. You'll need to meet up with the men. They have a map that shows the location of the monastery, and a vellum paper that's the key to the location of the galleries there. The men won't know what to do with that vellum. The boss said Dante is the only one who will know how to use it. Even I don't know. So the kid is essential to us. As for the men, you must convince them to let him figure it out and see that they don't harm him."

"Then what? Once I find the collection, they'll want their share."

"You will handle them," said Otto. "They're fools."

"What if the police—?"

"If anything goes wrong, it's easy enough to say you stumbled upon a robbery." He told her he would send a van to the monastery, that she should choose some smaller pieces from the collection first, and that he would arrive soon to help her.

"Otto, I doubted you earlier. It's turning out better than we could have planned, yes?"

"Yes. It's time. We can now tap the collection sooner."

"And be free from them. Me, from my aunt. You, from the old man. Still, I worry. They're cunning."

"I'll handle the boss. I'll see to it that he makes no announcements. I'll handle the baroness, too. I have to hang up now."

"Wait. And down the road? When he finds out?"

"He'll never know what's missing. He's not involved in the details anymore. Neither are the other members, frankly."

"All right. Now, how do I contact those men?"

"I'll text you a cell phone number. Their names are Jerrie and Riggio. Tell them to wait for you before they do anything. Tell them they won't get into the monastery without you. I'll call you when we land in Katakolon."

"Oh, Otto, I can taste it."

"And I. Just slip off the ship quietly. And don't let on to the baroness that you're leaving."

He ended the call and walked to the car that would take him, Ancient Light, Alison, and Professor James to their helicopter.

· ✦ ·

MODESTINE BUMPED GENTLY AGAINST the pier at Katakolon as the baroness, Marshall, and Dickenson watched from the pool deck.

Marshall had been quiet, his thoughts turning to Dante as he looked aloft at the ship's now-motionless radars. He missed him. And missed the calming vibrations of *Modestine*'s engines, her heartbeat. The taste of the sea's salt air, too. And soon, the camaraderie of the crew and the people he had shared the voyage with would be just a memory.

"I get such an empty feeling at the end," he said. "Always happens. But especially this time."

The baroness nodded. "And I had hoped that Doctor Ali would join us up here."

"He told me he preferred to be in his cabin. In case Miss Deuss had arranged another travesty, as he put it."

"I'm not sure why he's stayed with us this long, actually," said Dickenson. "He could have left at Rhodes, or Bodrum, or Ephesus."

"You might say I insisted," said the baroness, without explaining.

· ✦ ·

MISS DEUSS WALKED OUT on deck, called the number Otto had given her, and introduced herself to the man who answered with a guarded "Yuh?" He demanded to know how she had gotten his number.

"I told you. I know Otto. Who do you think Sackville worked for?"

"Go on then," he said warily. "What do you want?"

"First, are you Riggio or Jerrie?"

"Riggio."

"Okay, you're being set up by Otto's boss. I know what happened last night at his villa. The boy you're holding is clever. He'll deceive you. Is he still with you?"

"Of course."

"I know how to handle him. We can share what's there, at that monastery. But without me, you won't get in and you won't get anything out. You'll have a problem with the police. You realize that, don't you?"

Riggio was silent.

"Let me speak to your partner. Which of you is in charge?"

"You'll speak to me."

"Look, I'm with the family that controls all this. If you cooperate, I'll see that you get some trinkets that will set you both up for life. You'll need papers for them, and I can arrange that, too."

Riggio agreed to meet her at the inn he was at near Katakolon.

She ended the call and began to make another.

· ✦ ·

THE BARONESS WATCHED MISS Deuss from the pool deck, only half listening to Marshall and Dickenson as they conversed.

"Gentlemen, I'm sorry," she broke in. "I have been terrible company. But, Marshall, listen for your phone. She will want a driver."

"Who will, my lady?" asked Marshall as his phone began to ring. He followed her eyes to Miss Deuss, who was standing outside her cabin, below them, phone to her ear.

"Put her on speaker, Marshall," said the baroness. "But lower the volume."

They watched Miss Deuss mouth the words that sounded from Marshall's phone a second later: "Get me a car. And don't tell the baroness."

· ✦ ·

THAT DEUSS TROUBLES ME, Regan," said Captain Nikkos. "Keep watching her."

"Yes, sir."

Marshall appeared at the door to the bridge, and Nikkos waved him in.

"I agree with you, Captain. Something is simmering. I came up to tell you she had me order a car. She's left the ship."

"For where?"

"She wouldn't say. I called the dispatcher after she left. They wouldn't say either. She must have told the driver to keep it private."

"Have you spoken to Alison or Professor James?"

"They're still not answering their phones. Sir, I'd like your permission to borrow Regan or Eyüp. I want to go after her."

"Except that we don't know where she's going," said Nikkos. "Or who she's meeting."

"I'll be able to spot the car. This is a small town."

"I'll remind you that I grew up in this town. There are dozens of roads twisting around those hills, and it's easy to lose someone if you've a mind to. Is the baroness aware of Miss Deuss's departure?"

"I believe she actually set it up, sir," said Marshall. "And something else. As soon as we docked, a courier delivered a package to me, with instructions to sign it over to the baroness. I don't know what's going on, sir."

"Okay, then. Best to stay put until the others arrive. I think the baroness knows exactly what she's doing."

"Just the same, I'm going to contact the police."

"I've done that," said Nikkos. "I know the chief. What I didn't know is that his department has a long-standing security arrangement with this group the baroness is apparently part of. He told me not to get in the way."

· ✦ ·

MISS DEUSS INSTRUCTED HER driver to wait when they pulled up to the white-stuccoed inn on a hillside above Katakolon. She marched to the door, ignoring the welcoming hibiscus, statuary, and phlox-filled urns. In the lobby, she advanced past a smiling desk clerk to a corner where a sullen man sat with Dante.

"I'm Monica Deuss," she told the man. "I assume you're Riggio. Let me see the vellum."

"Here."

She acknowledged Dante with a wordless stare, then scanned the lobby. "Where's your partner?" she asked Riggio.

"Gone. Swallowed up in the Delta this morning." He looked away, his face blank. "It was some kind of witchcraft this kid did. He's dangerous."

"Then you see why you need me," she said, displaying no empathy or even curiosity about what had become of the man. "So?" she snapped at Dante. "What's this vellum for?"

He returned her wordless stare.

"Says he won't know until he gets to the monastery," said Riggio.

"My car is waiting," said Miss Deuss.

I shouldn't be surprised to see her, Dante thought as Riggio pulled him to his feet. *And Ancient Light is allowing it. He's trusting me. Or using me. To do what?*

In the taxi, Riggio handed Ancient Light's map to Miss Deuss, then leaned his head back and closed his eyes. Still shaken by what Jerrie had endured, and unsure of his capacity to lead the rapidly changing mission, he willingly deferred to his new partner. But after the taxi had meandered through the hills for more than half an hour, they had begun to grumble.

"I'm sorry," the driver told them. "Your map is not helping me."

"Well, I'm not paying you for a tour of these damn hills," said Miss Deuss. "What's wrong with your GPS?"

"It doesn't show such a monastery, miss. I will try this road again," he said, sighing.

But it was another hour before they came upon a wiry monk in his late seventies walking behind the gates of a secluded property.

"Stop here," she ordered.

"Welcome to the Monastery of Saints Constantine and Helen," the monk called.

She sent the driver off and pulled Dante close. "You do what I tell you. You figure out where the collection is kept, and fast."

"That man kidnapped me," he shot back, "and now you're part of it."

"Don't be dramatic. Just do as I say."

The monk walked to them and introduced himself as the monastery's abbot.

"I'm Monica Deuss, the grandniece of Baroness Renate von Weber."

"Mercy," he laughed as he opened the gate. "We met when you were a child. You visited here with your father and mother. I recall that you loved handling our collection of old coins in the library."

"I don't remember that, Abbot."

"Oh, I thought you might have. The coin boxes were lighter after you departed."

"Well," she said, looking off, "anyway, this is Dante, a student on holiday with me. And my colleague Mister Riggio."

"Welcome again. Have you come to see our gardens? Our coins?"

She produced the vellum.

The abbot gave a shrug and a smile and invited them to his study.

As they walked, Miss Deuss told him she had permission to borrow objects from the Ancient Wonders collection, and that her friend Otto from Alexandria would be arriving later to meet her.

"We will, of course, document what we take," she said. "But we're rather in a hurry now."

"Bless you," he said cheerfully. "And how is Otto?"

"I'm sure he's well."

"That is wonderful news. It has been too long since I last saw him."

Now Dante felt the familiar energy that told him a picture might come. He slowed, his eyes drawn to his right, to a columned, domed pavilion just visible through a grove of olive trees some forty feet from the monastery. But at a sharp push from Riggio, his unformed picture was lost.

"Please, come in," said the abbot. "Now, you spoke of some objects?"

"Yes, lead us to the galleries, Abbot, so we can look at what we need."

"Pardon my puzzlement. You see, I know nothing of such rooms or objects. We have holy objects—relics, paintings, icons. But wonders? A collection of some sort?"

"Don't be coy, Abbot. This place is visited by some of the world's most prominent people."

"I suppose they come for the serenity offered by our chapels and gardens. But if there are treasures here—worldly treasures—they are unknown to me. Our treasures are those that derive from God, His glory, the boundless and priceless beauty of nature—"

"Yes, yes," she interrupted, as she slammed the vellum onto his desk. "Tell us," she ordered Dante as she unfolded it. "What does it mean?"

Now Dante saw, more clearly than he had at the villa, that the vellum had seven Greek letters, and that their spacing indeed corresponded to the geographic positions of the Seven Wonders. But this was not a map or a plan. It showed no natural features, no manmade boundaries. Only the seven letters. *What am I supposed to do with this?* he asked himself. *What am I supposed to see?*

He felt the stares of Miss Deuss and Riggio and was relieved when a monk entered, carrying a small package and several bottles of water.

"What is it, Father Dominick?" asked the abbot.

"A package for you. The courier told me it should be opened immediately."

The abbot placed the package on a refectory table, opened it, and removed an object wrapped in cloth.

"That's what Sackville hired us to find," Riggio growled when the abbot unwrapped it. "The snake," he sneered, reaching for it. But Miss Deuss grabbed it first.

"Show some manners, sir," she told Riggio. "Abbot, this is one of the objects we're seeking for our project. It's Queen Meritites, you see, and she's part of the collection."

She waved it at them, then quickly rewrapped it and thrust it into her bag.

"Miss, I protest," challenged the abbot.

"That's Alison's!" Dante shouted. "Give it back."

"It *was* Alison's, you mean," said Miss Deuss. "It has apparently been purchased from her by Ibis. How interesting. Abbot, you saw the accession number on the tag attached to it? And Ibis's stamp on its base? Yes, all quite in order." She placed her bag on a chair out of Riggio's reach.

"Here is water, gentle guests," said Father Dominick. "If you would like some."

When Miss Deuss declined, he placed a bottle in her bag. "You may want some later, miss," he told her. The monk then withdrew, patting his stomach and smiling to himself. Only Dante noticed, and he tried to understand what had amused him.

Now, as Riggio repeated his claim to the statuette, Miss Deuss took him aside, telling him he would be wise not to implicate himself in Sackville's murder and reminding him that, with her help, he would have much more to choose from.

While the two bickered, the abbot whispered to Dante, "The one you call Ancient Light has contacted me. The situation is quite as expected. We must remain calm."

"I don't know what to do, Abbot."

"Nor do I, but he has told me about you—that you have the ability to know things, and that it is best if you determine how to proceed."

"I'm trying." Dante spoke the words bravely, but the abbot saw his distress.

"What is wrong?"

"I didn't try to kill the man in the Delta, Abbot. I didn't—"

"What are you saying, child?"

"Riggio's partner. He was, like, stricken there by something . . . some kind of energy. All of a sudden. It almost killed him."

The abbot brought a hand to his mouth. "An electrocution of some sort? It happened without any cause?"

"Yes, unless I did it somehow."

"Be at peace. There are accounts of phenomena like this. Spontaneous combustions, even. Science can explain it, I suppose. Some would call it karma." He winked. "In any case, you must not blame yourself."

"I don't know. An ibis was there—like it knew . . ."

"You must move on now. But draw from it." He paused. "I have been told by certain visitors that the African sacred ibis was honored by the ancient Egyptians for its courage. Perhaps the one in the Delta protected you? There is a legend that they battled the snakes that came into Egypt each year from other lands. And that they could kill a crocodile with just a touch of a feather." He gave Dante a contented nod. "You will see something here. You will be guided by it. Ancient Light told me. But you must promise you will not reveal it, except to your guardian, and not write about it until he sees you again. This is what he told me."

"I promise."

"And now, you must keep your nerve."

Miss Deuss turned away from Riggio and picked up the vellum. "I asked you what this means," she snapped.

Dante ignored her and put his hand in his pocket, feeling heat again from the stones in the pouch. In a silent challenge to her, he walked outside.

"What are you doing?" Riggio shouted.

"Let him go," she said.

He approached the domed pavilion, sensing now what was there and feeling overcome with anticipation, until—almost laughing with relief—he realized that the destroyed mosaic at the villa was a copy. Knowing what he would see next, he closed his eyes, drew up to the edge of the pavilion and opened them to see a large, rectangular terrace tiled in the same rich blues as the Ishtar Gate, and at its center, the mosaic itself, the African sacred ibis in flight. His mind raced. *Who*, he wondered, *would have designed this, a bird, in Nebuchadnezzar's Babylon, which honored his strutting lions, bulls, and dragons?*

Now he gazed across the terrace's yellow-glazed border wall. It was two bricks high, just as in his pictures, and its top bricks were inlaid with little mosaics, as on the Hillwood Stone. But there was more—something he hadn't seen in his pictures. Set into the terrace, spaced evenly around the outside perimeter of the wall, were six squares, each measuring about three feet to a side. To his disappointment, they were not mosaics—they appeared to have been filled in with plain terra-cotta tiles.

He brought his eyes back to the mosaic. It was larger than he had expected, more than eight feet across. But missing was the bird's bright eye, the feature that had seemed to flash at him from the mosaic at the villa. Here it appeared empty and dull.

He stepped toward it.

"Slippers, my son," he heard the abbot call.

He looked down. Next to him was a wooden cabinet stocked with bulky canvas slippers. He put a pair on over his shoes and walked to the lower wing of the ibis, feeling its energy, and he was compelled again to look up to the sky, where he saw two more hieroglyphs forming—eyes, and a half disk.

He knew that a single eye meant "see," but that two meant "observe." And that the bowl-shaped hieroglyph meant "all."

Observe everything, he told himself. *The whole.*

"Oh," he said softly, pulling the pouch from his pocket. He made a cup of his hand and poured the little stones into it. There were seven, and now he saw that they were cut so as to fit together. He flattened his palm to arrange them.

The shape they formed was some three inches across.

An eye.

He ran to the ibis's head, scraped the clay from the eye socket, and replaced it with the seven stones. The eye completed the mosaic, giving the bird life and a presence as profound as that of the ibis that had engaged him in the Delta. He silently thanked Ancient Light, then took several slow breaths, allowing himself a moment of satisfaction.

"Hey!" Riggio shouted. The man began to approach the mosaic but pulled back abruptly.

When Dante looked up, he saw Riggio wincing in pain. He saw Father Dominick standing in front of the man, feet apart and arms folded in a protective stance.

"That bird . . . that mosaic!" Riggio cried to Miss Deuss. "They're evil. Murderous!"

"I remember this tired old patio from when I was a child," she said. "So, is this the great mosaic you wrote about in your blog?" she called to Dante. "I thought you said it was in Alexandria. Never mind," she shouted. "I'm not interested in it. Too big. Come here."

He ignored her. There was more on the terrace to observe. He

scanned the entirety of the wall in search of the place once occupied by the orphaned Hillwood Stone. Seeing no gap, he walked to a corner of the wall that was obscured by pots of mint and sage. He pushed back the dense vegetation and saw that not one but six or seven concrete blocks had been dropped into the wall in place of the original bricks.

Missing, he thought. *Or removed. Taken away, along with the Hillwood Stone.*

"An empty pursuit," he recalled Ancient Light saying. "Theirs is an empty pursuit."

He turned and saw the abbot standing behind him.

"The rooms, Abbot."

"The rooms," the abbot repeated earnestly.

"For the wonders collection. The galleries. You don't know?"

His question brought a blank look to the abbot's face and sent Father Dominick jogging back to the monastery.

"You're wasting time, young man," Miss Deuss called.

"All right," he answered. "We need to go back inside."

He turned to the abbot as they walked. "It's okay, Abbot. I think I know what to do now. Do you have a floor plan of the monastery?"

"There is one in my study. We had some renovations done a few years ago."

When they reached the study, the abbot led them to a file cabinet and pulled out the floor plan.

"No, Abbot, do you have an older plan? One the same size as this vellum?"

He scanned the walls as the abbot pondered. Amid the icons and old prints of saints and cathedrals, he spied a framed, top-view drawing of the monastery's foundation. The drawing extended out to the right, to the mosaic terrace, which was represented by a large rectangle.

"That one!" he shouted. He took it down and brought it to the table. "Look, it has grid marks on each corner, just like on the vellum. They're for aligning the two documents."

He placed the translucent vellum on top of the drawing.

"We should find the galleries in these areas," he said evenly. "Here, where the Greek letters are. But I only recognize a couple of the letters. What are they, Abbot?"

"This is the Greek letter phi. This one is pi. This, beta—"

"For Pharos, Pyramid, and Babylon," Dante guessed.

"Forget about Babylon," said Miss Deuss. "The Hanging Gardens are long gone. What are the other letters, Abbot?"

"Here, chi, and here, mu. And alpha, and finally, this is zeta."

"Colossus, Mausoleum, Artemis, and Zeus," said Dante.

"But these areas under the Greek letters are not galleries," said the abbot. "The entire floor space of the monastery is occupied by the monks' rooms, and our chapel, and library, and dining room—"

"They're underground!" Riggio shouted. "Like Sackville said. There must be a basement. There must be stairs—"

"I know of no cellars here," said the abbot.

"Well, this area marked with a pi is the closest to us," said Dante. "Maybe there really is a basement, Abbot, and that's one of the ways down to it."

"That is Father Dominick's room."

When Miss Deuss asked if there were keys, the abbot thought for a moment, then rifled through a drawer in a cupboard, at last pulling out a ring of large skeleton keys.

"My predecessor, Abbot Gregory, mentioned these to me, but neither of us knew what they were for." He handed them to Dante.

"There's six," said Dante. "That makes sense. I guess there wouldn't be one for the Hanging Gardens. This one has a pi, for the pyramid."

"Take us to that room, Abbot," said Miss Deuss.

"Father Dominick is a private soul," said the abbot as they walked. "He will not be pleased with the intrusion."

As they approached his room, Father Dominick could be heard singing "Ah! Vittoria! Vittoria!"

Riggio kicked the door open.

"Blessed Mother!" the monk cried. "You interrupt a man when he sings Puccini?"

"I'm sorry, Father Dominick," said the abbot. "You see," he told the others, "Dominick is the principal baritone in our choir. He is acclaimed throughout the Peloponnese, especially for this aria from the little opera *Gianni Schicchi*."

"Move," Miss Deuss ordered as she pushed past them. "What's this monk up to? Why did he run back here when we were at the mosaic?" She turned to Riggio. "I see a door behind this big wardrobe. Move this thing away."

She took the keyring from the abbot.

"But the keys are rusty, miss," Father Dominick told her. "They will not turn the locks like that. Let me scrape and oil them."

He took the keys to his desk, keeping his back to them. Miss Deuss gasped when he turned back to them, clippers in hand, and snipped the tip off the last of the six keys.

"Foul monk," snarled Riggio, as he stared at the solid steel door. "I'm going to look around. There have to be other ways down."

To Dante's surprise, Miss Deuss didn't direct her ire at Father Dominick or at anyone else present.

"Damned Otto," she cursed, and pulled out her phone.

Dante looked at the placid abbot and the bemused Dominick. *What now? How do I see the rest? Ancient Light said only I can reveal the catalog of treasures here. Catalog, he said.*

He sensed Ancient Light's meaning now and threw Miss Deuss the bait.

"Maybe there's another way."

"Say it," she demanded, as her call to Otto went unanswered.

"I'm guessing," he told her, trying to give weight to his words, "that there's a record of what's here. Yes, a catalog. An inventory."

"What good is an inventory to me?"

"Well, with those papers, you could claim the objects later. They'd be proof that you own them."

"Produce the inventory!" she commanded, her eyes darting between Dante and the abbot. "I mean, if you please, Abbot. We don't have a lot of time."

"We have centuries of files," said the abbot wearily. "You see," he said, pointing to the wall of boxes and cabinets lining the hallway. He stared at them as if trying to remember if there was a filing system at all. "But I believe the foundation drawing came from that old oak cabinet when one of our guests took it out for framing."

He approached the cabinet and, in time, pulled out a carbon-copy document. Miss Deuss seized and read it, finding row after row of numbers and letters but no descriptions. Looking more closely, she saw that each line entry also contained a Greek letter.

"We might be getting somewhere," she mumbled, as her phone rang. It was Otto.

"Where are you?" she snapped, moving away from the others. "All we've found is some papers dated nineteen forty. There's hundreds of items, but in code. And the rooms are locked tight."

"Look, stay calm," said Otto.

"Stay calm? A monk just destroyed the keys. Why didn't you know any of this?"

"Okay, we were a little delayed, but we've just landed in Katakolon."

"Get here fast," she told him. "Sackville's man . . . I'm afraid of him."

"Where's the other one?"

"I don't know. Wandering around in the Delta or whatever. Just get over here."

"Okay, tell him I'm bringing him cash."

Seeing Riggio return, she ended the call and stuffed the inventory into an outside pocket of her bag.

"Who were you talking to?" Riggio demanded.

"Someone who will compensate you. He's on his way. It's a bust here, okay?"

"You're lying. All of you." He snatched the inventory from her bag. "I'll have this."

"Give it back. It's nothing."

"Oh, it's something. And I'll figure it out. Keep the statuette. It's cursed, like everything with this kid." He grabbed Dante by the arm. "But I'll keep him."

"Wait, at least until Otto comes. I told you, he's bringing money."

Riggio gripped Dante tighter, then brandished a knife until Father Dominick backed into the foyer. "You two will figure out how to get into those galleries," he told them. "And you will stay there," he called back to Miss Deuss and the abbot.

"Do not do this," the abbot pleaded.

But Riggio forced Dante and Dominick back into Dominick's room, cutting the monk's arm when he resisted.

"How am I supposed to help you?" Dante yelled. "I can't get you in without keys. I can't walk through doors and walls."

"Then you will rot in here until you figure it out," Riggio grunted as he shoved Dante into the wardrobe and locked it.

· ✦ ·

A LIMOUSINE STOOD READY at Katakolon's heliport when Ancient Light's helicopter landed. Otto took the wheel, telling Alison and Professor James that they would be at the ship within minutes.

"Forget the ship," said Alison. "We're going straight to that monastery. Call the abbot, please."

"There are no phones there, ma'am," said Otto.

"Then we need the police. Give Professor James back his phone."

"As you wish."

"Please, Miss Fine," said Ancient Light. "It would be unwise to confront the kidnappers. We will proceed to your ship, and then Otto will go to the monastery alone. He knows what to do."

"Well . . . all right. If you're certain."

Marshall raced down *Modestine*'s gangway when he spotted the limousine approaching.

"Oh, Marsh," Alison called from her window, "Dante's been kidnapped."

"We know. I got the package you sent. What was it?"

"Queen Meritites."

"Okay, I signed it over to the baroness like you wanted. But why?"

"Dunno, Marsh," she said as she stepped out of the car. "No choice?"

Professor James stepped out next, followed by Otto, who then helped Ancient Light out. When Otto got back in and sped off, Marshall asked, "You want to tell me what's going on, Alison?"

"That's Ancient Light, and he's telling us to trust him. Dante's up in those hills somewhere, Marsh, with Sackville's men."

"But, Otto . . . ?"

"He's going up to save the day or something. And like Dante said, he works for Ancient Light."

"Well, I arranged a car for Miss Deuss a while ago, but she wouldn't say where she was going. Maybe to church," he joked, "because she put on a headscarf as soon as she got in the car."

"What?!" Alison exclaimed, turning to Ancient Light as he climbed the gangway. "You knew Deuss would be there at that monastery with Dante and those kidnappers?"

Ancient Light ignored the question. "And now I must see the baroness and the captain."

"As if nothing's happened!" she cried. "As if a kid isn't missing and being held by her poisonous grandniece and two murderers. Trust, you say, in your supreme—"

"If you interfere, you endanger the boy!" Ancient Light shouted, his body shaking. "And the monks. Would you have that, Miss Fine?"

He turned to take another step up the gangway, but stopped when he saw Doctor Ali coming down.

"You do not look well," she heard him tell Doctor Ali as he passed.

Doctor Ali simply shook his head. Their eyes had met, but neither man had been able to hold his gaze for more than an instant.

"What's with them?" Marshall whispered to Alison.

"Good question." When Doctor Ali reached them, she asked, "You know him?"

"Once."

"He tells us that Dante's been taken to a monastery nearby. He says we can't interfere."

"Of course not," said Doctor Ali. "It must be done his way. But I'm glad to see that you're safe." He watched Ancient Light greet Captain Nikkos, then heard him ask to be taken to see the baroness. "Ancient Light and the baroness," he muttered. "Zeus and Hera. All bow to them, the all-powerful."

Alison looked up to the sky. "Does anyone understand what's going on here? Have you been listening to any of this, Jasper?" she asked, seeing him fumbling with his phone.

"I've been trying to get the police."

"That will not change the outcome, Professor," called Ancient Light.

· ✦ ·

INSIDE THE LOCKED WARDROBE, Dante found the matchbook and candle stub Father Dominick had tossed to him before Riggio slammed the door shut. He lit the candle, but it produced only a sputtering, feeble flame. His discoveries of the ancient mosaic, the inventory, and the galleries seemed meaningless now.

He watched the flame die out.

Outside, he heard Riggio and Father Dominick argue, and all at once the night when he was three washed over him again, bringing back his anger toward his father and his guilt that he had done nothing to help his mother.

He began to kick the door.

No, he told himself, *clear your head*. He slowed his breathing, cleaned the candle of its built-up wax, and relit it. And now the amber beads from his necklace absorbed the light from the candle and filled the wardrobe with a light and energy of their own. And he heard his words gush out in a voice so clear, so commanding, that when it was over he was as surprised at himself as he was winded: "If I were you, Riggio, I'd leave with all that money you got, and you know Deuss is in this for herself and she has no use for you, so don't be a loser, leave now with the inventory, it's everything!"

"I know what I'm doing," Riggio shouted back.

But Dante heard the uncertainty in his voice. "My ship is here by now," he called. "The police will be looking for me. Looking for me here. Okay, there's no way I can get you into those galleries, but if you let me out, I can figure out those papers for you. They're important. It's a list of treasures from the Seven Wonders. Once I tell you what's on it, you can use it against Ibis. They don't want it to get out. It's worth a fortune to them."

Riggio was quiet.

"I just need a closer look at those papers and then you can leave and you can demand whatever you want from Ibis."

The wardrobe door opened.

"Hurry, then," said Riggio. He pointed his knife at Dominick and ordered him to move to the corner, then handed Dante the inventory.

"It's not very clear," said Dante as he pored over the document.

"I may need some time," he said, hoping the police really would come.

Riggio grabbed it back and put it in the inside pocket of his jacket. "Devil," he barked as he patted Dante down. Dante resisted, and in the tussle he snatched the inventory from Riggio's jacket and stuffed it into the back of his jeans.

"Where's that pouch you had? What's in it?"

"Just some old stones," said Dante. "I put them into the floor out there in the pavilion. Look," he said, producing the pouch. "It's empty."

"No, no, you're not fooling me!" Riggio raged. "We're going out to that pavilion. And you're going to find a hatch or whatever to the gallery under that mosaic. Or we're going to smash through it, and you're going to dig, and all the monks are going to dig, and we're going to see what's under it!"

"No," said Dante. "The Hanging Gardens washed away two thousand years ago. That's just a tired old patio, like Miss Deuss said." Seeing Riggio's confusion and sensing that he was now capable of anything, Dante looked at the man with an intensity that he hoped would rekindle his memory of his partner's agony in the Delta. "If you go back out there, you know what will happen . . ."

It was enough to unnerve Riggio to his core. He cursed at Dante and Father Dominick and ran out of the room, bolting past the abbot and Miss Deuss in the foyer and out the door.

"Where's he going?" she shouted. "He has the inventory. Stop him!"

The abbot didn't move—nor did the group of monks who had assembled outside the door. "Useless people!" she cried. After retrieving her bag, she kicked off her heels and gave chase.

"I have business at the gate now," Father Dominick told the abbot.

"Wait," said Dante, as he tore off his T-shirt and wrapped

Dominick's bleeding forearm. "I don't think you'll catch Riggio, though."

"Oh, I know a shortcut," he answered as he took off.

Dante looked at the abbot, who offered a serene smile.

"I think I know what Ancient Light had in mind, Abbot. How he saw it playing out."

"Yes, I suppose. But what did play out, exactly?"

"Well, I think I did what I could. I hope Ancient Light handles the rest. Anyway, Riggio didn't get the inventory." He pulled it from his waist and held it up. "He wanted the little stones, too. He probably thought they were jewels."

"Those little stones," the abbot mused. "Ancient Light has always said he would be back with them when it was time. Oh, could this be him?" he said as a limousine moved up the driveway.

"I see you've taken care of Dante, Abbot," said Otto as he got out.

"He has taken care of himself. And rid us of at least one criminal. Mister Riggio."

"And where is Miss Deuss?" asked Otto.

They turned to find her limping toward them through the olive grove.

"Police out front," she panted. "My feet are torn up. So nice you could make it, Otto. Riggio took the inventory."

Dante was confused. *Are they working together?* He turned away from her to stuff the inventory into his pocket.

"I saw that," she said. "Give it to me!"

Dante handed it instead to the abbot, who made it disappear into the abundant sleeves of his robe. After shaking his head at Miss Deuss, the abbot took Otto's hands.

"You were Dante's age when I last saw you, Otto," he said, then reached back into his sleeve and handed Otto the inventory.

"Abbot!" Dante cried, throwing up his hands.

"I think you can trust me with this," Otto told him. "It's Ancient Light's, after all, no?"

But Dante bristled when Otto gave Miss Deuss a look of re-assurance. "What's going on? Why are you helping her? She has Alison's statuette, you know. How did it get here? She took it."

"Well, then," said Otto, "let us each be content with our prizes here. I have the inventory, Miss Deuss has the statuette, and you have had the honor of placing the little stones in the mosaic."

"How did you know I did that?"

Without answering, Otto gestured for him and Miss Deuss to get into the car. "We'll be returning to the ship now, Abbot."

As Otto drove, Dante looked at him and at the scowling Miss Deuss next to him, wondering who he worked for and what would become of the inventory and of Alison's statuette now.

When the car approached the monastery's gates, he saw lights flashing from a cluster of police cars and motorcycles. It cheered him to see Father Dominick grinning and holding Riggio against a tree as an officer handcuffed him.

"Please hold the cash you find on him," Otto called to the police lieutenant. "I will give you a statement at your convenience about this man's crimes: breaking and entering, extortion, kidnapping, attempted robbery. And the murder of Doctor Peter Sackville in Cairo."

"And assault," said Father Dominick, holding up his arm. "And damaging my door. Victory, my boy!" he roared, laughing, and then shook Dante's hand and lumbered back to the monastery, again breaking into the triumphant aria.

Victory? Dante wondered. *How? Miss Deuss has the statuette. Otto has the inventory. And what if they're not taking me back to* Modestine?

"You may go," the police lieutenant told them.

"You wisely did not mention the statuette, Mister Dante," said Miss Deuss as they drove away.

"And you'll regret taking it, Miss Deuss." To rattle her, he added, "It isn't kind to thieves and kidnappers."

She looked at him uneasily, recalling Riggio's insistence that it was cursed.

"Put these on and turn up the volume," Otto ordered as he thrust an iPod and headphones back at him. "I'll be watching you."

He was glad to have the music. It calmed him, even as he worried about Alison and how Ibis got the statuette from her. Now, as they neared *Modestine*, a picture came—one so odd that he thought it impossible it could become real. It was the statuette, but in a barely recognizable state, an amorphous state. He dismissed the picture and pushed it away, then eased the headphones from one ear enough to pick up the end of Otto and Miss Deuss's conversation.

"So this didn't work out," Otto told her. "Stop worrying. You have the statuette—"

"And you'll arrange for its sale. Quietly, and in a way that's not traceable to us." He saw her turn to Otto with an avaricious smirk. "And we know enough now to arrange for pieces of the collection to appear on the market, as and when we like. Yes?"

"There may be a monk that will help us," he answered with a rare smile.

"We'll bleed it, Otto. No one will know."

Otto gripped her hand. "We just keep up appearances for the next day or two."

"What about Riggio, though? What about the boy?"

"Riggio will be put away forever," Otto assured her. "After tomorrow, we can be on our way to Paris, or Miami, or wherever you want. As for Dante, the old man will deal with him. He's already told me that."

· ✦ ·

WHEN SHE SAW THE limousine approach, Alison grabbed Marshall's arm and hobbled down *Modestine*'s gangway. Dante emerged first, followed by Miss Deuss, who leaned down to speak to him.

Alison watched, struggling to contain herself as Miss Deuss strutted past her up the gangway. Thinking better of confronting her just yet, she limped to Dante.

"Oh, you're safe," she said, hugging him. "Those men—"

"They're history," he said.

"What did she say to you just now?"

"She told me to keep my mouth shut about the statuette. She has it, Alison. Did you sell it to Ibis?"

"Of course not."

"But someone had it delivered to the abbot—"

"Yes," she said.

"You knew?"

"It was Ancient Light's idea. He says things are under control."

"You've talked with Ancient Light?"

"I have. He's here, incidentally. We did go after you in Alexandria, you know. No more questions now. You've been through a lot."

"Oh, it was all worth it, though. I saw it—I saw the mosaic there at the monastery. It was amazing."

"But the mosaic was at the villa," she said. "I emphasize *was*."

"That had to be a copy. The real one is at the monastery. But you can't say anything."

"Okay, wow. Well, just go get cleaned up. We brought your bags and your laptop back."

"But—"

"What? Everything's okay now."

"No, there's something about Otto. We shouldn't trust him. There's something between him and Miss—" He stopped, seeing Otto approach, and changed the subject. "I lost your phone, Alison."

"Heavens, is that all?" She hugged him again and greeted Otto. "Well, you kept your promise. You brought him back."

Otto nodded. "I'll walk him to his cabin."

Dante spoke to him only when they reached the door to officers' quarters.

"Remember, I know you have the inventory, Otto."

"I do have it, yes."

"And Miss Deuss has Alison's statuette. What if she leaves with it? I don't trust either of you. I have to talk to Ancient Light."

"Of course you must. But not until tomorrow. I'll be taking him back to our hotel after he's finished with the baroness. Miss Deuss won't go anywhere. Now, get some sleep."

Dante flopped onto his bed and let go of his urge to see Ancient Light. *Otto said he'd "deal with" me, after all,* he worried.

He began a sketch of the ibis mosaic, then pulled himself up and walked to his desk, thinking he should at least check in with Nora. He opened her latest email.

> Why won't you reply? Alison doesn't answer her phone. Grandma and I are worried now.

When he replied that they were safe and on the ship in Greece, she wrote back instantly.

> I found more in the *Sun-Times* archive about Papa. After the police questioned him about Mr. Mishky's death, he was released and then he was supposed to appear for a hearing, but he fled. I can't find anything more on him. Did he change his name? Did he leave the country? Are you coming home on time?

Dante allowed his head to drop, his thoughts rolling over the news from Nora, over Otto and Miss Deuss, over the statuette . . . and over Ancient Light, how angry at him he might be, as angry as Zeus . . . until sleep came at last and fashioned the vast churn of discovery, deceptions, and questions into dream.

12

OLYMPIA AND THE STATUE OF ZEUS

T HERE IS A TEMPLE *bright white before a twilight sky all royal blue.
And inside there is Zeus ten times my height on a throne of ivory
and ebony and he looks down at me stern and curious. And his
white beard and mane of hair begin to flutter in the wind but he
stands and walks away without speaking. And now there is just the
throne on the plain of Olympia but it is human size and there are
chairs in a semicircle in front of it. And a screen painted with Greek
gods and goddesses drops down near the throne and the baroness and
Otto peer out from behind it. And a minibus arrives making no sound
and people from the cruise begin to file out . . . And I want to tell
Alison her statuette of Meritites is in Miss Deuss's bag but she points to
the crescent of chairs and says we must sit. And Otto calls, "All rise," as
Ancient Light walks out from behind the screen. And he is in a white
robe and his hair and beard are like Zeus's. And the baroness walks out
in her navy suit with all of her brooches and a gold band on her head.
And Ancient Light says, "I want a thunderbolt!" and orders Alison to
give him her stick. And now Alison lights a torch that sends up fire and
black smoke and she hurries back and tells me, "He says there will be
a trial." And I say, "Then it must be for me . . . for trespassing at his
villa and for all the stuff I wrote this week and for what I didn't do to*

help my mother when I was small." And I stand but I cannot speak or move. And a door closes on me and all is blackness.

Dante stirred but did not wake, and his dream returned, reformed.

Now Zeus is on his big throne and the six other wonders appear and they are filling the sky and towering up like Chicago skyscrapers. And around them the air is visible like all of time and history . . . all energy all around pulsing dark and bright. And the wonders royals and gods and goddess begin to speak about me. And Pharaoh Khufu in front of his pyramid says, "He was in my chamber and he was overcome by haunted memories, but in his dark hours Thoth informed him. He will come to know the bonds and fates of ancestry." And Poseidon from atop the Pharos says, "He discovered the ancients who would be his beacon. And oh how that bird stirred him in the Delta." And the Pharos Tritons trumpet through their shells and say, "He could not blow out his cake's slight candle, but here he did not founder nor sink. Nay, he reckoned well his set and drift and his course was made good." And the Colossus Helios says, "Aye, the weight on him was great and I feared he might crumble under it." And he laughs and he says, "Oh, how brief was my handsome statue's time. Good that the boy holds on through his quakes and storms even if I could not. And good that he had a sound ship to carry him. Yet it is clear that he remains at sea." And Nebuchadnezzar from high up in the Hanging Gardens says, "I am suspicious of him and have no use for him. What is his interest in my lonely princess? What is his interest in my marshes and my gardens?" And Princess Amytis from her ibis mosaic terrace says, "Nay, husband—my gardens. They were overrun by men and beasts who in the great haboob ripped away my mosaic. . . . Oh, all insist my gardens are lost, but the boy disbelieves that and will make art of it. For he knows well the spirit of that sacred bird which does prevail." And night falls but her mosaic terrace stays bright under the moon and constellations. And there is solemn music from a bassoon and Mausolus from his chariot says, "The boy is wounded and struggling inside, I suppose. I observed it from my rooftop. But who is not battling a heavy stone? He begins at least to understand it." And the goddess Artemis steps from her temple and she is wearing her giant beads and gourds and pendants and she is glowing with the light of ancient amber. And she looks at me and with her eyes holds me in a gaze that warms me and I am no longer anxious. And she says, "Now, Zeus, this boy is impulsive and complex yet looks hard and deep at things . . . like Mister Wood Turtle at my temple." And she laughs. "So, Zeus, you decide. How will you classify or steer him? For there is much still that he does not know." And Zeus says from his throne, "I confess I am amused when watching him, and would rather let him find his own way."

Dante stirred once more at a ping from his laptop, but the dream found its way back.

And we are all seated in the semicircle of chairs on the plain and Father Dominick brings us bottles of water. And I see the water become the Nile and the Euphrates . . . and the rivers flow toward us and wash over us but we are not harmed . . . And the ground swallows up the water and now green shoots of papyrus plants and reeds rise up past our chins. And an ibis flies toward us low and I feel the breeze she makes. And her wing grazes a snake near my feet and I see her look back at me with her crescent beak turned up in a smile. And when I feel my ear the bandage is gone and my wound is healed. But Ancient Light is watching and I wonder how he will deal with me . . . And he says, "For is the young man not like papyrus plants and reeds and all that is vigorous and green? Shall we cut him down or watch him grow?" And he turns to Otto and says, "There is more pressing business today. Bring Monica Deuss from her chair." And when she will not move he roars, "Monica Deuss!" and he is holding up Alison's stick and its ebony veins grow into dark clouds and its silver knob is lightning stabbing the air. And he says, "You have disrespected the Seven Wonders and you have sought to exploit them. You have committed theft." And she demands, "Where is your proof?" and she looks to Otto for support but his face is blank and she cannot read it. And Ancient Light commands, "Hand over the Meritites statuette," but she tightens her arm around her bag and she lies, "Riggio took it." And Ancient Light calls, "Someone search her bag." And she says, "All right, all right, I intended to return it. Look." And she reaches into her bag and she scowls and moans and fishes out a sticky dripping cloth that held the statuette but it is dissolved. And Father Dominick walks over to us and he is smiling and the guests sing "Ah, Victory! Victory!" from their chairs and I say, "But I don't understand." . . . And now Queen Meritites appears and she is as tall as me. And she looks at Miss Deuss but does not speak to her and turns her back to her. And she walks to me and says, "Do not assume that you were not beloved of your father too." And she shrinks to three inches in the baroness's hands. And Ancient Light's voice rumbles through Olympia's hills as he calls, "Dante Rivera, do you recognize this statuette?" And the baroness presents it to me and asks, "Your answer? Do you recognize it?" And I say, "Yes, it's Alison's." And she asks me, "What, then, is that sticky, soggy rag that Miss Deuss is holding?" And I answer, "I don't know." And I hear laughter and I say, "Why does everyone else know?" And Ancient Light says, "Enough. Must he know everything?" And he asks me, "Did Monica Deuss conspire to remove objects from the monastery and did she take you there against your will?" And I say, "Yes, sir." And Doctor Ali appears and he looks angry and hurt and unsure and Ancient Light looks the same and they stare at each other, shaking. And the baroness's eyes dart between them and she tells them, "Only you two have the power to heal this bitterness of these many years." But Ali is gone and Ancient Light turns away and I see his pirate lamp shattered on the ground . . . And I see my father running and running and I call to him but I can make no sound . . . And now I hear the baroness say, "Dante Rivera, do you wish to exact revenge on Monica Deuss?" And I say, "No." And she asks, "Why not?" And I say, "Because karma?" And I see a battered taxi that says VIP on its door and Riggio is driving it in circles. And Ancient Light points to the taxi and says, "Monica Deuss, you are banished from Olympia and from the other wonders now and forever." But she is staring at her hands and they become reptile claws that try to scrape and rub the stickiness away—

Dante felt a nudge to his shoulder and awoke, his head still resting on his laptop. Alison, Marshall, and Captain Nikkos stood over him, but he closed his eyes again to hold the dream.

"Someone wants to see you," said Alison.

He raised his head and saw the baroness at his door with the Queen Meritites statuette cupped in her hands.

"It was loaned to us by Alison," she explained, as she placed it on his desk. "So that Chef Werner could create the marzipan copy, which we rushed to the monastery. And now, I return it. So. Are you awake yet? You look dazed."

He rubbed his eyes and felt his bandaged ear as he processed this news, then rapidly recounted his dream to them before it was gone from his head. "But now I need a minute to remember more. Please don't say anything."

· ✦ ·

"OKAY," HE SAID, LOOKING up at the baroness. "Miss Deuss's trial . . . That felt real."

"Well," she said, "I cannot explain the part of your dream about your loquacious Seven Wonders, but we did confront my niece—Ancient Light, Otto, and I. Privately, in my cabin, while you were sleeping this past hour. I must say, you judge well our heartache with her. And with Ali."

"And the wet cloth . . . I don't understand. There was water in her bag?"

"Oh, yes. The marzipan statuette was quite dissolved when we ordered her to produce it. A sugary, liquidy paste."

"And the water got in there how?" asked Alison.

"I suppose we shall never know. My grandniece instantly blamed Otto, of course. Why is Dante grinning?"

"Because now I remember," he said. "Father Dominick offered us each a bottle of water at the monastery. Miss Deuss didn't want one, but he put one in her bag. I bet he loosened the cap . . ."

"Ach, that Dominick. Always der Witzbold."

"Jokester," Marshall translated.

"I'm beginning to understand the rest now, too," said Dante. "Otto and Miss Deuss—that was fake, right, how Otto pretended to love her and help her?"

"Oh, yes," said the baroness. "Otto told us earlier that he had suspected her intentions even a year ago. I was certainly fooled by her when I invested in all this."

"But Doctor Ali's anger—" He fell quiet, overwhelmed by the dream and wishing it had gone on, wishing it had brought more answers. "I got an email from Nora before I fell asleep. My father was questioned about Mishky's death in Chicago. He didn't show up for his hearing. He might be a fugitive even now."

"Oh, Dante," said Alison. "I'm so sorry."

"You must believe we had no connection with your father," said the baroness.

"Okay," he said, still not sure if he could. *But why else would he have fled after Mishky died? Or did he run because of what he did to my mother?*

Now his thoughts returned to Doctor Ali, who had seemed so troubled, even in his dream, and who had said he had been to Chicago and knew of the Hillwood Stone. *Clear your head*, he told himself.

"Well look at this," called Marshall.

They went to Dante's window and watched Miss Deuss make her way down the gangway to a waiting taxi.

"We can't just let her leave—"

"Not to worry, Marshall," said Captain Nikkos. "She'll be stopped and charged. I arranged a call to the police earlier. We've given them a statement. They'll be here shortly to take one from you, too, Dante."

"She'll soon be in the slammer with Riggio," said Alison.

"I will leave you now," said the baroness. "Until tomorrow, then, for the interview. Again, Dante, I am sorry about your father."

"You're on a lot better terms with her, I see," Marshall said to Alison after the baroness and Captain Nikkos had left.

"She's redeemed herself," Alison answered. "For the most part. I'm hoping we'll have a clearer picture of all this after the interview. And Dante, I'm going to take her word that she and Ancient Light didn't know your father. For now, at least, it's their show. So let's just watch it play out tomorrow. Okay?"

He nodded.

They walked out to the pool deck and saw another taxi pull up. A woman with tousled hair and a rumpled pantsuit emerged.

"Dyllis!" Alison called.

"Ahoy or something!" Dyllis answered, startled to see Alison's bandaged hands and ankle. "What did you do to yourself?"

"Slipped and fell when we disembarked from this nice ship the other day. We'll come down and meet you."

"Hold the railing this time."

When Dyllis had boarded, Dante thanked her for her help and for her reporting, but his gaze was distracted, his voice mechanical. "Is Doctor Ali still here?" he asked Alison. "Does he know Ancient Light was here?"

"Ali is still aboard. And yes, they did meet, briefly. There was friction between them, like in your dream. Have you seen Doctor Ali, Marsh?"

"I just saw him aft, in the bar," called Professor James as he joined them.

"I have to see him," said Dante.

Alison told him that it could wait. She looked in turn at him, Marshall, Professor James, and Dyllis. "I just want the five of us to sit for a while, to catch up."

"I'll start, then," said Dyllis. "I got a curious email from an Egyptian boy named Med. He said he was following my stories. Said he and Dante met up with trouble in the Delta. There wasn't much I could do. You weren't answering your phone, Alison. And, Dante, he said you had vanished."

"Oh, I better call him. I put him in a lot of danger . . ."

Alison took a long breath and drew a finger along an ebony vein of her stick. "In the Delta," she said. "Okay, fill us in on what happened there, in the Delta."

His account was perfunctory. His thoughts were on Doctor Ali, on what happened in Chicago.

· ✦ ·

AT BREAKFAST, CHEF WERNER surprised Dante and Alison with a pitcher of the same yogurt concoction he made daily for the baroness.

"Very nice, Chef," said Alison.

"And nice job on the marzipan Meritites, too," said Dante.

"An hour I spent, working furiously to copy your statuette. Only to have it dissolve," he sighed. "But the baroness has told me the outcome was satisfactory."

"Chef, there was a monk at the monastery . . . and he smiled when he saw it."

"A large monk who sings?"

"Yes."

"Then you met my friend Father Dominick. He is very fond of

my desserts, and especially my marzipan. He recognized my work, no doubt," he added, and scurried back to the galley.

Now Otto approached with an offer from Ancient Light to drive them to the monastery for the interview. The others—Professor James, Marshall, Dickenson, and the baroness—would meet them there, he explained.

"Didn't you invite Doctor Ali?" asked Dante. "Or Captain Nikkos?"

"They declined," said Otto. "I suspect they've had enough of us."

"We'll be ready, Otto," said Alison.

She thanked him again for recovering Dante and apologized for distrusting him at the villa, then joked that she was glad that he hadn't sent the real statuette to the monastery.

"That would have been foolish," he said plainly.

"Well, our Otto was even stiffer than usual," Alison said to Dante after he left. "I'm beginning to think he's a Vulcan. But I suppose his mind is on the interview. Dyllis was an investigative reporter. I wonder if Ancient Light has thought this through."

"I don't think he's worried," said Dante. He took a gulp of the yogurt drink. "I tried to find Doctor Ali this morning."

"You can talk to him later. The baroness told me he's staying until tomorrow morning. Anyway, when we ride with Ancient Light, let's keep our powder dry—about your father, I mean. Like I said to you last night, I want to be in observation mode. Let's see what's on his mind and where he's going with this interview."

"Okay."

"And during the interview, best if you just observe, and let Dyllis do her thing."

"What if I can add something?"

"Then speak up. After all, you're an authority on all this. You'll be taken seriously now."

Dante finished his drink and held up the glass. "Yes, taken seriously."

"Okay, but you might want to lose the yogurt mustache."

· ✦ ·

OTTO OPENED THE LIMOUSINE's passenger door for Alison, but Dante waited, fixing his eyes on the tinted rear window. When it lowered, there was Ancient Light, whose expression was less severe than he had feared. Relieved, he recited the lines he had rehearsed.

"I know I've upset things. I couldn't let go of all the things I was trying to piece together. And all the stuff in my head. And then trying to help." To ground himself, he had been staring at the back of the seat in front of Ancient Light, at a black panel six inches square.

"Slide it," Ancient Light told him after waving him in.

Dante leaned forward and slid the panel on its track. Behind it was a mosaic crest with a large letter *I*, flanked by two African sacred ibises standing victorious over a swarm of snakes.

"You did no wrong," said Ancient Light. "I expressed my confidence in you, no?"

"So, you're not angry?"

"You did what you had to do," he said, as he signaled Otto to drive. "And in the process, you stopped some aggressors like those on the crest, no?"

"The abbot told me about the legends of the ibis. I witnessed it . . . I directed Riggio and Jerrie into the Delta after we left your villa. There's an ibis reserve there."

"You found my property."

"Yours? I first saw it from the train. Sackville's man, Jerrie . . . he was overcome there—"

"The keeper informed me this morning what happened. The ibis is a powerful protector. It can dispatch all manner of snakes and reptiles with ease."

Dante told him that Riggio, too, was nearly overcome when he approached the mosaic.

"It is well for Riggio that he did not advance onto it," said Ancient Light. "He would have suffered the same fate that Jerrie did, or worse. The ibis is a powerful protector even in its mosaic form." He leaned forward and tapped Alison's arm. "I apologize for the trouble at my villa, Miss Fine."

"But that was my fault," said Dante. "I guess you knew I would come, though."

"Yes."

"Wait," Dante suddenly called to Otto, thinking he had missed the turn to the monastery. But Ancient Light said they would be visiting the site of the Temple of Zeus first, and that he wished to speak with Dante for a few moments alone there.

"Did my words at the villa equip you well enough at the monastery?" he asked Dante as they walked.

"I remembered you telling me that Riggio and Jerrie were on an *empty* pursuit," Dante answered. "Then you said the vellum would reveal the treasure *rooms*, the *galleries*. You didn't say the treasures themselves."

"Good."

"And the last thing you said—you shouted to Riggio and Jerrie that only I could reveal the *catalog* of treasures. That made me think there must be records, which uncovered the inventory. So . . ."

"Yes?"

"The galleries are empty then, right?"

"Yes," Ancient Light confirmed, with a matter-of-fact shrug. "I could not allow your kidnappers to know that, of course. But I knew that you had begun to trust yourself. I thought it best for you to be occupied. To work out a puzzle." He smiled. "It was also a convenient way to get you back to your ship."

"I had a dream about here," Dante told him, as he looked across the plain where Zeus's temple and statue once stood. "You were Zeus."

"My powers are overrated. Yours are impressive. But you have not spoken of the pouch."

Dante told him the tesserae had drawn him to the pavilion, and that hieroglyphs had come to him there.

"Hieroglyphs, you say?"

"Yes, eyes. And a bowl."

"Ah, then you observed," said Ancient Light. "Fully, no? And without bias?"

"Yes, I saw the pattern of the eye the little stones made, and I began to put your clues together. And when I discovered the patched section of the wall, I figured the Hillwood Stone must have been sent away, and probably the rest of the collection, too. But, why?"

"You will have to wait for the interview."

"So I figured there was no harm in telling Miss Deuss where the rooms were."

Ancient Light beamed. "That certainly drew her in. She revealed her intention to loot the collection, a treacherous move on her part. You exposed her and outwitted Riggio. I had hoped you would direct things that way."

"I almost didn't, though. We almost didn't find the monastery at all from the map you gave us."

"Did that irritate them?"

"A lot."

Ancient Light laughed. "I marked the monastery's location a few kilometers off. Chef Werner needed time to make the marzipan, after all."

From the car, Alison watched them. Fifteen minutes, twenty, and still they paced the ruined site, talking.

"Shouldn't we get to the monastery, guys?" she called. When

they returned, she apologized for rushing them. "I'm just anxious to see the legendary collection."

"It's not there, Alison," said Dante.

"So, no wonders at the monastery?" she mumbled. "After all this? No Ibis collection at all? Only the mosaic?"

"You will learn more at the interview," said Ancient Light. "Let's go, Otto."

"I've been thinking about Father Dominick," said Dante. "There's a door to the Great Pyramid gallery in his room. He stopped Riggio and Miss Deuss by snipping off the ends of the keys."

"Did he?" laughed Ancient Light. "I had forgotten about those keys."

"He's more than a monk, right?"

"Dominick has worked for us for many years, yes. But he also longed for the monastic life."

"He asked to be placed at the monastery to protect the collection," said Otto, as he took the car through the monastery's gates.

"So he didn't know the galleries were empty, either?" asked Dante. "Because, like I said, he snipped the keys."

"Correct, but he takes excellent care of the mosaic." He explained that the steel doors in the monks' rooms were used only during the construction of the underground galleries—that there was nothing behind them now but wall.

The abbot was standing in the monastery's driveway when they arrived. He embraced Ancient Light, then took Alison's hands.

"Welcome, Miss Fine," he said. "This way to my study." As they walked, he gestured toward two CNN vans and then at the pavilion, which was now shrouded by a scrim. "Alas, my monastery has come to resemble a movie set, and already it has begun to attract crowds."

In the abbot's study, Ancient Light spoke first, telling Dante, "You are here because you had connected with the wonders, each of them, and so deeply that you would inevitably encounter me . . . and therefore adversity."

"I kept thinking about something Alison told me from a book. About ibises foretelling gales."

"From *In Patagonia*," said Alison.

"I see," said Ancient Light. "And about seasons changing . . . and about living and dying. So be it. We push on. And if some day you read another of Chatwin's books, about the indigenous peoples of Australia, you will discover the spirit and threads that guide them. You will learn about the songlines that weave through space and time, invisible, connecting them to their land, to their sacred places, to their ancestors. . . . I have imagined you grappling with your gift. At first, it may have caused you to worry, and to block and repress it, then confront it and put it to use. Perhaps we gave you a push?"

"Yes."

"You helped another find his way."

"How? . . . Who?"

"You made me examine my life, my purpose. My legacy, no doubt. I thought about my own youth. And further back, to the days and nights of Babylon itself. And as I imagined you placing those little stones in the mosaic, I was there. You wore the slippers before you walked, I hope."

"Yes, and the ibis did come alive to me then. It stirred. It filled out like it would yelp and pump its wings."

"Yes," Ancient Light said with a laugh.

The abbot's mantel clock began to strike noon, followed by a tall clock in the foyer and the great bell in the monastery's tower. When a monk reported that the guests had arrived, and that Dyllis and her crew were ready, Ancient Light drew a long breath and walked to the foyer.

Alison watched him greet the baroness and sensed that he was at peace with what he was about to announce. In the baroness, she saw relief. She saw Otto, ever stoic, standing near the camera, poised to intervene if necessary. She handed him the nondisclosure agreements that she and Dante and everyone else present had been required to sign.

"How was your ride with him?" asked Dyllis.

"He's a charming man," said Alison. "I didn't press him about Chicago and Mister Mishky. I really should have."

"You know I will."

· ✦ ·

"OKAY, EVERYONE, TAKE A seat," called Dyllis. She introduced herself to Ancient Light, sat down in a chair opposite him, and nodded to her crew to begin taping.

But Ancient Light called her back.

"I must insist on an embargo of this interview, Miss Kirby."

"You never mentioned this," Dyllis protested.

"It is for just a few months. We will let you know when you will be free to air it." He handed her a typed agreement. "Unless you sign, we cannot continue."

"That's a long time. I can sign only if you agree to do no other interviews before then."

"That language is in the agreement."

"Okay," said Dyllis as she signed. "Now may we begin?"

"Now we may begin, Miss Kirby."

"Welcome, then, sir. Your organization and your collection have been the subject of much speculation. For centuries, but especially of late."

"Our achievements have been exaggerated by many. And underestimated by most."

"Well, I hope you can illuminate some of the history for us, but first, you told me that you have an announcement."

"I want to say that I have disbanded the Ibis organization. It exists no more. That being the case, we shall divest the collection—"

"Divest?" Dyllis interrupted. "Please tell me how. By auction? Will it be done transparently?"

"That is not the subject of this interview."

"Then, are you prepared to reveal the collection today? It's here, presumably, or you wouldn't have brought us all this way."

"I have invited you here for two other reasons, Miss Kirby. First, so that the world will know that the collection is *not* at the monastery. This is to preserve the monks' peace." He looked off. "I have not seen the collection in nearly eight decades," he said softly, forgetting to mention his second reason for arranging the interview at the monastery.

"You're losing me, sir," said Dyllis. "Was it ever here?"

His eyes searched for the baroness, who gave him an encouraging nod.

"Yes, it was here. But it was moved to another location in nineteen forty, to protect it. This was at the start of hostilities between Italy and Greece during World War Two." He paused. "You see, our love of the great monuments, through the generations . . . our members . . . people of refinement . . . each of them a curator, a guardian . . ."

An uncomfortable silence filled the foyer as his voice trailed off.

"Are you okay?" asked Dyllis.

"Yes. I'm sorry."

"You were saying you haven't seen the collection since nineteen forty. Why?"

"Because, madam, the objects are still in storage. Elsewhere. Crated up. I will say no more about this, but I assure you that they will be relocated appropriately, in time."

"You say the collection was moved, but I have information that you and others have visited this place many times. Are you being honest with me?"

Now Ancient Light looked down, overcome by memories and

by the enormity of his decision to let go of a secret he had pledged to guard for all of his life.

Seeing his distress, Dante called out to Dyllis, "He's trying to tell you."

When Dyllis motioned to him to come forward, Dante leaned over to Ancient Light. "The second reason for calling us here, sir," he prompted. "You know . . ."

"Yes," said Ancient Light. "It is so that the world may see the one piece from the collection that was *not* removed. Yes, Miss Kirby, we visit this place, and for good reason."

He rose and led everyone to the pavilion, where he called on the monks to remove the scrim.

"You see in front of you," he announced, his voice strong now, "the only object known to be from the Hanging Gardens of Babylon. This mosaic terrace—"

"Yes, a true mosaic!" Professor James burst out, as he ran to the edge of the terrace. "I would have expected a bas-relief. This is so ahead of its time. Remarkable!" he gushed.

"You are correct, Professor," said Ancient Light. "There was nothing in Babylonian art like what we see here. The mosaic represents a thorough break from tradition. A monument in art history. We believe that Nebuchadnezzar's wife, Princess Amytis, designed it herself. It was, of course, too fragile to be moved with the rest of the collection during the war."

As Ancient Light spoke, Dante directed Alison's attention to the low wall that surrounded the mosaic.

The baroness had followed them. "Yes," she said quietly, "each top brick has a little mosaic. So, thirty different plants and trees— there a cedar, and there, a date palm, and farther down, bamboo. There, a tulip, a hollyhock, hostas, papyrus, and more. You see, the princess cataloged it all, and so beautifully. And here, Miss Fine, just here in front of us," she whispered, "your calamander, the wonderful tree from which your stick was made."

"No way!" shouted Alison.

"Alison," Dyllis implored. "Professor. This is chaos. Can we get on with it?"

"Now," Ancient Light continued, "we associate King Nebuchadnezzar's Babylon with its gods of intimidating strength— the lions and so forth. So why did the princess choose to honor the African sacred ibis? We believe that she had visited Egypt."

He looked at Professor James, who had made a questioning sound under his breath. "I see you are skeptical, Professor. Yes, there were hostilities between Babylon and Egypt at the time. But what if she went on a mission of goodwill? What if she developed an admiration of Egypt's culture and deities? The ibis was plentiful there, and also in the great marshlands near Babylon. So, she would have known the bird, and perhaps going to Egypt gave her an appreciation of its wisdom and, yes, power—notice the unsuspecting snake—power as great as any of the beasts on Babylon's Ishtar Gate and Processional Way. How glorious that she gave it a central place in a terrace of the Hanging Gardens, and that she conceived it in this mosaic form. And in her peaceful retreat," he added, pointing to the wall bricks' mosaics, "she also created a little encyclopedia of botany, perhaps the first."

He allowed himself a satisfied smile before concluding, "For if the Hanging Gardens are gone, the essence of that wonder stands perfectly preserved before us."

He pulled on a pair of canvas slippers, motioned for Dyllis and the others to do the same, and then walked to the ibis's head. "Here, the eye. It had been blank and incomplete. But Dante saw it and knew."

When he asked Dante and the abbot to help him bend down to it, a monk rushed forward with a low stool for him to sit on. Father Dominick followed with small bowls of fine sand, lime, and water. He placed them next to Ancient Light and gave him a fourth bowl, which Ancient Light used to mix the ingredients into a mortar.

Now he removed the seven tesserae that Dante had loosely placed, and, in consultation with the baroness, arranged and reset each with permanence. When finished, he stood and stepped back to admire the bird and the arresting brown eye with its deep-red outer band.

"With this, you complete your work," said the abbot.

"A chapter," he answered.

"I meant to give this back to you," said Dante, as he handed Ancient Light the pouch that had contained the tesserae.

"Please keep it," he replied. "To hold the thing I gave you earlier."

Alison overheard, and wondered what he meant, but dared not disrupt the interview again.

Next, Ancient Light pointed to a group of easels that had been set up near the terrace. "These are enlargements of pages from the archaeologist's journal from our expedition to Babylon in seventeen hundred."

"Doctor Ali knew about that dig," Dante whispered to Alison. "Why didn't he want to be here for this?"

She drew her forefinger to her lips. "Best to listen, now."

"You may be curious about the six squares outside of the wall," Ancient Light continued. "They are blank, even in the archaeologist's sketches. We installed them here as placeholders for what we believe must have been more mosaics. Unfortunately, they were not excavated during the dig. What they depicted remains a mystery."

Now he turned and pointed to the monastery. "The galleries for the six other wonders are inside."

How convenient, Alison thought. *Barely a mention of the wall around the mosaic, and not a word about the Hillwood Stone that was part of it.*

The group followed Ancient Light along a path that led to the rear of the monastery and a pair of armor-clad double doors, each six feet wide by ten feet high. He produced a key and handed it to Father Dominick, who opened one of the doors and led the party down a wide ramp. Murals of the Great Pyramid and the landscape around it decorated the hallway leading to the first gallery, as though they were approaching the site itself.

"Oh, you were right," the abbot whispered to Dante. "We had always thought there was merely a stable behind these big doors."

"Just ahead, the gallery of the Pyramid of Khufu," said Ancient Light.

"So many empty niches," said Dyllis as she entered. "So many pedestals and plinths, displaying nothing. Just nothing." She waited, hoping Ancient Light would feel compelled to fill the silence and reveal something of what had been in the gallery. The tactic nearly always worked when trying to draw out a reluctant interviewee, so she waited some more.

"There being no questions," said Ancient Light, "we will proceed to the Pharos of Alexandria gallery."

They passed more murals, of the lighthouse and of seascapes stormy and calm, before entering the gallery. Ancient Light walked to the center of the room and placed his hand on a plinth some eight feet in diameter. There were many more, along with a deep circular niche nearly ten feet in diameter cut into the far wall, but again he revealed nothing.

"That niche," Dante whispered to Alison, "it has to be for the polished metal disk that would have reflected the beam out to sea."

"We will now proceed to the library," said Ancient Light.

They entered a large room lined with bookcases, their shelves empty, but the room still held its original library table, chairs, and settees.

"Oh, the Biedermeier," Marshall whispered to Alison. "I'd kill for that furniture. I can just see it in my condo."

Ancient Light overheard. "Are you Marshall? Dante has spoken favorably of you. You may have it. Now, to the four remaining galleries. Come."

They passed still more murals and peeked into the empty galleries of the Colossus, the Mausoleum, and the Temple of Artemis, then took a long hallway to the Statue of Zeus gallery. As they walked, Ancient Light spoke of the architect who had designed the spaces.

"He was an American. A general. In the late nineteenth century he created a design that would connect the galleries in a pattern that mirrored the geographic positions of the sites." Thus, he explained, a walk through the galleries would have evoked a sightseeing journey to the Seven Wonders.

"What about those amazing murals?" asked Dickenson.

"They are in the style of the great Scottish painter David Roberts, whose work the general admired."

When they reached the Zeus gallery, Ancient Light lowered his eyes and spoke so quietly that he could scarcely be heard. He did not go inside.

"This was the last gallery to be cleared—" He stopped when his eyes landed on a piece of drawing paper on the floor. It was folded and yellowed with age.

Dante picked it up and handed it to him. He had not looked at it, but he saw that when Ancient Light unfolded it, he was moved, and the baroness as well when she drew up next to him.

"May we see?" Dyllis asked.

"It is nothing. We will leave now."

"Well, the sheer size of this," Dyllis reflected. "I do wonder about the methods Ibis employed over the centuries. And how you must have steamrolled over your competition to accumulate on such a scale."

He shook his head. "*Accumulate* implies hoarding, Miss Kirby. Ibis was selective. As to methods, much worse was directed at us. We were the target of predators of every stripe. Even to this day. You have seen it." He waved his hand, as if to brush it all away.

"Do you think you led effectively?" asked Dyllis. "Do you want to comment on your stewardship?"

"Others may judge my standing among the Ibis principals."

"If we knew who they were," she challenged. "It's rumored to be a line as colorful as the British monarchs or the popes."

"You are prone to hyperbole, Miss Kirby."

"We must wrap this up now," said Otto.

"Not before I ask about the wall around the mosaic outside." Her eyes flashed to Alison and Dante, then back to Ancient Light. "Sir, those wall bricks resemble one that turned up in Chicago fourteen or so years ago—the so-called Hillwood Stone. I wrote about it. What was it doing in the States?"

Ancient Light didn't answer.

"I'll remind you that an employee of the Hillwood Estate in Washington got his hands on that brick. It was marked with the letter *I*, so it was part of your collection. How did he obtain it?"

"The man must have stumbled upon it. We have had thefts in the past. I cannot tell you how he obtained it."

"Cannot, or will not?"

"You are unfair, Miss Kirby."

"And you disappoint me. In bringing me here, you were prepared to confirm the existence of Ibis and of your collection. Yet, you won't say what it is or where it is. If the world must wait, all right. But the Hillwood Stone has a checkered history, one involving foul play maybe. *That* you won't talk about. And *that* is not all right." Her words echoed down the long hallway.

She was not finished. "Sir, did Ibis attempt to retrieve the Hillwood Stone from Raymond Mishky on the day he fell to his death in Chicago?"

Ancient Light wouldn't engage.

"Are you aware," she pressed, ignoring Otto's calls to end the interview, "that the police in Chicago and Washington may now be cooperating in reopening the Mishky cold case? Mishky worked at Hillwood. Is that where the rest of the collection is? Do you still wish to deflect my questions on this, sir?"

"We are done here," declared Otto. He took Ancient Light's arm and led him away from Dyllis and into the Zeus gallery. The baroness followed.

"Don't press him so hard, Dyllis," said Dante. "He has to do this his way."

"Ibis's criminal acts, if real, need to be addressed," she told him. "That's central to all of this. And if there was one murder, there were probably others. How dirty is this organization?"

Several minutes passed before Ancient Light, Otto, and the baroness emerged from the gallery.

"We will provide you with some additional background, Miss Kirby," said Otto. "The embargo of this interview will remain in effect."

"We may continue filming?" Dyllis asked.

Ancient Light nodded. "As I told you earlier, we needed to remove the objects from the monastery for safekeeping because of the war. Mrs. Post agreed to allow us to store them—"

"You are referring to the heiress Marjorie Merriweather Post? From Hillwood?"

"Yes, the collection was crated up and shipped to her Florida estate, Mar-a-Lago."

"So Mrs. Post was a member of Ibis?"

"I discuss the shipment only, Miss Kirby." He explained that the crates were never unpacked in Florida, nor later, when they were moved to Hillwood in the late fifties when Mrs. Post purchased the estate as her primary residence. He revealed that she had offered to build a new home for the Ibis collection there, but that there was little agreement about it among Ibis's members.

"In nineteen seventy-three," he said, "Mrs. Post died. It was a blow. Time passed. Her estate became a museum. Our membership thinned. The prospect of returning the collection to Greece became ever more daunting."

"But when Hillwood became a museum," said Dyllis, "surely every inch was surveyed and every piece of art cataloged."

"We saw to it that the building holding the collection was kept off limits. But there was a curious Hillwood employee . . . the unfortunate Mister Mishky." He paused. "We are in communication with the authorities in Washington and Chicago, by the way, Miss Kirby. You have broken no news. As for Mishky, he apparently explored the contents of at least one crate. He removed the object you call the Hillwood Stone and then tried to sell it."

"Would you like to comment on his death?"

"I will not speculate."

"Did anyone from Ibis visit Mister Mishky at that time?" she pressed.

"I resent the implication that there was foul play on our part. I will answer no more questions about this."

"All right. I wanted to give you an opportunity to address the man's death, sir. But thank you. We'll move on. But I find it odd that almost a decade and a half has passed since Mishky left the brick with the Tribune Tower. Why didn't you ever come forward to claim it?"

Ancient Light shook his head. "No more questions about it, Miss Kirby."

"Then, can you tell us anything about the collection and where it will go?"

"We are in conversations with the governments of the countries of the wonders' origins. We will have more to say in a few months. Can you not wait?"

"Except that you're apparently still in the business of acquiring," said Dyllis. "I speak of the statuette of Pharaoh Khufu's wife, Queen Meritites."

Ancient Light raised his hand to the camera.

"Turn it off," Otto ordered.

"My statement has concluded," said Ancient Light. "I will say that we made attempts to acquire the statuette. Clumsy ones. But Meritites is where she belongs, with Miss Fine. And I will say that Ibis did acquire other things since the collection was sent to America. These few things are kept elsewhere. They, too, will be divested."

"All right, but you've left many questions open. May we continue later? Or tomorrow?"

Otto shook his head.

"Just one more question, then," she said, closing her notepad. "I'm puzzled by the bad blood that I understand exists between you and the Babylon expert, Doctor Ali Khalil. And that you seem more upset with him, an unassuming academic, than with the associates of Doctor Peter Sackville or with Monica Deuss, the people who betrayed you."

Without a word, Ancient Light slammed the Zeus gallery's door and walked with Otto, the baroness, and the abbot to his car, where he scribbled a note.

"Please give this to Miss Fine, Abbot."

"We're to join him for dinner," Alison told Dante as she read Ancient Light's note. "Hotel Europa at seven. Sorry, guys," she told Professor James, Marshall, Dickenson, and Dyllis. "He doesn't mention any of you."

"Of course he doesn't," said Dyllis. "He didn't deny sending an Ibis agent to see Mishky. I'm sure they'd like to convince you that they had no involvement in any of it. Then there's his emotional state, his reaction to my question about Doctor Ali. I'd be very wary—"

"No," said Dante. "He saved me from Riggio and Jerrie and Miss Deuss, didn't he?"

"Dyllis has a point, though, Dante," said Alison. "We don't really know him. He dispenses information in little spoonfuls, and always on his terms. I'm not sure I want us to be used—"

"He just wants to talk," said Dante. "Without the cameras. He must want to get something out."

"Are you seeing anything? Just to put me at ease?"

"It could be something more about the collection, I guess. But maybe something about his family . . . even if he doesn't know it yet."

"All right, we'll have dinner with him. But I want one of you there, too," she added, looking at Marshall and Professor James.

"Take it, Professor," said Marshall. "I got the furniture."

"Then I'll be heading back to Istanbul," said Dyllis.

"And I'll say my goodbyes as well," said Dickenson. "But, Dante, you're right, there's more. Draw them out."

· ✦ ·

"I'M SORRY TO CRASH," said Professor James, as he approached Ancient Light's table with Alison and Dante. The baroness and Otto were there as well.

"Nonsense," said the baroness. "Please sit."

"Soon, the world will know our plans," Ancient Light began. "It is fitting that you know first."

"Your nondisclosure agreements remain in effect," said Otto.

"Until such time as you receive your invitations," said the baroness.

"To what?" asked Dante.

"To the opening of the Ibis collection exhibition at the start of the new year," said Ancient Light. "It will be in your country."

"At Hillwood," Dante guessed.

"In your capital city, yes, but not at Hillwood."

"Are you going to give us a preview tonight?"

"No, but some history at least." He outlined the organization's rise and influence across six centuries, but revealed no names or methods.

Dante asked the question that he knew was preoccupying Alison: "Was there anything criminal, though? I guess we have to know."

"If being ruthless is a crime, and if exerting influence is a crime, then my predecessors acted so for the highest purpose."

"Which was?" asked Alison.

"To rescue and protect the wonders from wars and vandalism and neglect. If some in the organization acted unethically, or covertly, it would have been in the pre-Ibis era. I cannot deny that."

"And under your leadership, specifically?"

"I acted decisively when necessary. I never condoned force."

"Did you condone Sara Gamal's tactics?" Alison objected. "She told us the statuette was modern. Not very nice . . ."

"My apologies for that," said Otto. "She was not authorized to deceive you."

Professor James cleared his throat. "May I? So when your organization changed its name to Ibis about one hundred years ago, your center of operations shifted away from Europe to Egypt. Why?"

"My ancestors were of the Ahwar," said Ancient Light. "Of the Mesopotamian Marshes south of ancient Babylon."

Dante leaned in. This was what he had been waiting and hoping to hear.

"In the eighteen forties, there was a terrible flood there," Ancient Light continued, his eyes moving from Professor James to Dante. "A boy—my great-grandfather—was separated from his parents. He was taken to Baghdad, where he was adopted by a prominent family. He was studious. An independent sort. He had wanderlust and in his early twenties found his way to Prussia, where he met a member of our organization and impressed him with his bearing and his knowledge of antiquities. He was employed by the organization and became indispensable. After many years of service, he was appointed secretary.

"My grandfather was elected principal next. He was drawn to the Nile Delta's marshes and to Alexandria—the city of the Pharos and the ancient Musaeum and the Library. He built the villa there in nineteen twenty, the same year he renamed the organization Ibis."

"This was a refreshment of the old order," said the baroness. "Ancient Light's grandfather wanted something different for the organization, to make it more, shall we say, relevant? He helped finance archaeological digs around the world. Quietly. We still do."

"Like you, Dante, my grandfather loved the night sky," said Ancient Light. "He wrote that on a winter night, while looking at the constellation Orion, he pondered the hunter's three-starred belt. Like you, he observed that the belt echoed the alignment of three wonders sites, and like you, he was struck by how the seven together resembled a bird in flight."

"I tried to get the stars and the wonders sites to line up perfectly, but they really don't."

Ancient Light smiled. "It was not precise, of course. It did not need to be. It was my grandfather's to define, as an artist would. He wanted to honor the sacred bird in the mosaic. He lamented that it had become scarce in the Delta. He lamented that the Hanging Gardens were lost."

"So he invented a star, too, for Babylon, like I did?"

"He may have, at first. But he was luckier than you. One night, he saw a light that was not there before."

"A planet."

Ancient Light shook his head. "Something rare. Do you know the comet Khalil?"

"Your grandfather discovered it?"

"Yes. The comet completed his constellation. It was the ibis's eye. It was Babylon and the Hanging Gardens."

When Dante guessed that he must have acquired the Vander Hoof map around that time, Ancient Light nodded, saying that it had delighted his grandfather to see the wonders sites on the map aligning with the stars and the comet, all connected through the ibis.

"Later," he said, "he recreated the mosaic in his courtyard at the villa. It was his touchstone, both for the wonders and for Babylon and the marshes. For home."

"How often does the comet appear?"

"Every twenty-four years. You will soon see it." He waved his hand, intent on finishing. "At the start of the Second World War, my grandfather stepped down and my father became principal. As I told Miss Kirby, he moved the collection to Mrs. Post's estate in Florida, and then to Hillwood, to protect it. Late in his life, in the nineteen nineties, he returned to Iraq with my mother. He was eager to renew the search for the Hanging Gardens, and to try to convince the government to reverse its policies that were harming the marshes. For their opposition to these policies, my parents were expelled."

Ancient Light went quiet, but the baroness took up the narrative, explaining that his father had decided that the time was approaching for Ibis to be dissolved, and had written so in his diaries and letters, which Ancient Light had begun to read.

"But that note you sent me," said Dante, "about the letter *I* on the Hillwood Stone, claiming it was really an *H*—"

"I acted out of habit, I suppose," said Ancient Light. "I see things differently now. I see what my father and the baroness wished for."

When Dante asked why the bricks had been removed from the wall around the mosaic, Ancient Light explained that his father wanted to preserve some of them to replicate the wall if it got damaged during the war.

"That Hillwood Stone was broken in half," said Alison. "Dyllis believes it happened in Mishky's hotel room."

"What does it matter?" answered Ancient Light, growing irritated.

"Please," said Otto, "do you have other questions for us?"

"When I looked into your courtyard at the villa," said Dante, "I saw a flash, a little spark of light."

"Crystal," said Ancient Light.

"From the mosaic's eye, right?"

Ancient Light nodded. "When the mosaic was excavated from the ruins of Babylon, the archaeologist feared that the tesserae would be lost, so he removed them and placed them in the pouch. They were put back in the eye after the mosaic went to Prussia, and again when it was moved to the monastery. But my grandfather wanted them with him in Alexandria when he built his villa. So he placed them in the eye of the copy of the mosaic there."

"But you removed them at some point," said Dante. "And put them in your safe. Why did you put the crystal in the eye instead?"

Now a deep sadness came over Ancient Light. "A perfect crystal for the eye," he said softly.

Dante changed the subject, not wanting to press him. He told him that when he discovered the villa, he had seen someone bend down near the eye when walking past it.

"Years ago," said Ancient Light, "I asked my butler to dust it each morning. But, over time, the older staff would touch it whenever they passed . . . perhaps to remember."

"Remember what?" asked Dante. But Ancient Light looked away. "Will you recreate the mosaic at the villa, do you think?"

"It is time to move past it. And who would care for it when I am dust? No, there is one mosaic again, and the little stones are where they belong. Ask me something else."

"Okay, the meaning of the 'Ancient Lights' sign on the wall at your villa?"

"Ah, that is a better question." He explained that it was once the custom for property owners to post the signs, giving notice that nothing could later be built nearby that would block the natural light from their windows.

"My grandfather wanted to preserve his view of the Pharos site and the harbor. The city was growing rapidly."

"The name suits you," said Professor James.

"To have Dante bestow it on me, in the singular, well, it pleased me."

Dante asked how the monastery was chosen to house the collection.

"Would it not make sense to move the collection to Olympia," Ancient Light offered, "if some of our members considered the Statue of Zeus objects to be among our finest?" He divulged that his grandfather had purchased the monastery, which had been abandoned. After restoring it and building the galleries, he leased it to the monks.

"For one drachma a year," the baroness noted as she adjusted her brooch, a seated Zeus in ivory with the goddess Nike and an eagle-tipped staff in gold. "The monastery provided excellent cover. No one suspected what it housed."

"How many members did you have?" Professor James asked.

"Only a handful in recent years," Ancient Light said. But when Alison asked if he would name them, or at least some from the past, he declared that he was not at liberty to violate agreements that had been made to protect their privacy.

Alison was not satisfied with the answer. "I'm sorry," she said, shaking her head. "You're entitled to that, I suppose, but privacy goes only so far. I'm troubled still about Chicago. And so is Dante. We can't just ignore—"

"What do you mean?" said Ancient Light. "Why is Dante troubled?"

"His father got caught up in that affair with Mishky."

Now a look of concern and of genuine surprise came over Ancient Light.

"You wouldn't answer Dyllis's question about whether you sent an agent to see Mishky," she continued. "And I still don't know what your relationship was with Sackville. I can't let you brush it all aside. You need to explain, or I can't allow Dante to have this association with you."

"And tell you what, exactly, Miss Fine? I know nothing about Dante's father." He looked at the baroness.

"Nor do I," she said. "And I have told Dante that. Dante?"

He said nothing, reserving judgment, though he felt relieved that Alison had finally decided to confront them.

"Maybe not," Alison continued, "but it seems there was *someone* with Mishky moments before he died. It was in Dyllis's story. And he's never been identified. She reported that the motel's housekeeper said he ambled down the hallway past her. Ambling on by, as if nothing had happened—just a little murder, maybe? Who was it?"

"Ambling," echoed Dante.

"What?" asked Alison.

"Wait, everyone."

He asked Professor James to call Dyllis.

"Dyllis. It's Dante. I'm putting you on speaker. The day Mishky died. The housekeeper . . . what did she say to you?"

"I talked to her mostly about the condition of Mishky's room. But she also said there was a man in the hallway. I only know a little Spanish, so it wasn't exactly an interview. When I called the police detective and asked for her description of the man, he told me she wasn't much help. He said she was saying 'ambli,' and repeating it several times, like the man was ambling past her. That's how I reported it."

"Dyllis, she was trying to say amblyopia." He waited for a reaction. "Don't you see?" he cried. "Anyone?"

"Let us be calm," said the baroness. She asked the professor to end the call with Dyllis, then turned to Ancient Light, saying only, "Please."

"Yes," he said quietly. "We did send someone to see Mister Mishky."

"So," began Alison, "your tactics do include—"

"No, Miss Fine. Our agent was instructed only to make Mishky an offer for the Hillwood Stone. Our property, I remind you."

"Why should we believe you?"

Dante was staring at Ancient Light, bursting to speak, but Otto broke in.

"Our agent did nothing to that man."

"How do you know, Otto?" Alison challenged. "You were probably a teenager when this happened."

Ancient Light held up his hand before Otto could answer, willing himself to speak. "That agent did not kill Mishky. That agent was my son."

"Doctor Ali," Dante whispered.

"I sensed that you suspected this, Dante."

"You suspected this?" Alison mumbled.

"It's been on my mind for so long," he said. "Doctor Ali said things to me when we first talked—about a secret dig, and that he had been to Chicago and was familiar with the Hillwood Stone. I knew Miss Deuss seemed to have something on him. But he wouldn't have 'ambled' out of the hotel after committing a murder in cold blood. I knew he couldn't murder anyone. So . . . did my father do it, then? How was he involved? No, this is too weird. No."

"Dante," said the baroness, "Ali told us Mister Mishky was in a paranoid state when he went to his hotel room. The man had been drinking. He panicked. It was just a fall."

"How do we know that?" asked Alison. "I love Ali, but just because he's Ancient Light's son doesn't mean he's innocent."

The baroness looked at Ancient Light, and when he nodded, she asked Otto to speak.

"As we have said, Miss Fine, we are in communication with the authorities."

"And?"

"We have supplied them with a video," Otto continued. "It

was taken by another of our agents who was shadowing Ali. This was standard procedure. The video shows Ali exiting the hotel and walking to his car. He is at his car when Mishky falls. This is captured clearly in the video. Ali could not have been involved. Monica Deuss only thought she had something on him."

Ancient Light seemed not to listen. "My son rejected his opportunity to lead Ibis one day," he said abruptly. "He abandoned me."

"You are harsh on him," scolded the baroness. "I looked for Ali earlier," she told the others. "I wanted to tell him that he no longer has to fear being dragged into what happened in Chicago. And then we were to have him here tonight to repair things—"

"You mean you knew he was clear," Dante broke in, "and you never told him?"

"I am not proud of that," Ancient Light answered. "However, you must understand his disapproval of us. You must understand that we could not take the chance that he might talk about Ibis. And maybe now you can understand why we opted not to claim back the brick from the Tribune Tower. All the questions that would have prompted, all the digging into our affairs." He brought a hand to his brow. "But it was we who reached out to the American authorities. In these past few days, and even hours, I have been in discussions with them. And, in turn, with our members. And the baroness. It is only now, tonight, that we are free to speak openly with Ali about this. I wish we could help you regarding your father, Dante." He turned to the baroness. "Of course, Ali would not have come tonight in any case. He has no interest in his father."

"But don't you know about his work in restoring the marshes?" said Dante.

"I do not wish to offend you, Dante, but this matter is private. Now, Otto, please address Miss Fine's question about Doctor Sackville."

Otto explained that his orders to Sackville were to have his men observe Alison and Dante, but that he had since learned that

Sackville had his own agenda, and that Miss Deuss had tried to engage him as an ally against Ibis, just as she had tried to engage Doctor Ali. And himself.

"And his death?" asked Alison.

"It came at the hands of his two hired men alone."

"Then, just one more question," said Alison. "For you, my lady. When we had tea in your cabin, you weren't straight with me about your desire for the statuette."

"I was, in truth, sentimental for it, but I was also deceitful. I am sorry. We are competitive, Alison. We wanted to keep others from acquiring it."

"I pushed you on that, Renate," said Ancient Light. "I wanted it. I wanted a success after so many years of failure. So many years . . ."

"You are tired, old friend," said the baroness. "Put it from your mind."

"Do you have any more surprises for us?" asked Alison.

"None," said the baroness.

"Wait," said Dante. "How were you going to loan anything to Miss Deuss if it was all packed away at Hillwood?"

"Ach, who knows?" scoffed the baroness. "I suppose we would have asked Otto," she said, grinning, as she turned to Ancient Light. But she saw that his eyes were fixed on his lapis lazuli ring, which he had been turning idly on his finger.

She rose, signaling an end to the evening.

"I tried to make it right!" Ancient Light burst out suddenly. "His eye. I could not . . . the doctors could not . . ."

"Couldn't what?" asked Dante.

"Correct it." He looked off. "So many years. The crystal . . . I placed it in the mosaic for him. For my boy . . ."

"Why?"

"Because he loved that my grandfather found the comet. I

thought it would please him. . . . I wanted him to believe that his own eye could be made right one day."

"So when your staff touched the eye whenever they passed, it was to remember Ali?"

"Yes. Yes." After a moment he brightened. "You say he keeps the marshes?"

"Yes," said Dante. "He does."

"It's time we retire, sir," said Otto.

Ancient Light rose and took a step, but then stopped and reached into his jacket. He handed the folded paper from the Zeus gallery to Dante, saying, "I made this sketch when I was a boy, on the day I helped clear and pack objects from the galleries."

"For real," Dante whispered, as he unfolded the drawing.

It showed the Zeus gallery before it had been emptied. In the foreground were two people of aristocratic bearing, a man and a young girl. He guessed them to be Ancient Light's father and the baroness.

"I am told that you sought to collect a memento from each wonder. Do you have one for the Statue of Zeus?"

Dante shook his head, unable to speak.

"Then you may have this drawing."

"The nondisclosure agreement remains in effect for this as well," said Otto.

"Yes," said Ancient Light. "You must keep this to yourself until the exhibition."

Dante promised he would. And as he watched Otto and the baroness lead the old man to the hotel's elevators, a sadness came over him, and a dread that deepened with each slow step he saw Ancient Light take, and it was all he could do to smile to him before the elevator doors closed and he was gone.

· ✦ ·

"SHALL WE HAVE A glass of wine after all that?" Professor James suggested to Alison as they returned to *Modestine*.

"Sure. Why don't you call Marshall and Captain Nikkos and ask them to join us? But give me ten minutes, Jasper," she said, waving to Eyüp to catch the boatswain's attention.

"Meet you in the pub aft, then," said Dante.

He raced ahead, guessing that Doctor Ali would be there.

· ✦ ·

WHEN EYÜP CONFIRMED THAT the baroness had returned to the ship, Alison went directly to her cabin.

"Come in, Alison. Have you more questions?"

"I wanted to thank you again for dinner, my lady, but yes, I do have one. First, though, is Ancient Light okay?"

"The day was tiring for him. Miss Kirby's style is rather . . . assertive."

"I guess mine is, too," said Alison. "I'm sorry. But you must have expected it. You must have known we would press him about the Hillwood Stone."

"We cautioned him."

"I'm just wondering why Ancient Light wanted to do the interview now, before the Mishky case is resolved. He could have waited. Why subject himself to such harsh questioning now?"

"Ancient Light is ill, Alison. He wanted to do it now, while he could. He wanted to introduce the world to that mosaic himself. And he was determined to gain back the Hillwood Stone—to see the wall and the mosaic terrace whole again. I would ask you not to tell Dante what I have said about his health."

"Of course. Please tell him I wish him well. I'll leave you now . . . though, have you had a chance to clear things up with Doctor Ali?"

"I am told he is in the pub, so I suppose I will have to see him in the morning. Now, I bid you goodnight. But when I am back in Germany, I am going to send you something that I think Dante will enjoy reading. You must mail it back to me, however."

When Alison suggested she could return it to her at the exhibition, the baroness said she did not plan to attend.

"I may need to be with him . . . with my old friend."

· ✦ ·

"COME AND PULL UP a stool," Doctor Ali called to Dante. "Tell me about your dinner with the moguls."

"The baroness said she invited you."

Doctor Ali shrugged.

"We learned a lot," said Dante. "About Ancient Light. Ibis, too."

"And the collection?"

"Not exactly."

"They shroud everything in secrecy. That's their way."

"They seem to want the best for it, Doctor Ali."

"You think I'm being too tough on them. Anyway, I haven't thanked you for what you did. For saving me from myself the other night outside Miss Deuss's cabin. And you must call me just Ali."

"Okay. We talked about you tonight. I know it was you that went to Chicago to retrieve the Hillwood Stone. That's what Miss Deuss was holding over you, wasn't it?"

"You think I killed Mishky."

"No, I don't. They cleared that up. They said you were at Mishky's hotel when he died, but there's evidence clearing you."

"Oh, sure," Doctor Ali scoffed.

When Dante told him about the video, and that it cleared him, he uttered a curse under his breath.

"So, they could have told me long ago, but didn't."

"I think they just never wanted any publicity around themselves," said Dante. "Or you. Good or bad."

"The scoundrels."

"They wanted to tell you tonight. They're even talking with the police to clear it all up."

"What else do you know?"

"That Ancient Light is your father."

"Alas," he said, tipping his glass.

"I told him you were working to restore the marshes. He was interested. Maybe you can talk to him about it."

"Now you sound like the baroness. I get enough advice."

Neither spoke for nearly a minute.

"My own father," Dante broached. "The newspapers said he met Mishky, and introduced him to someone at the Trib. . . . So do you know anything about him? The baroness and Ancient Light told me they don't. But you must have talked with Mishky. I have to know."

"Forgive me, Dante. I didn't want to keep this from you. I suppose it's safe for me to tell you now." He took a sip from his drink and began. "All right. So, a person connected to Ibis on Hillwood's board contacted Ancient Light about a theft from the building where the collection was stored. And when we learned that Mishky was trying to sell the brick, we tracked him to Chicago. Ancient Light chose me to visit him. The man feared me. He thought I was a Hillwood detective or the police. I told him I just wanted to buy the brick. He wasn't coherent. He staggered out to the balcony. I didn't see the brick, so I left. I heard his scream from my car, so I assume he lost his balance. I saw people run to him. . . . I drove off."

"What else?"

"There was a note on Mishky's nightstand—a reminder to meet someone later at a tavern. I took it, thinking that it would lead me to the brick."

"That person was my father, then. Tell me!"

"Yes. Again, I'm sorry."

Dante bent forward, saying nothing.

"Dante, listen. The name Rivera was written on that note. When you wrote your name and address for me the other day, it hit me that you were his son. I could see him in you."

"What happened at that tavern, then? You went there?"

"Yes. At eight o'clock, like the note said. There were just a couple of people there. I introduced myself to him. I told him I had seen Mishky earlier. I told him I would pay him for the brick if he had it. But he told me Mishky had already taken it to the Tribune Tower. He said he was waiting for Mishky, to get his commission."

"Commission for what?"

"For telling Mishky the Trib might be interested in buying the brick. That's all. I told him that Mishky fell and was probably dead."

"So they had met the night before, like the papers said?"

"Yes, at the same tavern. He told me Mishky was bragging about the brick. He said he saw Mishky drop it and break it later at his hotel."

"What was he like, my father?"

"He was anxious. He told me he had to leave the city. He said he didn't really expect Mishky to show up."

"So that's when he left us—my sister and me. I was three."

"I'm sorry."

"Did he mention my mother?"

"No. He seemed troubled. Overwhelmed, somehow. Wounded inside." He pushed his drink away. "That visit to Chicago led to my final break with Ancient Light and Ibis. I told him I wanted no more of this business."

"Tell me so I'm sure, Ali. Did Ancient Light or the baroness know any of this? Did they know it was my father who helped Mishky?"

"No. I reported my meeting with him, but not his name."

Dante went quiet. When he saw Alison and Professor James walk in with Marshall and Captain Nikkos, he motioned to them to take a table away from him and Doctor Ali.

"What's wrong, Dante?"

He had been absorbed by a thought that now worried him above all else.

"My sister found some information," he began. "She said the police questioned my father about Mishky's death. So could he have been there when Mishky died? Like, between the time you left Mishky's room and the time you got to your car and he fell?"

"I would have seen him in the hallway, or in the lobby. I pulled Mishky's door shut when I left. Only seconds passed before I got to my car. Your father couldn't have been there."

"Then you have to call them, the police in Chicago. You can clear his name."

"Of course."

"Did he talk about me?"

"He talked mostly about you. He talked about how you loved the stars when you were small. How you always wanted him to hold you up in the air to look at them—" His voice broke.

"What, Ali?"

"This has brought back something."

"About what?"

"Of my own child."

"I didn't know you had a family."

"I lost them. . . . My daughter. My wife." He looked away. "There was a bomb blast. In Baghdad, during the war. Twelve years ago."

"I'm sorry. I don't know what to say . . ."

"Let me go on. . . . Your father told me how you would point up to the sky and say 'stars,' whether it was night or day."

"I did?"

"Yes. He said he was not there enough for you. He was an emotional guy, in the best way. Not like my own father."

"No, he was emotional tonight. He opened up."

Throughout their conversation, Ali had mostly kept his head

down. But when he looked up, Dante was struck by the color of his eyes, the same deep lapis lazuli as Ancient Light's ring.

"He was upset about your eye, Ali."

"He sent me to doctors when I was a boy. They did nothing that helped. Then he went away. Traveling. Always traveling. He didn't care. He abandoned responsibility."

"But he said you abandoned him."

"I see that you're exasperated. Don't be. We clashed over everything and nothing. Who knows why this is? But I wanted no part of Ibis. I knew that. I ended the long drama. So what? I'm only glad that I could tell you about your own father. He loved you."

"You don't think Ancient Light feels the same? For you?"

"Maybe once. Not now."

"He keeps an old photo of you in his library. I saw it when I was at the villa."

"I'm a disappointment to him."

"He placed a crystal in the eye of the mosaic at the villa. He said it was for you."

"For me? Why? Listen, I'm fine with my eye now. It's me. If it bothers him, well then, good."

When Dante asked if he remembered a pirate lamp at the villa, Doctor Ali told him it had been in his room when he was a child.

"It fell and broke," said Dante.

"As should Ibis."

"What do you mean?"

"Well, they should be broken up. And gone . . . them, and their pirate ways."

"He told us he never used force in building the collection."

"Still, for him, it's the love of things, of collecting. Not of discovery, or of people."

Dante told him that Ancient Light had decided to give everything back. He told him how Ancient Light had held the broken lamp and Ali's photograph, even as Sackville's men were shouting at him, even as they were destroying the mosaic.

Doctor Ali listened guardedly, then shook his head, his face locked in a stubborn stare.

"She was right," said Dante.

"Who?"

"The baroness. What she said in my dream. That it's up to you and Ancient Light. So, I'm going to leave you alone."

He walked to Alison and the others.

"Talk to him," Marshall was telling Alison. "We'll leave."

"He doesn't want anything to do with Ancient Light," Dante told her.

"From over here, he certainly looked like he was blocking something," she said. "Maybe someday he'll try, but not tonight."

"He said he met my father in Chicago. He said my father talked about me, and cared about me. And he's sure my father didn't kill Mishky. But did my father kill my mother then? He left. . . . How am I supposed to forgive him? When will it stop pulling me down?"

"You'll keep trying. I wish I could offer you more than that. You'll get there, and maybe Ali, too."

"I don't think so. I don't think they will. And my own father—if he cared, why did he leave?"

"I know it frustrates you. It's been a long day."

"It's messed up. I don't care if he's gone."

"People disappoint you, then. I mean, when they do, you can't get past that?"

"When they let me down, I can't."

"I hope I haven't," she said.

"No."

"Because if you cut people off who disappoint you, that will narrow you . . ."

She saw his face cloud over. It seemed not to matter to him.

"I'm closing out my blog tonight. The trip is over. Probably my writing is, too." He told her he would deal with it. By himself, as he always had. And though he saw the disappointment in her face, he let his words stand.

"I can't let you talk like that. Dante, a trip is never over. You remember it, and call it up the rest of your life. There's the wonders exhibition coming up, so you'll extend your blog. Or you can work on something new."

She knew that he had come to embrace his ability to foretell things, and that he had learned vastly more about what had happened when he was a child. But now she realized that there was something else, and she struggled to understand it. For all his goodness, there was a detachment about him. And not just now, as she reflected back, but at other times during the trip as well.

"How are you feeling, Dante? I mean, about what's next after this. On the plane last week, you said you weren't sure about college this fall. Do you still feel that way . . . ?"

He shrugged, then took Ancient Light's drawing of the Statue of Zeus gallery from his pocket. "I'm not supposed to show you this yet," he said.

"That's okay. I can wait. So you're thinking about all the stuff that was in that gallery?"

"I'm thinking about how Ancient Light drew his father. . . . They were close."

"Dante, I'll just say that nothing is forever messed up. No matter what feels missing. Will you just promise me one thing? Your writing . . . I've seen how it focuses you. It's direct, and it's honest. Will you promise me you'll keep at it?"

"I guess."

"And college . . . if you haven't decided, just stay open to it, will you?"

"I'm not open to starting now. January, maybe, if my head is clear. Not now."

They heard the rumble of a stool and watched Doctor Ali leave the pub. They soon followed, returning to their cabins within the safe, strong hull of *Modestine*, where each would reflect, or stew, or wonder. And, in the morning, leave for the airport and home.

· ✦ ·

TOO RESTLESS TO SLEEP, Alison left her cabin and walked up to the pool deck. She took in *Modestine*'s superstructure, remembering Dante's climb at the start of the cruise. "What are your radars and antennas saying to you now, Dante?" she asked aloud.

"Alison?" she heard Professor James call.

"Jasper? I'm worried about Dante."

"Why?"

"The thing with his father, mostly. He's a little bit at sea. . . . Wants to put college off, too. I just don't know . . ."

Professor James took out his phone and scrolled through his emails. She caught a glimpse of a map on the screen before he began to walk the perimeter of the pool, the whole time absorbed in his phone.

"You don't have any reaction to what I said?" she asked when he returned.

"Oh, I do. How do I get in touch with his grandmother?"

13
———

WASHINGTON, DC

IN THE FIVE MONTHS since her interview with Ancient Light, Dyllis had honored his news embargo, while Dante, Alison, and Professor James had kept secret his plans for the wonders exhibition. But none had spoken with him, nor had he commented publicly on the rising speculation in the media about Ibis and its collection.

Finally, in mid-November, the first credible report of an exhibition appeared in the *Washington Post*: "In recent weeks, the unmarked tractor-trailer truck has been spotted several times, moving at a crawl in the predawn hours under escort by police and private security vehicles. . . . The convoy travels from the Hillwood Estate in northwest DC to a loading dock at the National Building Museum downtown. . . . The Great Hall of the museum has been reserved for a major, but as yet unannounced, exhibition that is expected to open in January."

By the time the story ran, four hundred guests chosen by Ancient Light and the baroness had begun to receive invitations to a private reception at the museum on January first, the eve of the public opening.

"We'll fly to Washington together," Alison told Dante's grandmother over the phone. "It will be good to catch up."

"I guess you've read that the police wrapped up that Mishky investigation?"

"Yes, and found no foul play. That must have been such a relief, Emma. I've been wondering . . . that thing I mentioned to you when we got back from the cruise in June, the conversation Dante had with Doctor Ali. Did Dante tell you about it?"

"Yes, in about four sentences. You know how he is."

"He's still resentful, then? About his father?"

Emma was slow to answer. "I didn't press him. It's a sore subject. For both of us."

"I understand." Alison let it go. But they shared a laugh when she mentioned Professor James's invitation to Dante to join a colleague's dig after the cruise. And laughed again when she explained that it was the baroness who paid for it.

"The experience suited him, then?" Alison asked.

"September and October in the forest along Lake Superior . . . yes. He said it's what he wants to do. Anthropology and archaeology. He'll start college in January."

"He's been writing, I hope?"

"He's been working on something, but he doesn't want to talk about it. Says it isn't far enough along. I think he worries he won't finish."

· ✦ ·

A WINTER STORM MADE the midday flight from O'Hare to Washington's National Airport two hours late. Marshall had arranged for a Mercedes Sprinter to meet Alison, Emma, Dante, Nora, and Professor James, who had been visiting Alison for the holidays. The luxury van, with its six big swivel seats, took them across the Potomac River and into DC to the Wardman Park Hotel, where Marshall worked part time. When they met him at his concierge desk in the lobby, he produced an envelope bristling with Egyptian stamps.

"A letter from Doctor Ali for Mister Rivera," he said, handing it to Dante. "Save it for later, though. Since you guys are late and the reception is only a few hours from now, I want you to check in fast and meet me back at the van."

"Why, Marsh?" asked Alison.

"We're going to Hillwood."

"I asked Marshall to book us a tour," said Professor James.

As a docent led them through the Hillwood mansion, Dante took in the view from each window, trying to guess where on the grounds of the twenty-five-acre estate the Ibis collection had been stored.

"Did you know a guy named Mishky who worked here?" he asked the docent.

"I know *of* him," she said. "We are allowed to say, now, that he removed a piece unrelated to Mrs. Post's collection."

"Well, duh," Nora whispered to Dante, "we already knew that." The docent raised an eyebrow at her, and appeared relieved when Professor James told her they were short on time and that he wanted to visit the orchid greenhouse.

"Orchids, Jasper?" said Alison. "In this weather?"

"You'll see," he said.

They dashed across the mansion's driveway and into the greenhouse.

"Incredible," she whispered, as she shook the sleet from her hat and coat and took in the hundreds of potted orchids hanging from hooks, crowding the floor, and filling the tiered benches that ran the length of the greenhouse. "Could the Hanging Gardens have topped you?" she asked the myriad blooms projecting from their spiky stems like inquisitive painted faces.

"You've gotten another picture, haven't you?" Professor James heard Nora say to Dante.

"Yes," he answered, looking at the professor. "But I'm not going to say anything."

Professor James leaned over to him. "Is it about something I'm carrying?" he asked in a low voice.

Dante nodded.

"Okay, it must be time, then," he said as he took a small box from his pocket and handed it to Alison.

"Oh, just look at this ring," she gasped.

"That's white gold with a setting of seven yellow diamonds encircled by rubies," said Professor James.

"It's like the ibis's eye in the mosaic," said Dante.

"And only slightly smaller," cracked Marshall. "It can't be real."

"It's a gift from Ancient Light," said the professor. "And, yes, it's real. Fabergé, he told me. I guess we have his blessing, Alison. Will you . . . ?"

Alison smiled, and when she nodded, he took his hands, framed her face against the orchids' plump green leaves and elemental blooms, and kissed her.

"Congratulations, Happy New Year, and we'll give you two some space," said Emma, as she herded Dante, Nora, and Marshall away. Marshall invited Emma and Nora to follow him to the more exotic varieties of orchid in another part of the greenhouse, and they wandered off.

"I guess I'll open this, then," said Dante, holding up the envelope from Egypt.

"Stay here with Professor James and me and read it," said Alison.

"We'll be back in ten," called Marshall.

The envelope contained a letter from Doctor Ali and an older piece of notepaper with writing on both sides. "He says he went to Alexandria after Olympia," said Dante as he read. "He says I gave him a push. . . . He's been working with Ancient Light on the exhibition all this time."

He held up the notepaper. "He says this is the note he told me about at the end of the cruise—the reminder my father wrote for Mishky. Look. 'Meet me. Vendy's Tavern—eight o'clock. Rivera.' . . . But he says he forgot about the writing on the back." He turned the paper over. "It's a crossed-out poem. He says my father must have written it, then probably crossed it out when he wrote the reminder on the other side . . . there's no title."

"We'll wait while you read it," said Professor James.

"No, I'll read it to you."

All is shifting, all around,
As I leave again, Serena.
I will go on lost patrol,
Mi amor. Solo.

Do they award a medal
For the storm inside?

But, Dante, will there be
A time when you will see
Beyond your memory
Of what I did to wound you?

And can I hope
That you will not know war,
But make the stars your company,
And from your heart create?

And rhyme of near and distant realms
In lines that will unfold for you?
And come to know
Your sister and yourself for me?

"Oh, Dante," said Alison. "He was in such pain."

"But he was thinking about us—Nora and me. He must have written it after he left us. After whatever happened to my mother."

He read it again, this time to himself.

"I don't understand what he means by going on lost patrol, or awarding a medal for the storm inside."

He read the rest of Doctor Ali's letter aloud:

When I returned to Alexandria, I told Ancient Light
I had blamed him for not fixing my eye when I was
young. I wore that resentment like a badge, and it was
small of me. I know now that he tried.

With our work on the exhibition concluded, he has
joined me in my own work in Iraq. You will come one
day, if it is to be.

"I'm glad for them. I'm glad I have the poem." He looked at it again, wondering if his own resentments would ever fall away.

Later, Alison watched him walk ahead with Emma and Nora to the van, where they took three seats together. And as it took them away from Hillwood, she heard him read the poem to them. She saw Emma pull out photographs from her purse to show Dante and Nora, and heard her speak her daughter's name, Serena.

"I never saw two people more in love," Emma told them. She showed them another photo. "I never told you that he was a soldier."

Now Dante began to understand the poem's allusions to war. "At the Mausoleum, a memory came to me of camouflage like that. Like he's wearing."

"Well, you were just sixteen or seventeen months old around the start of the Iraq War in two thousand three," Grandma explained. "Your father was sent there right away. And he was sent there again for another tour . . . and when he returned, he was not the same."

"What do you mean?" asked Nora.

"He had trouble concentrating. Trouble coping. He wouldn't talk about it. I can't imagine . . . I tell you this to help you understand."

She let her words sit, the better for Dante and Nora to process them.

"Enrique," she said finally. "I haven't said his name to you ever. I'm sorry."

Dante asked her to go on.

"It was hard for your mother, caring for you mostly alone. And when he was back, between his deployments, they had so many arguments. They were too young to know how to get through them. And the night it happened, he had just come back from Iraq. Dante, you were three. He had just been discharged. Earlier in the day, your mother called to tell your grandpa and me, but she also said they had begun to argue."

Alison swiveled her chair away, knowing that Dante and Nora would finally be told what had been kept from them for so long.

"No, Alison," said Emma. "I want all of you to hear this." She looked at Dante. "At some point that night, your mother must have gone into labor."

"Is that how she died, then?"

"Yes. We knew that she was having complications. And there was the stress from the arguing . . . but I don't think your father ever struck her."

"I thought it was something worse, that he did something to her. And I did nothing to help—"

"No, you couldn't have done anything."

"I could have. But after he led me into the cupboard . . . that marble stone was too heavy. Why do we keep that thing?"

"Because it reminds me of the good in him. I told you he wanted to sculpt something from it. It would have been something from the sky, he told me. A star, he was thinking. It would have been for you, he said. But, no, you couldn't have done anything to help your mother that night."

Nora was trembling. "Then it was my fault she died."

Her grandmother reached over to her. "No, child, it wasn't your fault at all. In his love for you and for your mother, your papa must have delivered you. And I think that moment between them must have been very good, and that when they saw you, they were for a moment happy again."

"But then he ran away."

"Yes, he was gone. But he called your grandpa and me. He said that we should go to the house at once. We found you both." She turned to Dante again. "You saved Nora for us."

"No," he said. "I couldn't have. I couldn't push the door open."

"Well, you must have. Because when your grandpa and I arrived, you were not where your father said we would find you. You were not in that cupboard. You were standing in the hallway, holding your sister. He must have washed and wrapped her before going away."

"Do you remember now?" Alison asked.

"I remember the screams. And then crying . . . I must have followed it . . . But I don't remember holding Nora or pushing away that doorstop."

"But you did it," said Nora. "You did, see?"

· ✦ ·

MARSHALL SUGGESTED A SHORT visit to Meridian Hill Park before returning to the hotel. The van took them south on broad Sixteenth Street and parked opposite an arched staircase set into the park's tall, tawny-pebbled walls.

"We'll meet you at the bottom," Marshall told the driver. "Everyone grab an umbrella."

They climbed the stairs into the park in the sleet, then walked to a cast stone balustrade overlooking thirteen terraced basins that ran down to a wide reflecting pool. The entire run of basins was flanked by hinoki cypresses and by water grasses now wintry-stiff and broken.

"It's how I've imagined the Hanging Gardens, except for all the ice," said Dante.

He turned to take in the big freestanding fountain behind them, drawn to it somehow, just as he had been drawn to the Hillwood Stone in the Tribune Tower's lobby and to the pyramid of Queen Meritites. Like them, it brought thoughts of his father. Thoughts, too, of his grandmother's words that he had not been the same after returning from Iraq, where he had seen suffering and suffered himself. And he wondered how this frozen fountain could have brought thoughts of him and of that distant, arid land.

"This way," Marshall called. "There's someone I want you to meet."

They followed a path that led to a twelve-foot-high bronze statue. Its pedestal of pale green granite read *DANTE*.

"I didn't expect to see him here," said Dante, as he looked up at the robed poet holding a book to his heart.

"Then maybe you're losing your powers," said Nora. "Because that should've been an easy one."

"Or maybe I'm thinking about something else."

Nora knew not to press him. "Okay. Do you want to go down to the reflecting pool at the bottom?"

"Go on ahead," Grandma told them. "We'll catch up."

As the adults walked, a blast of frigid air swept across the park, changing the sleet into snow. At the bottom, they joined Nora and Dante and watched it coat the terraced cascade.

Marshall told Dante, "If it were summer, we'd see water spouting from the top and flowing down into the big lower basin, and this reflecting pool would be shooting up eight jets of water. Those urns, dolphins, and grotesques shoot water too."

Dante said nothing. Marshall repeated, "If it were summer," but Dante had been turning over in his head his father's question. *Dante, will there be a time when you will see beyond your memory of what I did to wound you?*

"Now, Papa," he answered, almost to himself. "Now, Papa!" he cried, his voice this time carrying across the reflecting pool and up the cascade to the top of the park and the fountain.

"You all right, man?" asked Marshall.

He nodded. "It's cool this way, too," he said, looking up at the frozen cascade. *It's not just about forgiving him for leaving*, he told himself. *It's about appreciating what was good about him. And understanding what the war must have done to him. . . . I'm at peace with it.*

He felt a tug to his coat. "Will we see him ever, do you think?" Nora asked.

"I guess we won't."

"Maybe he'll read about you," she said. "Or see the interview."

"I don't know . . . but he wrote that poem for you, too. You can think about that, okay?"

They heard the driver call and saw him point to his watch. But Dante pulled Nora close. "I'd like to see him, too," he told her. And when he closed his umbrella to let the snow crystals dance and fall upon them, Grandma did the same, and then the others. And no one was in a hurry to leave.

· ✦ ·

THE RED-CARPET ENTRANCE TO the National Building Museum teemed with photographers, arriving guests, and onlookers as spotlights beamed skyward into the falling snow. When the Sprinter pulled up to let them out, Dante said, "Why not?" and put on a pair of bulky tortoiseshell sunglasses, a gift from Captain Nikkos.

As they walked the carpet, Marshall explained that the building was constructed after the Civil War from more than fifteen million red bricks. "It was the Pension Bureau," he said, "and it handled benefits for the war veterans and their widows and orphans."

"All those soldiers," said Emma, looking up at the terra-cotta frieze above the building's entrance.

The others slowed as they, too, took in the long tableau of figures from the Civil War.

"That frieze wraps around the whole building," said Marshall. "It shows people from all parts of the military. And a formerly enslaved person freed by the war, which the architect insisted on. That's him above the door."

"Where?" asked Emma.

"He's the teamster driving that supply wagon."

Emma steered them to the side to allow the stream of guests to pass. "Let's rest our eyes on them for a while," she said. "All of them up there."

When they entered the Great Hall, they craned their heads up again to take in the eight seventy-five-foot-high Corinthian columns, the tallest in the world when they were built.

"This building became a museum about forty years ago," said Alison, reading from the program. "'Of architecture, design, engineering, construction.' No wonder Ancient Light chose it."

"I think it's more than that," said Marshall. "I remember him saying the galleries at the monastery were designed by an American general. I think it must have been Montgomery Meigs, the architect of this building. He was Lincoln's quartermaster general during the Civil War. He died on the same day and month Ancient Light chose for the grand opening tomorrow—in eighteen ninety-two. I emailed the baroness's office a few weeks ago and asked."

"Did they answer?" Dante asked.

"Sort of. They said, 'We have long thought General Meigs's building in Washington a modern wonder.'"

When an announcer called for the guests to take their seats, Dante looked around, hoping to see Ancient Light.

"Don't give up on him yet," said Alison as Otto walked to the lectern.

Otto introduced himself as an officer of the newly formed Ibis Trust. He said that the chairman was unable to attend.

"He's saving his strength, probably," Alison told Dante. "For his work in Iraq with Ali."

Otto announced that all of the treasures displayed would be returned to their home countries after the four-year run of the exhibition, giving each country time to build or dedicate an appropriate space for displaying the objects.

"I think I already know what the big ones are," said Dante.

"Oh, geez, you mean you've seen them all in your head already?" she said. "It's not possible. Really it isn't."

"It's not that. I just figure the main pieces will match the brooches the baroness wore. . . . Actually, she only wore six. She didn't wear one for the Hanging Gardens that night on the ship when Ali spoke. I think it would have shown the mosaic. Maybe she sensed that I'd found the villa earlier in the day. Maybe she suspected I knew she was with Ibis even then. There's one thing I don't get, though."

"What's that?"

"Her Statue of Zeus brooch. It showed the statue whole. Ancient Light's drawing did, too. That can't be possible."

Now the lights dimmed, and the tall curtains at the far end of the Great Hall opened as video streamed live on jumbo screens around them.

"Before you explore the exhibits," Otto announced, "here is a preview. From the Great Pyramid of Giza, you see the magnificent gold mask and painted coffin of Pharaoh Khufu. These were obtained by Ibis from the Mamluks in Egypt. Next, these two tall, red granite statues of Khufu and his wife Queen Meritites, which we acquired from associates of Napoleon during his Egyptian campaign. They had no appreciation of their value. Ignorance was often our friend in collecting." The camera zoomed in on a tiny statuette. "Compare the large Meritites with this less-stylized little portrait of her. The statuette was loaned to us by Alison Fine, who, with her student, found her in a shop in Cairo last summer."

"And she'll go back to Egypt after this," Alison said to Dante. "My gift to the new Grand Egyptian Museum they're building. She belongs with the little Khufu."

They grinned for the next several minutes as the objects Otto highlighted from the Pharos, Colossus, Mausoleum, and Temple of Artemis were indeed those depicted in the baroness's brooches. But they gasped along with the audience when the camera moved to a close-up of the head of Zeus, then slowly panned out to reveal that the statue was entirely intact.

Otto announced that it was an exact but half-scale copy of the original wonder, which had been destroyed by fire. He explained that it had been commissioned in the fourth century AD by a prominent Greek family who feared the original would be moved away from Greece or destroyed by the Romans. There was also a broad marble basin that had served as a reflecting pool at the base of the original statue. It was all just as in Ancient Light's drawing.

"Finally," said Otto, as the ibis mosaic appeared on the screens, "we have applied three-dimensional printing technology to produce this copy of a mosaic terrace from the Hanging Gardens of Babylon. And in this display case, you see the brick known as the Hillwood Stone, which was part of the terrace's wall. It has been returned to us from the Tribune Tower collection in Chicago. The actual mosaic terrace will soon be taken to Iraq. It was discovered there in seventeen hundred . . ."

But Dante only half listened as Otto described the dig, raised his eyes only slightly when he heard him mention his name, and felt only emptiness at the announcement that Dyllis's interview with Ancient Light would air internationally later in the evening.

"What a full, full day," Alison reflected as the ceremony ended.

But he could only say, "It's no good without him here."

· ✦ ·

Exasperated by the crowds, Dante rushed through the exhibits and rejoined Alison at their table.

"That was quick," she said.

"It's a lot of stuff. I don't know . . . I prefer thinking about the wonders when they were whole."

"Well, I think your drawings accomplish that. Did you ever finish the Hanging Gardens?"

He had, but he told her that he'd had to imagine what might have been in the blank squares around the outside of the mosaic. He had been thinking about how hard it must be for Ancient Light and the baroness and Ali to have wondered all their lives what the six squares represented, and what else had been left behind from the dig.

"Ali told me he pictured himself at the Hanging Gardens a lot," he said, "and imagined himself talking with Princess Amytis there."

"You've reminded me." She reached for her bag and pulled out a large envelope made of thick Florentine paper. "It's from the baroness. A loan, she told me. Something she wanted you to see."

From the envelope Dante pulled a worn, leather-bound journal. He read the handwritten title aloud: "The Excavation of a Babylonian Mound in August of the Year Seventeen Hundred, Volume the Second."

"It's the archaeologist's notebook," she said. "The baroness told me her Prussian great-great-grand-someone-or-other led the dig. She tabbed a passage she wanted you to see. It's at the end."

Dante opened to it and read. "O, back two millennia, through the timeless haboob, to Babylon . . .'"

"She made a point of telling me you must never brush away the particles—'the particles from the haboob,' she said. Whatever that is."

"A sandstorm," said Dante as he touched the weathered page. He read the archaeologist's final words. "From this air, I hear the songs and conversations of ancient nights and days and the fountain that invites them. May others listen, too, when passing this way, this place of peace."

"There's this from her as well," said Alison, handing him a small envelope. But he set it down without opening it. "What are you thinking?" she asked.

"Just that it's strange . . . the archaeologist's reference to a fountain. When we were at the park this afternoon, at the top, there was a fountain, and all of a sudden I thought about my father over there in Iraq."

"You told Nora that you had other things on your mind. Was it that?"

"Yes. But Ancient Light, too." He closed the journal slowly. "This is hard."

"Go on."

"When I was walking with him at the Zeus site, he told me he had a lot of work to do. He must have meant all the work to plan the exhibition. Then he said he wanted to come here. And go to Iraq, too, to look at the ruins of Babylon. I guess probably to pick out a site for the mosaic when it's returned there. He said, 'Will there be time to do both?' I thought he was just thinking out loud. But he wanted me to answer. I couldn't tell him."

"Go on."

"I felt something. I knew there wouldn't be time. I shouldn't have let him see me worry. But he just smiled and held up his hand. Then he gave me an Egyptian amulet. He said, 'Take this. Wear it, for joy. He has lifted me. Let him lift you.'"

"What was it?"

"A little baboon. It's just over an inch tall and made of ancient Egyptian glass. Green faience, he called it."

"Ah, so when he told you at the monastery to keep the pouch, he meant you could use it for the amulet?"

"Yes."

"So, are you wearing it? May I see it?"

"I didn't want to travel with it and risk losing it, but it has a feature I didn't understand at first—a sun disk that sits on the baboon's head. I'd never seen Egyptian baboons depicted that way. Then he told me he felt he had to go home while he still could, to Iraq. And that he'd never given up."

"On what, do you think?" Alison asked.

"Finding the last wonder. He said more, too. I memorized it and then wrote it all down before the interview started. He said, 'You know well enough of Thoth, who wore the crown with the moon disk as he coursed the evening sky with Ra. Such a serious fellow, Thoth. Oh, my boy, it is good that you hold close the night and its mysteries, but did you know that the ancient Egyptians also depicted Thoth as a baboon? Yes, the baboon sun god Hedjwer. That is him in your amulet. Egyptians esteemed the exuberant creatures, who chattered and sang and danced to greet the sun as it rose each morning. So should you also want to greet each day with joy. And if you infuse your life with that joy and light, it will touch others, and it will never expire.'"

"Well, he said it better than I ever did."

"It took a long time for it all to sink in. And what you said, too, at the end of the cruise, when I was upset with Ali, and my father."

She smiled. "You had quite a bit going on at the time, as I recall. But the troubling parts—about your parents and now Ancient Light's last days—that's the deal in life. But you'll have an outlet all your own through it. Do you know what I'm saying? What that is?"

"My writing, like you said."

"Even if it's a struggle sometimes."

"Like composing," he joked.

"Yes. Well, we try to work through it. And imagine a wonderful result."

"I've made a start."

"Your grandmother told me."

"I don't know if it's going anywhere." He paused. "I took the amulet with me to the lake last fall, to the dig. I watched the sunrises there. I felt close to the people that were there for thousands of years before us. And the wholeness of things. It's the work I want to do."

He looked up at the image of the ibis mosaic on the big screen above the lectern, and as he thought about Ancient Light half a world away, the din of the crowd began to give way to the sound of water splashing impatiently.

"I'm going to sit over there for a while," he told her, gesturing toward the wide, circular fountain at the center of the Great Hall.

He moved his chair close to it and opened the envelope from the baroness. Inside were a letter and a black-and-white photograph. He heard her voice as he read her account of the last hours of the dig, as passed down to her through generations of her family. She wrote of the great haboob that had moved in, the archaeologist's crushing disappointment that more could not be excavated, and his carelessness in losing the journal with his maps of the dig.

"They found the Hanging Gardens of Babylon," she wrote, "and they lost it. They lost it." He smiled as he read her remark in parentheses: "But we have the mosaic, and of course another stunning brooch."

He looked at the photograph. She was young, in her twenties, and wore the brooch, which she described as "the sacred ibis in white opal and unpolished black onyx inside a floral border of carved jade."

Her closing words at once saddened and warmed him. "I am sorry to tell you that Ancient Light has become more frail. But he asks you to watch for some things he will send to you in Chicago. He speaks of you."

He opened the archaeologist's journal and passed his fingers over its pages, feeling the sands of a haboob from more than three centuries past and remembering Ancient Light's words about the Chatwin book, *The Songlines*. He had read the book over the summer and believed it must be possible for others to pick up the signals and signposts around them if they were open to them, or at least tried.

Resting his hands on the old journal, he imagined the dig and the camels and the men laboring in the haboob. "Every wind must carry memories and dreams and stories," he whispered. And now a tableau of pictures came to him—first, a great haboob advancing across an arid land, and next, closer in, its particled air curling over the top of a curved, half-exposed object massive in size. And although the object would soon be shrouded by the storm, he had seen it clearly and knew it to be part of the ancient mosaic terrace that invited conversation, poetry, and song.

The fountain.

He stared into the journal, thinking about Ancient Light, thinking it would be dawn in Iraq now. He stared until the page went white, even as his picture of the fountain coursed through his heart to his distant friend.

· ✦ ·

ANCIENT LIGHT DREW HIS face close to the window of his chartered plane. The sun's first rays had touched the languid Euphrates, and he was imagining the vibrant city of Babylon that once crowded its banks.

"The area seems to have been spared damage from yesterday's earthquakes," he said to his son.

"For the most part, yes," said Doctor Ali. "Although I see signs of a small fissure there, past that village. There, near the date palms."

Ancient Light seemed not to hear. "Dante and the others will be viewing the collection now," he said. "At General Meigs's big red barn, as some disparaged it. I suspect Dante is thinking as much about what is not there as what is."

"I'll call Otto later to see how things went—"

But Doctor Ali was interrupted by an update from the pilot about the mass of sand and dust that had been moving in from the west toward the ruins of ancient Babylon below them.

"I should alter course, gentlemen. The haboob approaches faster than I expected."

But Ancient Light stared ahead, his expression quizzical and then expectant. "How remarkable," he whispered.

"What is it?" asked Doctor Ali.

"Something. . . . How remarkable." He looked into the haboob and pressed his hand to the window. "Go in," he ordered the pilot, jabbing at the window with his finger.

"But, the storm," said Doctor Ali. "We should turn—"

"No, go in," he called again to the pilot. "The quake has damaged some of the excavations. There is something new. I feel it. Oh, I hear it, Ali. Steer right, ten degrees. Keep going. Keep your eyes on that area below, Ali. Oh, yes, there," he said, pointing to a feature that would soon be obscured by the haboob. "Mark it. Mark it."

"I have it," answered the pilot.

"Do you see, Ali? A beautiful curve. It's as if the boy—"

"Turn now!" Doctor Ali called to the pilot.

Ancient Light looked at his son and laughed quietly. "A spot to investigate. One that would have been protected by Babylon's walls from the dry westerly winds. A spot ideal for a garden." He turned to take another look from his window, hoping to see more of the fountain. "There the mosaic will go, Ali. And there she shall return."

"Who shall?" asked Doctor Ali.

"The sacred ibis, of course."

"Do you still wish to continue south?" called the pilot.

"As we planned, yes."

With the storm behind them, they soared over the canal-laced marshes of southeastern Iraq.

"A promising dawn," Ancient Light reflected. But he had begun to stir uncomfortably in his seat.

"You must rest now," said Doctor Ali.

"No doubt. But first, tell the pilot to drop altitude."

He brightened as he made out the narrow boats filled with bundled reeds and propelled through the marshes by young men clothed in loose, cooling cotton. "Closer," he said, and the plane took them over an island-mound with a group of arched reed houses. A smile creased his parchment face as he watched the children look up with happy shouts and waves. A group of wading birds stirred and took flight. One, an ibis, turned its head to meet his eyes, its broad, black-tipped wings propelling it forward, parallel to the plane.

"Closer," he whispered to the sacred bird.

"What did you say, Father?"

Ancient Light turned. "Oh," he said, seeing Ali and the morning sun in his face. He grasped Ali's hand, clenching it with all his strength. "All right," he said, a quiet summing-up before the light went from his eyes.

14

LYRIC STAGE

O N THEIR RETURN FLIGHT to Chicago after the exhibition, Dante had asked Alison if she would show him the Lyric Opera House. She found it intriguing, after taking him through the building several days later, that he had seemed most interested in the set-design and set-building spaces backstage.

"So, any particular reason you wanted to visit?" she asked, as they wrapped up the tour in the orchestra pit in front of the stage.

"I'll be too busy to come once school starts next week," he answered, thinking he might say more later if it felt right. "I have a photo to show you." He took out his phone. "These are the globes Ancient Light sent me. They're from his library. I was hiding behind this one when we met." His smile lasted only a moment. "I miss him."

"Let's sit." She leaned in to get a closer look at the pendant he was wearing. "What's this little creature? Is it the baboon amulet from Egypt he gave you?"

"Yes."

"I see the sun disk on his head."

He told her that Ancient Light had said it was found during the dig at the Hanging Gardens, and that the archaeologist had discovered it when sifting the soil near the mosaic.

"Same way Khufu's little head was found," she said, delighted.

"Yes. And he said it's the same age as the Hanging Gardens, so it's more evidence that Princess Amytis visited Egypt. He believed it was hers. Do you remember him saying she was a peacemaker?"

Alison nodded, then closed her eyes, imagining the princess's times and travels, her gardens, her soul. "You know, I wish the tour had taken us to Iraq last summer, to see Baghdad and to drive out to the ruins of Babylon."

"Yes, but then we might not have met Ali or learned anything about my father. Or seen his poem."

"Right. I feel better. Are you still writing?"

"A lot since we got back from DC."

"And does it feel now like it's something you're meant to be doing?"

"Yes, it fits with what I want to study."

"Professor James told me you have the archaeologist's gene. He said he got feedback about your work at Lake Superior last fall—about your insights into the ancient cultures and people there, and their artifacts and symbols."

Her remark brought to mind the hieroglyphs he had seen on the cruise, and it came to him that they might inform and guide him in all that he did. "I want to help tell their stories."

Alison nodded as she retrieved a small box from her bag.

"Did Grandma tell you she took me to a doctor?" he asked.

"No. Is everything all right?"

"It was to a psychologist. To help me understand things from when I was little. But, I'm good. No one needs to worry."

"I'm glad." This news brought back her concern about his detachment, but when she remembered what Nora had first said to her, that he was just in his bubble sometimes, she had to smile. *Nothing wrong with being self-contained*, she thought. *Imagine having that perspective . . . soaring above it all.* She held up her hand and allowed the sunlight to catch the stones in the ring Ancient Light had given her. *Like a bird—taking in everything, the good and the bad, as he said to me on the plane at the start of our trip. What a view.* "Glad, too, that you're writing," she added. "I've been meaning to give these to you." She handed him the box.

"Wooden pens. Cool."

"I made them from the marsh reeds that Ali brought to *Modestine* for his talk."

"Using your tools for your bassoon reeds?"

"Right, so you now have pens like the ancient Babylonians and Egyptians had—except for the ballpoint cartridges I stuck in them," she laughed. "You know, I love what Gloria Steinem said about writing—that it's the only time she feels like she shouldn't be doing something else."

"It's true. I feel peaceful and charged at the same time. And when I wake up in the morning, ideas come, and I have to put them down. I'm writing about . . . something. I haven't talked about it with anyone."

"No worries," she said. "Writers mostly don't until they're done." But she felt certain that he had too much to say now to hold back.

"Do you remember," he began, "after we were all back on *Modestine* in Greece, when you woke me from my dream?"

"Yes. You said the wonders appeared in it. You said they spoke to you."

"About me. They were characters, like in a play. Princess Amytis spoke, too. About her gardens and the ibis."

"I remember. So your story is around her?"

"Well, I imagine Amytis having to deal with things she couldn't control, things that would have upset her more than just being homesick. Like palace politics, and the weight of her duties. And wars. But like Ancient Light told us, she traveled to Egypt. And maybe she was drawn to the African sacred ibises because of their legends there, and because they were also in Babylon. And that inspired her to design her mosaic."

"Go on."

"So there she was, living in a palace in the most powerful city in the world." He paused, his expression serious, but Alison detected a trace of a smile when he resumed. "I see her hosting the wonders characters there, on her mosaic terrace. Khufu and Poseidon and Triton. And her husband, Nebuchadnezzar. And Helios the Colossus and Mausolus and Artemis. Zeus. All of them."

"And then?"

"I'm giving her the words I think she would have spoken. The words that all of them would have said. And sung. All the wonders and their personalities, like I felt when you talked about your buildings on the *First Lady* and how you brought them to life."

"I like that you felt that, I have to say."

"So they'd all be there, like in my dream, on a big stage, rising up and moving around . . . and they debate things, and talk a lot." His smile broadened. "I'm just not sure what they do yet. But they're important, and big, like—"

"Yes, mighty," she said. "But also flawed?"

"Right, because some of them weren't angels. And maybe they're vain, too, some of them."

"A little eccentric?"

"Yes. Not ordinary. Not mainstream."

"I'm feeling it. Is there more?"

"A lot. So the wonders were built at the peak of all those civilizations. But they all came to see war and broken times. Like a lot of places today. . . . And I think about all the troubles in Iraq and what the Iraqi people went through. And about Ali losing his family in the war there. And when I felt the sand in the archaeologist's journal, I imagined my father in the haboobs of Iraq—because I believe he was there, near the ruins of Babylon. And I wonder if he felt what the archaeologist felt during the dig, or if a person can feel anything good in war. . . . But the ibis—Ancient Light told me it was a powerful protector. The abbot did, too. And I remember witnessing that in the Delta. So, what if the ibis has the power to do bigger things? For the land, the sea, the marshes in between . . . and for people, people oppressed. Anywhere. I don't know. It's a lot."

"And big, like you said."

"But also small. I mean, personal. At least, I think it should be. So Princess Amytis . . . she's made something that's her own in the Hanging Gardens. She has everything, but she's in an arranged marriage, so maybe she doesn't. But she has the African sacred ibis. Not just the real ones around her—the one in her mosaic. And it grounds her, and gives her inspiration, too, and hope. And she's connected to the other wonders, sort of like they're all part of something together. But then . . . I'm not seeing where things go from there. How it should end."

When she assured him that he would find it, as surely as Mister Turtle Wood had found the Temple of Artemis, he opened his notebook and showed her the drawing he had made of the Hanging Gardens.

"So that would be Princess Amytis," she said. "Beside a fountain. I like that image."

"Because I got a picture of a fountain when we were at the exhibition in DC. It came to me when I was looking at the archaeologist's journal. It was big and it was there, where the mosaic was excavated. So I drew it that way. But . . ."

"What?"

"The archaeologist wrote that he imagined hearing a fountain, but I've read his whole journal and he made no other reference to it and he made no sketch of it."

"If you got a picture of it, then it's there. I know that much. Likely the whole party involved in the dig back then was sworn to secrecy about it."

"Well, I want it to be there, because I think that terrace and fountain would have been a place where things happened. That's her place. Princess Amytis's place. And as I write, I'm thinking that what makes her feel less isolated and what fulfills her would be about doing good where she can . . . and just finding someone she's comfortable with. Just complementing each other could be what's right for her. For them. And that would be a happy life, wouldn't it?"

"There must be a thousand paths to happiness," she agreed. "So, I'm thinking about what a challenge your story presents. I mean, all the decisions you have to make about location and timeline and—"

"Yes, but it's not a story like a novel or something. I'm putting it down like . . . I don't know."

"I won't say a word to anyone."

"Okay, it's like, a poem. Like, lyrics."

"A libretto?" she said, her eyes getting big.

"Well, I said I'm giving Amytis and the others words they'd speak and sing . . ."

"Yes, you did. So, it's epic stuff. Operatic, yes?"

"It could be, I guess. A modern one though, a fresh one."

"Well, you have all the elements, I'd say. And you have the freedom that verse gives you. The ending will come, like I said."

"I think so, too, because ideas come even when I'm not thinking about it. And I see the shape of it. And the rhymes. They move around, until they seem right. Like in my father's poem, about the lines unfolding . . ."

Alison nodded, allowing his words to pool around her, beguiled by the artist's ability to create something that could be no other way—to observe and to assemble the parts and pieces of all that had streamed to him, no longer fragmented, but put into place and made whole.

"It's just without the music yet," he said, knowing she would pick up his meaning, his invitation.

They sat quietly now, their bond so comfortable that there was no requirement to speak, no need to explain. And when he took one of her reed pens and opened his notebook to capture a thought, she closed her eyes, attuned to his heart and to what he was seeing.

It was Doctor Ali, in a narrow flatboat propelled by a young man through the Mesopotamian Marshes, his face calm as he examined the fresh growth of the reeds near the village he had flown over with Ancient Light just days earlier. And him leaving afterward in a caravan of SUVs, traveling north to the ruins of Babylon, and putting binoculars to his eyes as he closed in on the curved object exposed by the earthquake. And running to it, and discovering it to be the fountain the archaeologist had alluded to more than three centuries earlier when the ibis mosaic terrace was removed. And his elation in uncovering the six smaller mosaics that had surrounded it, which, taken together, would give a panoramic view of ancient Babylon—the city, its walls and its gates, the boat-filled Euphrates, Nebuchadnezzar's grand palace, and the lost wonder itself, the Hanging Gardens.

"He'll go there, Alison. He'll find it."

"Yes," she affirmed, "It would be Ali."

"It's all he's wanted. He'll tell us to come and be part of the dig. I know it."

"I'll go and pack," she said with a laugh. "I'm thinking you'll postpone college again . . ."

"I'll have to, right?"

"I'm thinking you'll jump straight to your PhD after this."

And when she saw him bring his hand up to the ancient amulet over his heart, she knew he was seeing more of his story, his libretto. And perhaps the ending.

All right, she told herself as he began to write again. *Now try to hear it. There . . . a major key, yes, D major. A triumph? A joyful something.*

He was writing of the return of the African sacred ibis—of her descent from the night sky, illuminated by the comet and the stars of her vast constellation. Returning this time from the marshes of

Mesopotamia, which she had wondrously healed, and alighting on the terrace of the Hanging Gardens to rest again, a mosaic, but remaining alert and poised to rise anew when the comet reappeared. To rise anew in another twenty-four years to protect or heal, or stop a war, or set a matter right in a different troubled place. And he was writing of the Council of Wonders, a lively body whose ancient members knew much, but who were given to opining on so much more. For they—Mausolus and the Colossus Helios and Nebuchadnezzar and the rest—needed every day of those twenty-four years to ponder, argue, and debate the ibis's next mission, though they would, in the end and as always, side with the sacred bird's decision because justice was her cause.

Moving now to the key of G, Alison told herself as she imagined the orchestra pit filling with musicians around them. *Something idyllic, something serene . . . An air of peace.*

He was writing now of Princess Amytis standing beside her fountain on the mosaic terrace, serving as host to the colorful council—but more often than not as its mediator, a role she had come to accept and then embrace. And writing of Doctor Ali, a kindred soul, standing with her, because everything would need to be chronicled, and because he belonged there.

Alison gripped her calamander stick and felt it stir as if to lead her forever-tuning orchestra into purpose. And as she watched Dante's pen form his words, she felt them pulse like notes into the near and distant air.

She heard his passage now—its line, and beat, and rhythm. Its voices, too. And saw its architecture. It was big, as he had said, at once lyrical and bold, like his drawings of the African sacred ibis in flight and of the Seven Wonders and the outsized beings they honored, Khufu to Zeus.

She pictured them all now, towering up and commanding her Lyric Opera stage, and above them the luminous ibis soaring. She imagined their powers and personalities and the lines and rhymes he might be giving them, and beamed.

I believe I can score this, she decided. And with her heart she told him. And on her music composition book she would write, *For Dante*.

Photograph by Paul Stannering

STEPHEN T. PERSON was born in Boston, Massachusetts, and now lives in Washington, DC. While serving in the US Navy, he circumnavigated the globe aboard the *USS Trippe*, and later worked as a magazine editor and corporate communications manager, with assignments that took him to England, Saudi Arabia, and Brazil. His writing is inspired by his travels. *Five Hieroglyphs* is his first novel.

StephenTPerson.com